HEADLESS
WORLD

Other works by Ascher/Straus

THE OTHER PLANET

LETTER TO AN UNKNOWN WOMAN

THE MENACED ASSASSIN

RED MOON/RED LAKE

ABC STREET

HANK FOREST'S PARTY

MONICA'S CHRONICLE *(ONLINE)*

HEADLESS WORLD

OR

The Problem of Time

A NOVEL BY

ASCHER/STRAUS

McPherson & Company
Kingston, New York
2022

HEADLESS WORLD

Published by McPherson & Company,
P.O. Box 1126, Kingston, NY 12401.
Designed by Bruce R. McPherson
First Edition 2022
ISBN 978-1-62054-049-7
1 3 5 7 9 10 8 6 4 2

Library of Congress Cataloging-in-Publication Data

Names: Ascher/Straus, author.
Title: Headless world : or, the problem of time / a novel by Ascher/
Straus.
Other titles: The problem of time
Description: First edition. | Kingston, New York : McPherson &
Company,   2022.
Identifiers: LCCN 2022030587 (print) | LCCN 2022030588 (ebook) |
ISBN 9781620540497 (trade paperback)|ISBN 9781620540534 (epub)
Subjects: LCGFT: Novels.
Classification: LCC PS3551.S33 H43 2022 (print) | LCC PS3551.S33
(ebook)
   | DDC 813/.54--dc23/eng/20220629
LC record available at https://lccn.loc.gov/2022030587
LC ebook record available at https://lccn.loc.gov/2022030588

Grateful acknowledgment to the editors
of *Exile* and *Your Impossible Voice*
where portions of this book first appeared.

To the nurses whose kindness I (Dennis) have known too well

To Beethoven's Diabelli Variations and Bagatelles,
and the late Quartets that were the complete sound horizon
for so much of my (Sheila's) chronicling

To the narrative innovators in film and writing,
from Melville and Dostoyevsky to Musil, Tarkovsky,
Broch, Ozu, Kieslowski, Zanussi, Kawabata, and Hou,
to name just some of those whose work sustained us

To Sonny Rollins, John Coltrane, Betty Carter,
John Lewis, and Abbey Lincoln

With love and gratitude

000

FOOT in the water: whole lake around the foot.
"David!"
On the far shore.
"Daaa-viiiid!"
From nearby, where blue spruce rise up along a green and brown and sunny knoll, a voice responds.
"David! I found you!"
(Not far away, but is it hers?)

·

Always from the outside, we feel life gather. Feel how life gathers. The completeness of life, but only from the outside and from a distance.

·

The little striped awning on the speckled slope.
Little awning with red stripes.
Children playing quietly in the sun and an elderly woman with a silky-skinned round face and pale cotton dress going up the steps of a house at the crest of the speckled slope, under the striped awning and through the door. Door bangs sharply, like the sound of a dog barking once, twice far-away. Bangs again and is suspended open by a sudden wind crossing the lake. Children playing look from their sunny knoll for round silky face and pale housedress but they've become invisible.

·

An infant sitting in its highchair on the terrace of the villa in the tropics bangs his chartreuse plastic cup against the greenish resin tabletop.

It makes a hollow tok-tok noise.

A little too weak.

Again, harder.

Tok-tok!

More satisfied, he burbles, "Bo!"

A few near-words, then "Bo! Bo! Bo!"

Tok-tok-toking of chartreuse cup on table, longish dribble of speech, then "Eep! peep! peep!"

"OH-BO!"

And a bit more Tok-tok-toking!

The child's afternoon passes pleasantly in this way as clouds cover the tropical sun and cut off the surge and sparkle of the ocean through the pines.

.

"Can any of these children be me?!"

00

ALL through his many lives he's felt something surging inside him: feels like a torrent of water forcing its way forward, spilling invisibly out into the atmosphere, but not completely. And this surging torrent was the wellspring of his strength. Except when something blocked its path. And then it pushed him with all its force toward death.

0

LITTLE boy with curly hair and oddly puffy eyes enters the room.

Warmth of his presence stimulates mutation of the image, like a blue spark that spreads through three-hundred-and-thirty-six acres of forest.

He approaches the mutating lines of light as if rejoining his soul.

HEADLESS
WORLD

He mourned ahead of time…,
ever since he was born….

ELIAS CANETTI
The Secret Heart of the Clock

1

FIRST thing he remembers is the smell of his buttered and toasted raisin bran muffin charring around the edges and sound of his vanilla shake churning in the blender. All around him people are eating their grilled sandwiches with fries and western omelettes with ketchup and drinking their coffees and sodas. He asks the waitress where he is, but, between the ZZZ of the stainless coffee maker and the ghostly nhnhnh of the prehistoric microwave, she can't hear him and goes on about her business. The quiet harmony between an indifferent human shoulder and the buzzing hardware it operates is familiar. Now the little flap comes loose. Little flap of skin that resembles memory — bunched like cloth between three fingers and forced under the humming needle. Needle makes its painful stitches, tears come to the eye, but memory evaporates.

2

THE law for everything is that once it starts it keeps going, there's no turning back. The world knows its own inevitable direction and, after canceling its silence, braids its noises into the tightest possible cable.

.

He thinks to himself that it's odd. If he holds his head at a certain angle (staring straight ahead at the waitress's back and at the tight, red-black pretzel loops fastened to the back of her head) the room is perfectly silent, only the quietest electronic hum at the boundaries. While, if he cranks his head to the right, he picks up machine noises, a conversation or two, the surge of twenty voices, and, when he's got his head just about screwed around toward the brightness of the windows with their long, squashed view of mountains so far away it's almost like being told they're there instead of seeing them, the noises of machines and voices have braided so tight they've become the drill that bores the hole that lets us know that experience has a boundary. (No matter how we reach out toward the real somewhere-else we feel nothing.)

From speakers positioned like little cameras in the ceiling corners, a young woman's voice suddenly becomes audible. A thrilling song that reminds everyone of his/her own stupid-stupid longings, though not of their forgotten object. An open-throated cry subsides into a quiet recitation charged with anticipation of the next meaningless eruption, nasal but heartbreaking.

Just as he's thinking, *while we listen all our atoms are*

aligned; we ourselves are up above our heads as we eat our burg-
ers, two fingers touch his forearm. Turns to see three faces,
one behind and above the other. Foreground face is the extraordinarily large face of a little girl, no more than nine, her
forest brown hair plaited in braids and pinned up in pretzel
loops, eyes wide and intelligent, brown with fiery green no-
vas, cheeks fat, forehead severe, the remains of a rare, giant
burger oozing ketchup through her fingers. Above her the
tranquil face of the older sister, profile turned just enough
to cast a watchful eye and ear. A smile of mysterious tenderness, but toward whom? And behind the sisters, the beautiful,
round and silky-skinned face of a white-haired woman bent
with serious pleasure over bacon, lettuce and tomato sandwich and a coffee ice cream soda.

The child says that this town used to be a mining town. The
element selenium was discovered in 1817 or 1818 by the Swed-
ish chemist Jons Berzelius, but it wasn't until the twentieth century that they found important uses for it and began to mine
it. It's quite rare, but there was a significant deposit of it right
here — basically in the middle of nowhere. The mines are long
since gone, of course, but the township is still called Selenium.
There's East Selenium, North Selenium, "Old Selenium,"
"New Selenium," and, where they are now, Selenium Center.

And outside of town there's Selenium Springs, Selenium
Falls, Selenium Grove and Selenium Wells, the older sister says.

The little girl's already lost interest in him and is licking
chocolate and raspberry off her fingertips.

The waitress is there, giving him his muffin and shake, not
on a plate like the others, but in a bag, as if he's being asked
to leave and eat in the parking lot. Being told to leave, yet the
waitress seems kind. Seems kind, yet her eyes are suspicious
and exhausted.

How can we ever know how another is looking at us? he
wonders. And why is it that our desires always give us delu-
sions?

This must be the moment he's supposed to say the password

and he says, trying to engage the intelligent little girl's interest without success: "In general, the persistence of an idea is a yardstick of its idiocy, but the idea that with humankind *time* was born...."

No one answers and in a second the sisters and their grandmother are gone and he's left with the feeling that he's lost his family one more time.

·

He's sitting alone at the counter, legs pretzelled around the polished steel stool post, draining off the last of his shake and eating his second order of spicy fries. While his grandmother and younger sister go off along the near edge of the sunny little plaza on some pleasant errand — an errand so pleasant he can't imagine what it is — his older sister remains behind in their white van, front door panel slid open, right foot on the ground, left up on the rim between dashboard and door frame, eating a fudge brownie and reading a book with a cover that's a blizzard of blue and red particles.

Seems to him that she sees him through the window. Top edge of her book dips down and his eyes meet hers. What is this look? What is the meaning of this look? Warm look of recognition? *Could* be a warm look of recognition, if only he could remember back to the beginning. But we can never remember the beginning, no more than we can know the end.

By the time he gathers the courage to risk losing her by going out to the van rather than losing her by remaining where he is, his grandmother's returning with his little sister. The girl's carrying a small box tied with blue ribbon and the grandmother is carrying a big sack of crinkly green paper.

Van starts up, turns right, immediately cuts left — straight across the local highway and onto a smaller road that splices through a stand of golden trees that have a spindle-like roundness only because it's late afternoon, when trees are spinning on their axes to catch the sun.

·

The waitress with the kind expression brings him another

vanilla shake. Sets it down, pushes it toward him. Immediately he begins sucking at the two thick straws. She smiles and lights a cigarette. The cafe's empty and she's in no hurry. Smokes three cigarettes before she says a word.

Has anyone ever told him that he's just about the twin of the woman who used to be on TV, the one who was so smart you couldn't understand a word she said and who had that terrible thing happen to her and was in a coma for a year or more? Now you don't see her anymore, but every once in a while somebody says something that seems startling and original until you remember that she was the one who said it first.

He turns to look at his reflection in the dark window, where only the blacker-than-black pine spindles are visible through the yellow-white flesh. His shirt is torn, there are smudges on his face, hair spiky and uncombed. And this is the face — this is the *blob*-face — that dreamed his sister was looking at him with anything but horror!

3

THE waitress has a neat but tiny apartment up some stairs above the ancient post office in Selenium Springs, a zip-through town not even five miles down the road to the west of Selenium Center. She brings out a bowl of buttered popcorn and they settle down to doze off together in front of the set. The program is unfamiliar, yet the characters bring back memories. At the end of the episode the son, who'd run away from home exactly three years ago, is in a phone booth out on an interstate somewhere, struggling to make himself heard over the noisy rumbling and explosive after-shocks of late-night truck traffic.

"I remember this, Mommy, but I need you to tell me if it's true. Three weeks after my eighth birthday, on the hottest August day on record on our planet, I won the sixteen meter swimming medal at the Athletic Union swim meet. Dad was in tears. You were there, Mom, and Gramma was there and even Valeria and little Flora. Valeria was the only one who looked normal. No twitches or tics, like Dad. Not doubled over like you, Mom, as if you were throwing up. Not desperate and rummaging in her bag for pills like Gramma or jumping up and down like little Flora. As I climbed out of the pool Valeria gave me a look I'll never forget. That's the look I carry with me as the measure of every other look.

"The very next day after winning my medal I nearly drowned. I began to swim and couldn't stay up, just like the first time you try and you can't keep your legs from sinking. Legs are like another drowning person pulling you under from the waist. Isn't happy till it gets your face under. That was the

16

great mystery of my eighth year. You and Dad couldn't figure it out. Or am I making all this up, Mom?

"You bought me a blue cloth wristband you told me was magic and when I put it on the arm stayed up, but the head went under.

"Months later, when we were on vacation on an island somewhere, they found me floating face down in the pool. You and Dad sprang into action as if I were still alive. I remember the flash of your oiled legs. Dad nearly fell in the pool grabbing me up. Gripped my little arm so hard he made me cry and come to life. I started screaming, scuttling along the edge of the pool and slapping the tiled ledge as I went. Tried banging my head on the top step leading into shallow water. You leaped too, but not so fast as Dad. Just behind him, hanging over the pool, arms at a funny angle.

"Two nights later I couldn't stay on the ground. I kept doing somersaults in the air over my bed like an astronaut, feet pushing off from the ceiling. I remember little Flora coming in and trying to catch my hand, but I kept rising and couldn't get hold of her. Finally I gave up and rested for a while against the ceiling, which for some reason smelled like yeast and flour."

The waitress, who's been dozing and mixing up the molecules of the boy on TV with the molecules of the son she lost thirty years ago, opens her eyes and says that this program only proves that our own lives aren't available to us. Available to others, but not to us, as if they're being broadcast on a service we don't subscribe to.

The boy on television, she says, talking to his mother from the last telephone of a bank of telephones near an isolated interstate toll booth, also looks a little like the woman who used to be on TV, the so-called Television Genius who came to a horrible end. One horror story blends into the next. Does that make each one *less* horrible? Or do they add up to one horror…?

He closes his eyes and can hear the voice of the boy's mother through the painfully cold receiver.

"'There's a chain that goes around the world,' she says,

17

'of people in love with people who aren't in love with them. There's a chain of longing, a current of letters and phone calls, e-mails and messages that flows in one direction only. So the more you dream about me, the more I'll be compelled to dream about someone else.'"

The waitress brushes aside the curtain, stares down at the dry dome of the post office lawn for a long time as if she sees someone there or out a hundred yards or so at the deserted intersection of three dark and vacant county routes and highways — someone who's also staring, transfixed by the pale, startled face and blue television illumination between parted curtains — and says that she thinks someone's come to take him home.

4

I T'S the middle of the night and he has no idea where he is.
The guy who calls himself Waldo Bunny is slumped way
down in his seat with his mouth open, his right hand resting
on the hard rubber runner and one foot thrust halfway across
the aisle for passing morons to break their necks on. Waldo
Bunny had said very little and that little bit didn't make much
sense. Called him Junior and apologized for the fact that Junior's mom hadn't been able to drive west as planned. It was
too long a story to go into, but Junior's mom Penny'd been in
the hospital for a while. She was ok now, home recuperating
and catching up on all those plot threads that unravel when
you're out of touch and his dad was still overseas, way out
on the Bakhmenev Peninsula, working on that huge, endlessly
looping interactive virtual reality park they've got out there
that Junior must'v seen on the news cause of all the billions
they've wasted on it. They can fiddle all they want, but for his
money it's the adjustment to the human brain that's always
lagging behind technology. . . .

So they had to send *him* to fetch Junior. And he fucked up,
as usual. Had to ditch the van in a hay field at the Bungalow
Ranch way out in the Snake River Valley, near Rigby, Idaho.
Another long story. To his way of thinking it'd all worked
out for the best, but he doubted if Junior's *mom* was gonna
think so.

That made him laugh at himself and go on babbling a while
longer. Then they ate from a picnic hamper Waldo Bunny had
brought along: enormous, spicy sandwiches and sweet drinks

so thick it was hard to suck them up. They settled into their seats and Waldo Bunny fell asleep at once, like someone who's been on the road for days, the double dromedary hump of his Adam's apple sliding up and down in his neck like a mechanical shuttle, eyelids flinching wildly from the terrible pictures his body's casting up against the narrow screen of the skull.

Junior leans his head against the window and wonders how he came to be called "Junior." Now things are one way, then they're another, and you always miss the little gate they passed through. Now your name is Junior cause someone says so. Now you're in one place, then you're in another. Without remembering if you've done this before, you know that when it's dark and the aisle lights are dimmed, ugly little towns will split open like black rocks that have nothing inside but one bluish path splashed with red. Long before there was the possibility of speeding up a loop of images to keep the eye from getting bored, there was the possibility of speeding through the world. An insatiable appetite for the next emptied image: where does it come from? The eye used to be content with sixteen images a second; now even sixty-four don't satisfy its urge to gobble and each image evacuates meaning from the last. He'd like to ask Waldo Bunny how looking out the train window is different from looking at TV, but Waldo Bunny's dreaming face has, if anything, grown stupider with sleep. He feels closer to the screaming thrust of particle jets forced into a straight line around every curve than he does to that face, dumb as it is long. *"Wherever we are we're alone and whenever we're alone a planet is being born and unborn."* Drifts off staring at dark fields and darker trees that roll all the way up to the blind windows that hold them at a distance like binoculars without magnification.

He starts dreaming and forgetting the dream at the same time, as if the dream includes a corrosive virus that eats it up as it goes along.

In the dream he's a child who's no longer certain his family is his own. They *look* like the family he knows, but they're acting strange, as if they were making a guest appearance on someone else's program, the horrible jelly of each overly-defined personality leaking out into the thin atmosphere through its porous boundary.

Someone tells him that his new dad is the murderer whose big, bearded head was just on TV. The body of the child they found on the mountain slope in the abandoned logging camp was buried there by his dad — and now he's hiding in the dark back bedroom and making animal noises. "How can my dad be a *murderer*," he says. "My dad is an *idiot!*" He just has time to turn on the light when his dad's teeth are at his throat. Knows he can't win. His dad's hatred is stronger and so are his hands. One of them is snarling and the other's yowling like an animal when its flesh is the first to get bitten. Pain always comes as a surprise and braids the body in a sickening way with the latent reality of reality.

Starts to explain to someone that there's a strange aroma when the terror in flesh acquires the force of murder — for the victim and for the murderer — and someone else asks if it's anything like the smell you get, which isn't exactly the smell of fresh laundry, when you fall from a small height and bang your forehead on the sidewalk — a smell that resembles the shock to the senses you get when your series is canceled and you step outside the building into cold bright air under a sky the color of mashed potatoes, wondering how you're going to spend your winter and who exactly you're supposed to be.

He wakes up with his forehead against the heated window's magnetic field, a scribbled manuscript of dust dispersed against it that would take a lifetime (between 21 and seventy-eight-point-ninety-six years) to decipher, mouth drooling into his dirty shirtsleeve. Waldo Bunny is across the aisle playing cards, drinking white wine and eating pretzels with a short woman with a grieving bulldog's face and featherduster hairdo.

"This is the way it works," Waldo is saying. "We have no more control over our own visibility than we do over our *in*visibility (or is it the other way around?). Therefore we have no control over our own existence. To exist and to be visible are now one and the same thing. Think about it clearly. Where are we when we're alone? Where are we really when we're not visible? And our visibility and invisibility are decided by someone else. One day you're canceled and you're not visible. And then suddenly you're supposed to exist again. And sometimes you're just not ready!"

"Complaining is the idiot's freedom, Mr. Bunny," the old woman says, taking a difficult, sidelong bite out of a thick, over-baked beer pretzel and dealing a hand of cards. "And listening to someone else's complaining is like going down to the edge of any dirty street in the world and chewing on the world's filthy paper that's always floating there. And chewing on the world's filthy paper is what makes us stupid."

"A lot of people must be chewing on filthy paper then. . . ."

For a second Waldo Bunny seems handsome and intelligent and Junior wonders who he really is. But as soon as it falls silent the face eases back into its former hangdog uncertainty — seems aware of the elongated ugliness of its look and starts talking again for no other reason than to prove it can.

"Last time I visited my mom down in Orlando," he says, "she had a dog that's supposed to look like my dad, only I don't remember my dad at all — so the only thing I know about my dad right now is that he looked like this dog my mom's got."

·

Before they go to sleep Waldo warns Junior to be on his guard. Junior's Gramma was supposed to join them on the train and this woman's claiming to be her, but he's afraid she's an impostor. She knows certain facts about Junior, but some of her facts are off. Something long and sharp is shining in the darkness at the bottom of her flight bag. It might just be a set of knitting needles, but it might be something else.

5

JUNIOR'S got his face flattened up against the glass, eyes shaded. Can just make out rows of mashed-down RVs by a lake. In the distance, the red and blue lights of a tavern broadcasting to outer space like the giant screen TV that's always on in the interior distance of someone else's front parlor, living its life indifferent to the human head that's watching it or not. Extra darkness gathers around the lights of the tavern and inside there's an unused dance floor, shiny and aromatic. Groups of friends are eating and drinking with the usual combustible mix of happiness and unhappiness. Windows are open and the ones whose bodies have slipped out of their protective amnesia sense the river of air that feels unearthly.

Junior is bent over a table, trying to write on a crumpled sheet of paper that can't be smoothed flat. He's covering one red ear, unable to block out the irritating noise of the merriment around him — and his clotted ballpoint keeps sticking in the irregular grain of the table.

"'What exists is absolute,'" he writes slowly and pronounces each word in his mind, as if it has nothing to do with the word before it or the word after it. "'Whatever has been brought into existence — no matter how synthetic or unwanted — joins the pre-existing reality of Nature on an absolutely equal footing. And the duplicated thing no less real than the original. The real world is full and total. We lie up against it and in some way feel its totality against our skin, even while something inward sinks away from it. Something inward is always sinking away. And our own particular velocity of sinking away from the fullness of the world is what we call the self.'"

These last words strike Junior and disturb him. He repeats them to himself, looking out toward the train that's passing slowly in an arc that doubles around on itself in the distance. And as he's murmuring to himself "our own particular velocity of sinking. . ." and feeling in his body what it means to sink down below everything you know as reality, he wakes up and finds the lights turned off with the exception of two or three individual high intensity reading lights. Here and there an exhausted face, a lifeless arm, a patch of lightweight blanket can't quite absorb the wobbly blue-green image cast there by the seat-back television monitors, the way the still water of a motel swimming pool sometimes feels the reflection a flowering tree has dropped down into it without enough weight to reach bottom and doesn't know what to do with it. Waldo Bunny's coiled up so tight Junior can't see his head. His black boots, black jeans and dark jacket turn the blue-red light of the television an oily purple. On the small screen a woman's face is barely visible through a blizzard of colored particles. Lips are moving, but the words are hard to make out through the boiling crackle of galactic broadcasting. Takes a minute to adjust the simplified controls.

"The world, clear and open on every side, is dense enough to press in on the sinking blob and give it shape.

"Another way: the world, no matter how stuffed with garbage, always appears clear and open to the crowded self.

"The pressure on the sensitive boundary of the blob is the push of an invisible river the hemmed-in self experiences in a melancholy way as time. Stationary movement of the body through what medium even while sitting propped up against pillows, legs stretched out, reading or writing. Body — even while sitting, getting nowhere but older — moves like wind passed from one tree to the other around the edge of a lake. And with the absence of pressure? The self leaks out into space, dizzy as someone stumbling out of a movie theater into the bright distance of an afternoon. We've grown comfortable at the weird intersection of abstraction and intimacy: what

once was farthest away and most alien is now our childhood play-mate. It isn't only looking that brings distance as close as the shake we've just sucked up through two thick straws. . . ."

Junior's face is close to the recessed television panel. The woman's face is beautiful, the voice as familiar as the lullaby sung to you every night by the one who stroked your hair, if not at home, then in a hospital by a kindly nurse. Face and voice are so familiar, so moving, it seems to him that someone he's loved and lost must be kneeling on the seat behind the clouded panel of glass, face close to his. Stands up to peer over the top of the seat, bumps into the long tip of one of Waldo Bunny's boots and wakes him up. Head pops up, hand goes inside his jacket for a weapon. Eyes seem to be suffering from the stroke of reverse genius that comes from wasting life's one brilliant idea on the wrong thing. Sees that everything's quiet and coils up again while Junior sinks down and stares miserably at the fresh image on the screen, where the molecules of his sister have become mixed up with the pixels of a young actress magnetically attractive season after season, from childhood to alluring near-womanhood, looking at you with sympathy beyond her years. Along your darkest curve, as if she were searching for you as well.

.

Hours later he wakes up again. The seat next to him is empty and he has a good view of his so-called Gramma. She's rummaging through her deep flight bag, making loud noises. Rummaging and rummaging through a crisp and crinkly plastic bag and, inside the crinkly plastic bag, other crisp and crinkly plastic bags. Hand goes in, paws around, comes out empty, goes back in, paws and paws and paws, pushes stuff around, pulls stuff out, looks at stuff with real curiosity as if it's someone else's, paws it, turns it over, unwraps and rewraps it, stuffs it back in, paws again for something else, makes a big show of packing it all up again before she waddles noisily down the aisle toward the exit door, bumping the heads and jostling the dangling legs of sleepers on either side.

As soon as she's gone he falls asleep. He's in a wheel chair, being wheeled quickly down the slick floor of a hospital corridor. Corridor shines darkly in front of him and he assumes that the figure invisible behind him is the kindly nurse with the round face and silky skin, the one who's always treated him like her grandson.

Figure behind him gives the wheels a hard forward spin.

Glides forward like a canoe moving in even thrusts across a dark lake.

What lake is this — and in what country? Head back, reclining in the canoe as if someone else were paddling, a helpless passenger with the naked length of his throat exposed, he sees that the sky is nothing but a reflection of the lake below him, except with the faintly glowing possibility of little cellophane-wrapped images blowing across it like candy wrappers across a school yard.

Hand goes to his throat, where he feels a small but painful injury. Now they're racing desperately toward the operating room, where a tube will be inserted through the tiny flap.

·

The false grandmother and all her things are gone and Waldo Bunny is returning from the windy space between two cars. He's combing out his disheveled hair, his cheeks are flushed and he's drying his hands on his jeans.

Drops down into the seat next to Junior and tells him that he's going to tell him a story, even though he always gets things mixed up and has to replay them again to get them straight.

"I don't think you were called 'Junior' when they abandoned you at the age of twelve. Your mom had been ill. She'd been in the hospital somewhere in Lee County, I think, for months and months, where the guy in the bed next to her looked an awful lot like Johnny Carson. *Why* they were in Lee County I don't know. I never knew that part of the story. But it didn't work out. Your mom and dad went into some sort of *oblivion*. They had hard times and your mom became ill.

"Every person who's had hard times assumes he knows the

story of every other person's hard times and anyone who hasn't had hard times doesn't have a clue about anything. Does that mean that every person's story is unknowable? Each person knows only his/her own story and no one else can (wants to?) understand it. The story that gets told is the story that's possible to tell. Every story is nothing but an account of what can be told, not what occurred. We can only tell what can be told and we can only know what we already know and that's why the world is such a dumb place. Everyone's got their life reduced to a story they know how to tell and everyone's always telling their own little story to someone trying to tell their own little story and if you listen sometimes you can't fall asleep because of all the little wheels that are flying into each other and gnashing their gears.

"We only know our own little plot summary and, as time goes by, we don't even know that.

"If I were you what I'd be thinking about is this: 'Why did my parents abandon me?' Was it because they never should have had you in the first place? Everyone's life has a certain consistency to it, no matter what kind of mess it looks like. It has a *shape* — you can feel when something doesn't fit in — and when you came along you may have been one of those things that didn't fit. The family may already have had its program going and you might have been this little alien character, this *intruder*, and no amount of fiddling could make it right. Or it sometimes happens that when we arrive we can tell that we don't belong. Can feel that we've arrived in a unit that's already complete and wonder what we're doing there and why we were sent."

After a while Junior and Waldo fall asleep, yet Junior has the feeling that somewhere, on another frequency or in a little cellophane-wrapped image broadcast long ago and drifting between the galaxies, his story is still being told.

•

Junior shoots the two stubborn bolts and stares at himself in the dirty bathroom mirror. His eyes have a look he recognizes and hates. Seems to him there was a time when he was beginning *not* to recognize himself and that he was happy then and that, in general, the times we're unrecognizable to ourselves are extremely pleasant and therefore unstable.

.

The light outside the city is gold, as it is everywhere. A golden light bristles in the brown rushes in the golden/brown waterways that bisect the layered plane of the past. Everywhere brown water washes a layered, purple rock and brown and purple surround the pale green twilight of the golf courses.

A level evening landscape of yellow lights and highways flows through the mind, which feels cleared by fire and ready for a fresh idea to get something going.

As the crust of detail is shorn away, laying bare the abstraction that makes it possible to live in the world, and the eye sees nothing but the external dome with its diagram of pathways between sites that are really functions, we succumb to the feeling of changing the world by speeding through it.

.

If we remember a lake and see it in sunlight — see others swimming, hear their voices, remember long and pleasant conversations on the shore — and then it becomes dark, is everything forgotten?

Dangle a foot in the water and lose it?

The meaning is clear, yet escapes him as always, flying away 625 times a second from the object it was attached to. ("Each object is a launcher that fires its own meaning as far away from itself as possible.")

He settles deeper into sleep and the dream begins to have its own dream that's fastened to the curve, bending and bending into view where he can see how it's pulling him along, like the marked date in next week's TV listings that makes the future happen.

6

ARTHUR! David! Daaa-viid! Ar-*thur*!"
Junior recognizes his mom's voice, always about to break
into a cackle. Mostly they've been calling him Junior, but
sometimes they forget. He opens his door a crack and puts his
ear into the opening to listen.

"There's a big pot of beef stew on the stove, honey. It's all
cooked. You might want to heat it up just a teentsy little bit."

"Stew?" his dad says, like it's something he's never heard of.

A strong smell of meat gravy and scorched onions, the smell
of life on earth, poisons the atmosphere all the way from the
kitchen to Junior's distant room and far enough out into the
universe through leaky windows for a brown-and-white mutt
across the way to lift its pinkish snout as if about to sneeze.

"I don't understand why have to go out."

"Jesus, hon, I *told* you about Waldo. Waldo's in the hospital
again. Big idiot nearly got himself *killed* yesterday! Van went
down the embankment all the way out where Rosing climbs the
overpass across Karolus. I think they did that new laser sewing
thing, honey, a miracle of modern medicine, and they sewed
his whole head back on."

"You're going to the hospital at this hour?"

"No, of course not. I'm going over to Junie's because I've
got to make plans with Ethel an' Freddy and everyone about
how to help Waldo. I'll be back real soon, hon."

"But," his dad's pouting and rubbing his eyes, "if you're not
here to heat it up for me, I'll have to wait to eat. Or else I'll have
to skip my shower."

29

"Whyever would you have to do that, hon?"

"Cause I wouldn't be able to heat the stew up till I get out. But I'm too hungry to wait to heat up the stew!"

"There's nothing for you to do, Arthur, but turn on the fucking flame."

"What about Junior?"

"He's going with me. If he ever gets ready! *Junior?* Get a move on!"

"*Junior!* J'hear your mother? Get going!"

That's Junior's cue to close his door. The room's a flimsy add-on to the west wall of the house, an enclosure of what used to be the wraparound section of the big porch that dates from the era when houses still occasionally brought on waves of nostalgia for older waves of nostalgia. There are two tall windows and already his favorite thing is to look out past the edge of the neighbor's low house toward the swirl of events at the near-distant point where one street intersects another. It's as if we can make what happens outside, because it has nothing to do with us, another self that can save us from the one we know.

"Put on your jacket and let's *go!*"

Junior wails back that he can't find his *cap.*

Arthur and Penny exchange glances: they've just discovered that what they say is true: distance, if it's great enough, is just the same as time skidding backward. The wailing voice doesn't sound like Junior *now*, but like the miserable little Junior they hadn't seen for five years or more, and who, to tell the truth, was a lot uglier than this one. *That* Junior was already beginning to look horribly like Edward G. Robinson, while this one looks touchingly like Tommy Rettig just before Tommy Rettig stopped looking like Tommy Rettig.

"You don't need a cap, Junior! *Fuck* your cap! I'm leaving with you or without you!"

There's no way for Junior to know that his mom's winking at his dad, pretending to be pretending to be angrier than she is, and there's no way for Junior's mom to know that he isn't looking for his cap at all. He's gazing diagonally across the street at a little boy in a blue parka who's just run screaming out of a house built in the same retrospective style as the one where his mom and dad are living. He stops and leans against a bound-and-tethered sapling to pull his shoe on. Walks down the street, looks this way and that as if trying to figure out where to go. Wanders to the corner and sits down on a low step in the sun's low rays, shaking his head with an idiotic regularity that shows that he's done a lightning scan of the street's possible entrances and escape routes and given up. The flickering coal of genius is always dying down into a moronic dullness. After a few minutes two girls come by with a big dog and he runs after them. Junior tries to follow them all the way across the bright gap of the intersection to see exactly where they slip off to, but the dark edge of the low house to the west clips them off just the way a scissor sends a useless margin of paper fluttering under the table.

Junior ambles sluggishly toward the brightness coming from the doorless kitchen doorway. Mom and dad are near the refrigerator, lovey-dovey, his thick arm around her scrawny waist, his hand spread out across her belly.

"If you aren't good — *are you listening to me?* — if you give your mother *any trouble at all*, you won't get that rocket gun! Not only will you *not* get the rocket gun, but you *will* get whacked! Understand?"

Junior catches the tiny movement of the muscled forearm giving the pinched waist a squeeze. Knows that he knows the meaning of that squeeze, but can't come up with it. Knows also that his father's eyes fixed on his are waiting for a "yes, Daddy" or an "I'll be good, Daddy, I promise," but his brain's too busy cackling at the pair of them to consider it.

"Okeydoke then," his mom says, "we'll be back in a jiffy, hon."

"Wait."

"Yep."

"Before you go, let me get one thing straight."

"Uh-huh."

31

"What's the menu?"

"The menu?"

"There's this stew that I've got to heat up."

"Correct."

"But what else is there?"

"Well, that's why I made a stew, honey, cause your vegetables and everything you need to have a complete, satisfying and nutritionally balanced meal are right there in that very same pot."

"That's it then? There's nothing else I need to know?"

"I think we've got a grapefruit, but you'll have to check that out in the crisper bin down at the left-hand bottom of the refrigerator, right next to the cold meat and cheese bin. *And*," she says, brightening in a way that makes her loose jaw and wild eyes snap into such a tight focus that she looks like she's come down from the high that comes from sniffing too much pine-scented cleanser, "even though there's *potato* in the stew, you could have some bread'n'butter! Bread'n'butter'n'stew sounds like a yummy combination to me!"

Junior's dad's hands have migrated to his pockets, chin in neck.

"Bread and butter."

"Mmm. Or you'c'n forget the butter'n dunk the bread right into gravy!"

"No crackers? You *know* I always put *crackers* in my stew."

"Gee, sweetie, I forgot."

"No crackers then?"

"Nope, no crackers. OK? Okey-dokey, we're all set then."

Junior follows his mom out into the total pitchblackness of the street.

7

As they're wandering the corridors, searching for Waldo Bunny's cubicle, Junior is overcome with the melancholy conviction that he himself spent time in this hospital as a child. If not in this hospital, then one just like it. Not one smelling of a cleanliness so absolute it brings to mind the illness it's meant to camouflage, assaulting everything that can't live up to its severity, but one where the pale green distance the soul has to travel from bed to window is exactly the same distance the body has to travel to recover.

Memory as powerful as it is uncertain.

No way to know if he ever actually had a fatal childhood illness from which he miraculously recovered. No way to know if it happened. No way, in fact, to know if anything's *ever* really happened — particularly if someone has a reason to want you to believe that it did. No way to know until someone devises an accurate test for the truth of memory. A way to distinguish, for example, actual memory from the real residue of what we haven't lived yet now is ours.

If the beautiful grandmother eating her sandwich in Selenium Center reminded him of a kindly, round-faced nurse wheeling him down a hospital corridor, does that prove that he was once wheeled down a hospital corridor by a round-faced and grandmotherly nurse?

Remembers being taken to a hospital, abandoned there, left for dead. Family leaves you there and disappears. Mother, father, little sister Flora, even your beloved older sister Valeria: no one remains by your side. Alone in a strange crib isolated by four glass walls rising up toward the pale green ceiling. In place of a loving hand stroking your head, the persistent smell of cooked beets, steamed potato and meat stewed for days with tinned string beans — smells so awful they penetrate the future as exterior memories, lying in wait for us to pass through them again.

What makes another mouth water gives you a dizzy headache when a serving dome is lifted and fragrant food-steam rises off cooked beets, boiled potato, dark and tender stew meat.

Wandering the hospital corridors with his mom reminds Junior of wandering and feeling dizzy on a railroad platform, one stuffed blue duffel, no more. A red baseball cap and a shiny blue jacket. Smiling with embarrassing friendliness at disembarking strangers, as if at departing loved ones.

Pretty young woman who shared your seat with you doesn't remember you at all, having slept 2058 miles curled up and headless as if murdered and dumped on the train to be shipped far from where it happened.

A middle-aged man you shared three or four sympathetic sentences with, drinking and eating in the club car, where two dozen people always fall together and tell their deepest, inmost lie.

The biggest liar, as always, an unhappy young man, head shaved close as a two-by-four, with eyes you take care not to look into, gathered up tearfully by mom & dad on the platform and whisked away home.

And another young man, a total mess, hair that can't be fixed by combing or even by heavy farm machinery, brain's drip pan like standing water below the curb where everything windblown ends its day, is kissed in the deepest possible human embrace by a young woman, body unnaturally pink and mushy in glowing green track shorts, standing on tippy-toe.

At the same time he's having what may or may not be memories, he's staring at his mom's bony back and feeling that the only thing that's keeping him from hating her for abandoning him is that he doesn't remember her at all.

Junior can tell that his mom's up to something. They've been wandering around the hospital for an hour or more, haven't found Waldo Bunny and aren't going to. She's ambling along, crabbing about a hospital system so fucked up it can't even locate a guy who's just had his *head* bolted back on, but she's acting. But, if she never expected to find Waldo Bunny, then why are they here?

Turn a corner and run into a red-haired girl with a face that's been crying on so many shoulders it's beginning to break down the way a nylon sponge breaks down after it's been in the sink too long.

"Oh god, Mrs. Anderson! Isn't it awful?"

His mom says that this is Tammy, their paper girl, a *wonderful* paper girl, a wonderful girl *in general*, an' Tammy's mom's the one who was pushed off the platform this afternoon and got her head sliced off by the express from Zworykin.

"Why is it that whenever any two people meet, one of them's always got a horrible story to tell?"

"Doesn't it seem like everyone you know is part of the *same* horrible story, Mrs. Anderson?"

"Who was it who said: 'The only thing that gives us relief is when things get even more horrible than they were before. Sooner or later everyone puts in an appearance in everyone else's nightmare.'"

"Well, I'm still a little too young to know about *that*, Mrs. Anderson," Tammy laughs.

Junior stares disgustedly through two layers of dirty window glass at a city he's only pretending to believe is there. While he's staring toward the dark smudges that could be the outlines of anything, he's listening to the buzzing of a fly caught between the two layers of glass. The inner one when raised functions as a trap, the fly escaping into the narrow slot between partially raised lower sash and permanently fastened upper, at first zzz-ing with excitement and then with a harsher buzz of desperation. The fly knows it's done something stupid. That's the meaning of its buzzing. It's the fly talking to itself about its own stupidity. Knows it's done something not only stupid but irreversible. "To know that your own stupid actions are responsible for your torment is the most hellish instant on earth." He feels a frightening kinship with the fly, yet has no impulse to set it free.

How come, Tammy asks, Mrs. Anderson happens to be here in the hospital at exactly the same second they're bringing in her mother's headless corpse?

They're here for the same exact reason!, his mom says. Her friend Waldo had his van forced off the Rosing/Karolus overpass. Plunged seventy-eight-point-ninety-six feet straight down into a ravine, had his head severed from his neck and only lived to tell the tale because one of those new emergency microsurgery vans happened to be passing on the lower roadway. Now the big dummy's disappeared from the hospital!

Tammy seems excited that all of them are here for newsworthy events and wants to go up to the lounge where they can watch TV together and relive their tragedies as many times as they want to, but Junior's mom is in a hurry to go out and search for Waldo.

8

TRAILS behind the woman who calls herself his mom and who keeps turning and barking at him as if he were a reluctant child, yowling and dragging its feet. She seems to be following a zigzag path both random and predetermined through streets so dark the light in a distant shop-front has exactly the same amplitude and luminosity as a faint star far overhead: casts no light outward, but only breathes in and breathes out an irregular sparkle for eye and soul to travel toward.

Mom seems to have some business inside the little TV repair shop and instructs Junior to wait outside, where he passes the time staring at the large-screen demonstration TV in the window, trying to make out the face of the beautiful woman made doubly remote and ghostly by the dirty sheet of window glass.

"I sometimes think about the things whose existence depends entirely on the nonexistence of something else," he hears her say clearly through a little speaker mounted on the wall. "What we experience as longing is the soul's geiger counter for the nonexistent."

Junior would like to stop and ponder her meaning but one idea quickly replaces another and evaporates into the dark atmosphere.

"How many are born and arrive at the table uninvited and starving? The starved and uninvited guest who didn't ask to be here but here he/she is anyway, with nowhere to go, longing for the thing that exists only as an object of longing. The starving soul is afflicted all its life with a craving for disappointment. The circuitry of disappointment is etched into desire for

37

the real but not-existent. Disappointment and hatred now more than ever the negative euphoria of the uninvited, starving guest at the table.

"One morning I woke up and knew that this was frozen death. I looked out my window instead of other windows with their blinds and curtains — other faces peeping out or staring openly toward the sunny little park with its image of strolling figures — and saw crows on the grass. . . .

"Now I'm somewhere where the barking of crows reminds me that there's a little hook in everything. The creature ripping a furry little creature apart with its little hook is at the same time listening apprehensively for the telltale rustle of a creature with a stronger hook.

"Two crows calling from a naked branch somewhere in the sunlit shadows at the visible perimeter of the dense evergreen forest frighten smaller creatures feeding in the meadow, but the crows are also uneasy, with one eye on whatever it is that's making glistening sunlight blink in the nearby woods.

"The enormity of the forest only makes itself known when the wind springs up. And sometimes it's hot and sunny, a shining rod that stirs insects up out of the quiet plane of superficial beauty.

"I'm somewhere far above the snowline. Snow begins early here, there are storms blowing around the peaks and the signals are weak coming in and going out.

"They've buried me up here in this so-called 'ski resort' and I have a feeling they're going to thaw me out for one more spasm of visibility. Or am I visible anyway in my twinkling orbit. . . ?"

A stinging slap to the back of the head gets his attention. Now she's dragging him forward again and cursing the fact that they sent her a son who's stupid enough to listen to that horrible ghost still yakking after all these years — as if we were on a distant asteroid in a distant galaxy and the satellite relay found us even though we traveled all that distance just to get out of reach of her drivel.

Junior's thinking that they always think a slap can stop you. If not one, then a thousand. And a thousand punches and lobster pinches too. But all the pinching and slapping can't stop you when something is pulling you, whether it exists or not.

9

WHEN Penny's gone Arthur showers then settles down in front of the TV with a deep bowl of stew, a stack of bread, a tub of butter and a bottle of dark ale crowded on the surface of his great-grandfather's childhood sea green rolling TV snack cart with colorful *Gunsmoke*, *Lucy & Desi*, *Ozzie & Harriet*, *Flintstones* and *Captain Video* decals. Knowing that Penny's out in the world while's he's alone, alive for others while he's invisible, makes the house feel like a capsule orbiting and isolated in space — and inside the isolated space capsule himself, small and shriveled as the last raisin stuck to the bottom of a little two ounce raisin box that's just been emptied into the mouth of an ailing child standing on the sidewalk and waiting to be driven to a hospital where he'll spend years isolated in a pod with food tray and television set.

Even Junior's not there to make him act like himself.

The reason you hardly ever see a human figure alone on TV (the isolated figure is immediately joined by another, talking loudly, making exaggerated gestures) is that without someone to cue you in to who you are you could be anyone. Without other personalities pressing in on the sensitive boundary of the blob, the blob remains a blob and not a personality. Each acquires definition from the other, but the definition is unstable and is in need of perpetual renewal. The self has to be invented over and over and the invisible goo of existence has to be kept flowing, otherwise it stiffens up prematurely into the horrible grimaces that usually keep themselves in check until old age.

He travels quickly through hundreds of channels and stops

when he comes across a scene from one of his favorite films, *The Invention of Time*, the one where the hero goes nuts when he discovers that time isn't a dimension. The movie's crackpot theory is that we ourselves are responsible for time: time reintroduced into the universe with every human birth. "THE HUMAN GAZE OUT OF ITS OWN BODY. . . ."

He can't remember how the rest of it goes and he's waiting in a rapture of anticipation for the dizziness that overtakes him every time the film gets into gear and heightens its pitch of senselessness when the door chimes sound.

He rushes to the door, hoping it's Penny, but it's only Penny's brainless friend Ethel with her gigantic Newfoundland, only a few weeks ago a yipping pup.

Dog's been running a fever for *days*, she says, she's gotta take it in for *shots*.

"I can't take it no maw, Arthur! No, I mean it, don't laugh! I'm *seeryus*! I said to Freddy, you gotta get me *outa* heah!"

Ethel's backed Arthur all the way out of the shabby entry hall into the big kitchen.

"You don't know what it's *like*! Junie's on my back twenny-faw-owas-a-*day*! I'm seeryus! Between her'n Freddy an even *Penny* sometimes, I can't *take* it! I mean it! I hate when people *criticize* me all'a'time! Don't you? I said to Freddy, next time you call me stupid I'm gonna get on a bus an get off the first time I see a lighted doorway an I'm gonna crawl *into* that lighted doorway an nobody'll eva see me again!"

"Do you ever think to yourself, Ethel, 'every little thing that happens to me, the eentsiest, teentsiest little thing, is more important than the worst thing that can happen to someone else'?"

Does he think it's a teentsy problem when you have to fuck someone to get to sleep? It's horrible to be built that way. No matter what she takes, it only makes things worse. She's on a million things and the tension is building right now to fuck somebody before bedtime.

They've moved far inside the kitchen, over by the sink, where water's plunking drop by drop into a full pot of water balanced on a stack of dirty stew dishes. The dog's hunting ravenously back and forth under the red formica table and chrome chair legs for savory little mummies of food, dragging its heavy leash.

Arthur has to admit to himself that Ethel has looks. Young as she is, this is Ethel's prime. The clock is ticking and before long it will go to mush. The kind of flesh that has the shelf-life of a banana. Overheated, her soft skin always has a little sweat to it, unlike Penny who wears her dry flesh close to the bone, whose jaw waggles like something's broken and who has a wild look in her eyes like a knocked-out fighter still taking weird steps this way and that way though the brain's already aligned with the horizontal about to arrive with a comforting smack.

"Maybe it's the fuckn *dog* that's makin me anxious, Arthur. Climbs into bed when I'm *sleeping!*"

Arthur doesn't say anything, but Ethel says, "Wait! I wake up an his head's on my thigh! "

"Well, Ethel, that's certainly no good."

"You're not kidn it's no good. Listen! He likes to grab holda my tits! Really! He does! He's always goin t'get hold'v'a *tit*, Arthur! Omna kick his *ass*, he does that any maw!"

Sometimes a dog gnawing on a bone is enough to make you drool. Ethel's body and Arthur's body are less than a foot apart, within range for the second self to come out and take a sniff. Ethel can see that Arthur is looking down into her scoop neck as if his animal's already drooling watching *her* body's little animal-on-a-chain gnawing on its bone. She knows that her breast is already in his mouth and that he's licking and sucking the nipple to make the breast bigger and more mouth-filling. She wonders if that means that he knows what she knows (and what Freddy doesn't ever seem to know): that the self has a self and that second self's self can emit a smell and send out other signals that let the second and third selves of others know that it's there and that it's aroused. Can even make the first or second self desire its own body and go sniffing after the self's self that's just waking up with a drowsy aroma. Fucking massages all the self's selves to a deep degree, but only when it's carried to its lengthy and difficult conclusion. That's why she can never curl up and go back to sleep after fucking Freddy. One of her selves is always still throbbing and on the prowl. . . .

Arthur is surprised by the thrill he gets when Ethel slips across the tiny infinity between touching and not touching and slides her arms around his neck. He's in bed with Ethel before he has time to imagine what it would be like. It's been so long since he's been with anyone but Penny, it's a shock to feel an unfamiliar body. Its unfamiliarity restores the strange superreality of reality. The flesh of another: get beyond looking at it and touch it: feel afresh its sheer fleshiness: the electricity in it adds to its unreality as much as to its reality.

Saw her belly and surprisingly big breasts with nipples as round and red as little hand painted roses for only one dazzling instant as they flew toward the bed and out of their clothes as if slashed free of the sealed spacesuit of the visual.

Now he's got one hand on one big breast, the other on her belly, the fat urn of the hips pressed against him: the lost continent of the physical, real beyond question, our realest reality, unmistakably ours — stolen from us so that now we have to look for it in the neighboring infinity in order to find it in this one — feels restored to him completely at this instant.

Rubs up against him, opens just enough to give him a taste.

How strange flesh is! The smells, the twisting pretzel loops, the ecstasy, the flood of moisture always latent in the thing that walks around dry and babbling.

She's getting wetter and wetter and he opens his mouth to say, "Jesus, Ethel!", but instead lets out a strange cry.

Slipperiness of skin from throat to thigh.

Struggles to get a grip, but burrows in like a crab in mud. Buries his face in her shoulder and feels waves parting. Parting of waves leads him forward. Hands dig into flesh, pincer-like and convulsive. Convulsive biting of elbows, knees, chin and prick. No matter how hard he bites she doesn't shrink away. On the contrary. Deeper bites make what's parting part further. Smells something pungent and penetrating, a gravy that's been cooking on the stove for a lifetime, hears himself cry out horribly for the third time and springs free to wash up while Ethel lies face down, wet and shining as a creature that's just crawled up on the shore, out of its shell.

The spotted medicine cabinet mirror over the shallow basin hangs open at an angle that brings Ethel's near-distant image right in front of him, a little thing thick as a clothespin, heels-ass-head compressed and miniaturized and oddly luminous alongside his tired face. While he's soaping his prick, he carries on a conversation with her image inserted as a darkly glowing little picture-in-picture running independently in a corner of the larger image before him, and he tries to express the feeling that you're either completely in it or you're completely out of it. When you're in it, it fills space the way green arcs of shadow sweep back and forth between the curved ends of a full bathtub. And when you're out, what you crash into — what kills you — is no more solid than the vacuum you drop into just after eating a big dinner in front of the TV.

"Let me ask you something, Ethel," he calls out, toweling off.

She turns her face over her shoulder and squints toward the over-bright light of the bathroom.

"Do you ever have the feeling you're being watched?"

"Oh, I was in a shitty motel once where they had these phony plastic ceiling panels. . . ."

Arthur re-enters the room and in seconds they're back in bed and he says that that isn't what he meant. And maybe it isn't a feeling of being watched, exactly. It's more like the sensation the hero has in *The Invention of Time*: that we're all given life by the attention others pay to us. Not a pinpoint of space remains on Earth that isn't a dazzling pixel for someone. The agitation of distant heads and the brilliance of the street on a sunny day now seem to have something to do with one another. Keep your eye on the late night News because sooner or later someone you know is going to stumble into the horrible spotlight.

Ethel's dog wanders over with the slow, bear-like restlessness big dogs have, a brand of unhappiness that makes it impossible for them to settle down peacefully on their tattered squares of oriental carpet. Rests its heavy head on the crumpled sheet and methodically starts lapping at Ethel's shiny skin. Ethel makes a feeble attempt to push the dog's hot muzzle away. He leaves off and wanders back into the kitchen and in a second Arthur hears him thump down onto the linoleum with a groan of deepest boredom. Then he and Ethel dig into each other with a frenzy, until their feet crack against the flimsy headboard like the hooves of an animal having a nightmare in its narrow pen.

10

THE smell of cooking builds up, gets thick and immediately disperses to the far corners of the world when Arthur dishes out two dark lakes of stew for Ethel and himself and some gravy and spongy vegetables in a yellow plastic bowl on the floor for the dog.

"Did I ever tell you the first thing Freddy noticed about me was my ass? Before he ever talked to me, he told the whole world that he liked my ass. 'Ethel has one sweet ass. I'd love to stick my wood in it.'"

"His 'wood' in it? I never heard that expression before."

"Then you must live in the same cave as Freddy. Waldo said to Freddy, 'you must live in a cave 'cause they stopped using that expression about 2500 BC when they started domesticating yaks in Tibet. "I have a woody." "Stick my wood in it," etc., etc.' Waldo said that once-upon-a-time they used wooden golf clubs and it had to have something to do with that. . . .'"

"But when did Waldo say all this, Ethel?"

"It hadda be last night or the night befaw."

"Well, it couldn't have been last night, Ethel, because Waldo was killed yesterday. Killed yesterday, alive today. That's why Penny went out: to visit the corpse they've got walking around down at the medical center."

He starts punching the tiny keys on his cheap video pager to see if he can find out where Penny is, but the screen remains a brackish green, as usual.

Ethel says that someone is in the hall, watching and listening, and Arthur goes out to look.

Across the threadbare square of blue hall carpet, through the front door and out onto the porch in white shorts and white athletic socks.

All he hears is the distant surf of moronic laughter, but he catches a rippling flash of far-off movement in the dark that's like the little curl of moonlight under a breaking wave and waits, staring blindly, while space develops the image of a boy in a glossy blue jacket and red baseball cap running across the intersection.

.

Later, when Ethel's gone, Arthur falls asleep in his deepest chair and finds himself embedded in a denser or thinner medium where others are always living in the thick and fertile inside of our thin and vacant outside or in the radiant and depthless outside of our thick and cluttered inside.

In this thicker or thinner medium he's someone else, young and thoughtful, sitting at a small, cluttered desk, trying to get his ideas about the confusing doubleness or quadrupleness of existence down on paper. And then he's unhappily awake in his deep chair again, almost completely merged with the self he knows, one that likes to sulk in its comfortable chair and chew over the bitter tobacco of life's disappointing unfairness, interrupted in its merging by another showing of *The Invention of Time*, not one second further along than he'd left it.

11

TAMMY the paper girl's mom has a new head and Tammy feels a little queasy about sitting next to her on the lookalike *Tonight Show* loveseat, watching TV and having a snack as if it were an ordinary night at home. This woman doesn't even *look* like her mom and has entirely different taste. Her old mom used to call everything stupid and kept whizzing through the channels, shaking her head. This mom likes everything, keeps talking back to the set and laughs so hard at every retarded punchline that she has to keep a good grip on her new head on its bandaged stem.

Tammy takes hold of the remote, but can't find an exit from all the things that make her miserable and her new mom happy, till she comes across the dark image on an obscure channel of a street that looks like a real street where nothing is happening in real time. Two remote figures, one a tall, lean woman wobbling on unstable shoes, jaw going non-stop like someone drunk and cursing, the other a boy with curly hair, running ahead or trailing behind like a dog off its leash, cross the screen at an odd angle and disappear through a sparkling, starlike speck of distance that may be the door of a faraway house that's suddenly opened inward.

12

JUNIE'S place is an old dump out on a rotten pier on stilts.
The water sloshing under it fills the atmosphere with the awful stench of vegetable slime. There's plenty of time for Junior
to listen to the slimy water sloshing and to sniff the rotten night
air because it's taking his mom forever to locate the keyhole
with her key. The metal of the key keeps scraping unpleasantly
across the flaking wood of the door and round and across the
keyhole and the metal lock plate.

She stumbles in when the door's flung open, goes "Oh, Jesus!" and starts cackling.

"Waldo, is that you? You aren't the one who did that poor
kid's mom, are you, you stupid fuck?"

Even from the shabby entryway Junior can see how over-
bright the interior of the house is, an even more bright and
amplified light in the studio Junior's mom is stumbling toward
— the small, noisy audience of friends and neighbors still min-
gling, not quite settled in the folding chairs facing the makeshift
stage and tower of nine illuminated tic-tac-toe squares remark-
ably like the original.

Once Junior's mom takes her place in the center square the
broadcast can begin.

Waldo Bunny's head (in the square diagonally below his
mom's and to her left) is longer than Junior remembers it and
has a different haircut, but otherwise he looks ok. Waldo Bunny opens a newspaper to its full wingspan and begins reading
"'BACK FROM THE DEAD: THE MIRACLE GIRL'S EXCLU-
SIVE SAGA.' This is the story of the beautiful six-year-old girl

who supposedly disappeared from her family's backyard barbecue and who became a famous milkcarton girl and a famous
postoffice poster girl and then a famous cable news unsolved
murder mystery girl — and whose dad was arrested and re-
leased and whose mom went into hiding. . . . Someone claimed
that she'd actually gone up on one of those stupid private space
excursions that never came back, but there were no records to
prove that. Then years later they found some clothes that may
have been hers in the woods not four miles from home, back
of her uncle's farm, and there were bones that may or may not
have been human. But there's been no proof and no solution.
. . . Well, now she's apparently been found alive and working in a bookstore and helping out in the communal kitchen
in a sufi retreat not far from New Lebanon, New York. They
don't know for sure if it's her (have to do DNA tests, etc.
etc.), but she's telling a story that doesn't entirely contradict
the crazy one her dad told when he was arrested. Listen to
this! 'I don't remember washing out a pair of socks or having
my usual Cinnamon Frosted Pretzel Loops for breakfast. *I
don't remember my mother or father, I don't remember if I had
sisters or brothers*, but I do remember flying under the ceiling
of a very big bedroom that was really a hospital room and I
remember that three or four children were in there with me. I
remember a little boy named David, whose face was terribly
swollen. . . .'"

Now Junior's mom can't stop laughing, drawing attention to
the center square, where it belongs. Everyone knows this skid.
It's one of the things they tune in to see: laughter that bubbles
up uncontrollably and that makes others laugh with her without
knowing why. For her part she's buoyed by the wave of recognition coming back at her as if from afar (the familiar sound
of returning laughter is the affirmation of something that's
been repeated so often it needs to be repeated again) but she
has a sharp inkling that when the car skids the railing's already
broken and the picture's already been taken of the shattered
windshield and the screaming mouth. She can't stop laughing,

doesn't know why she's laughing and has no desire to stop laughing, yet feels absolutely separate from the laughing of the self's insane little toy self let loose while the sober first self is thinking guiltily that the little girl in Waldo's story could easily be the child she abandoned long ago by the side of a wooded road somewhere in the region of Selenium Grove or it could even have been in the so-called Silicon Valley.

"Wait!" Waldo says. "It goes on. 'I feel as if I've already lived my whole life, but not in order. I crossed it the way a basketball player dodges across the court trying to get to the basket. I stepped, I ran, I skipped, I took a fast step sideways and then I ran again, not in a straight line but in a half-circle, and then I jumped. I remember all that, but nothing in between.'"

Junie (in the square to Junior's mom's left and diagonally above her) thinks she's heard someone ask her the question she's been waiting for, struggles to remember the cute answer she's supposed to give and says instead that yesterday she knocked on Ethel's door to ask if Ethel needed anything in the market and Ethel yelled back, "'Wadya want!'

"'I'm going out, Ethel. Can I get you anything?'

"'Well, ahm in bed! Ahm in bed with Freddy! Ahm getn a good fuck from Freddy for a change! Get adda heah an come back layda! Come back layda, Junie!'

"'Fuck you!' I said."

Junior's mom feels the loss of life-giving waves bundled as particles and particles that act like waves of attention from visible and invisible audiences (what's beaming vitality into Junie is draining vitality from her) and picks up the color-coded blue telephone each panelist has in the lower right corner of his/her square and calls or pretends to call Junior's dad, no one can tell for sure.

"Hi, honey," she says. "*Really?* Your boss really said that? Gee, if you're the one who made that whole big system start up again, that kind'v makes you a *hero*, right? The whole nation owes you a round of applause, honey. I SAID THAT I'M PROUD TO BE MARRIED TO THE MAN WHO GAVE THE WHOLE COUNTRY

ONE MORE UNINTERRUPTED NIGHT OF BRAIN DEAD CRAP. Listen, I hate to change the topic, but I'm afraid we're gonna have to have those yummy fish balls again for dinner. And some curly fries. OK? Yup — the same yummy fish balls and fries we had last night. Cause there's not much grocery money left, hun, that's why. Huh? Of course I understand that you work hard. I'm sure it's no fun at all being shipped out to those ugly satellites every other week to keep that stupid thing running, but I'm not feeling all that great myself. Dr. Quatermaine wants to operate, but, in my opinion, it's safer to lose your head nowadays than it is to lose your spleen. Don't you agree, honey? It's almost as difficult as the decision I'm facing with this leukemia thing. Do I want the leukemia or not? When I'm home and frying your fish balls or picking your underwear up from wherever you've let it fall off your ass I really don't care if I have this thing or if I survive this thing. But when I'm away from you and the house and I remember that it really is possible for a human being to be happy and to accomplish something, I become frightened and remember that a little ambivalence about living is what kills you...."

She's out of breath and knows that no one's laughing, that next time she'll find herself in the bottom middle square next to Waldo Bunny, but can't shut up and says that the reason she's dying is that laboratory tests prove that Arthur's voice is one more thing that causes cancer to grow on the skin of rats. Voice poisons the body through the ears the way a virus climbs up the nose. Over the years the dripping of Arthur Riley's voice into her ear has poisoned her spleen. Every word he's ever said is false. Even more so now that he knows some of the right things to say. As life goes on, if we aren't *complete* cretins, we learn the right things to say. The language that was our own, that was natural to us, we find out is the *wrong* language and we figure out what the right language sounds like.

That's our job in life. To learn the right language that isn't our own.

That's why Arthur Riley, the good little monkey who thinks

he's the hero of whatever comedy he's plunked down in, is loved by his bosses.

The question of who loves Arthur Riley is an interesting one. He's loved by his bosses because he's the good monkey who's learned another language, but does he love himself? Seems to love himself, but what does that mean? What does it mean to love your self? What is this "self" the person supposedly loves? Consider the fact that Arthur Riley is only Arthur Riley while there's somebody awake and watching. But the times when no one's watching and Arthur Riley has *no good reason* to be Arthur Riley and he's just the blob that might *turn into* Arthur Riley if someone started watching? It's too horrible to think about! We're afraid to see that blob. Every image is just a blob forced into activity because someone happens to be watching. We're compelled to look and we live in fear of seeing too much.

She herself is no different: follows Arthur Riley with fascination and has her own favorite Arthur Riley episodes.

One of her favorite episodes is the one where Arthur Riley is writing a report for the lowest boss of all his bosses. He's got all his crappy papers spread out and he's laboring over them with a moron's huge concentration. She's over on the other side of the room, staring at him, taking notes and laughing. *Looks* like she's taking notes, but she's got her favorite fish-filleting knife and she's writing on her stomach with the point. Arthur's getting mad, because dummies like Arthur are *always* getting mad — they're stupid and always getting mad for the wrong reasons — but every once in a while they get lucky and a correct reason for being mad accidentally lines up with their condition.

Arthur Riley looks up, focuses, figures out that it's a knife — a knife, therefore *not* a pen, therefore *not* a drawing pad, therefore what's dripping is *blood* — does his famous triple-take. . . .

Now it seems to Penny that she has everyone laughing just the way she hoped, but can't laugh herself: the itch that can be scratched by everyone but you. While they're laughing she's thinking about the children she's abandoned across the States in the course of her life. "Abandoned" probably isn't the right word for what she was forced to do. Some of those "abandonments" are too horrible to think about, but that was her mission. The sense of having a mission in life is said to be the gift that gets us through, but doesn't everyone have a mission? And yet so many are unhappy. Certainly the mission of "abandoning" a child never made her happy. And after the ugly event, the distance you were made to put behind you — new city, new cast of characters, new time slot — never proved to be the foundation of happiness.

Now she tries to remember where she got the idea that "everyone has a mission". It used to be a popular slogan. The genius who thought it up lost his job long ago, but an idea is like a public space whose grooves and openings shape the human flow for centuries.

·

While his mom is talking, Junior is rubbing the flattened bulb of his nose as if memory is making it itchy and he's trying to wipe it out with the back of his hand. Remembers crying and screaming as an infant, nose running. Trying to fight free of his mom's painful grip while his dad made a laughingstock of himself up on stage, drawing a blank on the two-part question: a) name the longest running prime time series with continuous characters in the history of the medium and b) name the character from that series who later re-appeared in so-called real life as a movie actor with the same name but no physical resemblance. What Junior can't get clear (what's making him rub his nose till it aches?) is whether the fool standing on the studio stage in memory, red-faced and frozen, is the same one whose house he's landed in now, like a shuttle that's missed its orbit and plopped down into some god-forsaken inland sea.

·

Penny hears herself say "okey doke then, honey, bye," and then, catching sight of her wild eyes and twisted mouth wobbling in the glass of a distant door panel, hears the first eruption of her own laughter — harsh, bronchial, shallow and endless

— the little itch that's also the dark lake, smaller and more hidden in the trees than the one with the floating dock and the bar where she once sat with blood on her forehead and left hand, on one side her husband of the moment, a fat dope with a small beard as tight into the folds of his chin as the knot in a necktie, on the other her boyfriend, more bloodstained than her, her usual type, bony and stoned in mismatched motorcycle leather, all three of them hanging low over their drinks, backs to the reddening sky, black trees and disassembled images in dark water.

·

Junie's busy banging glasses, plates, cups and saucers, rattling knives and forks, with the idea that one of the figures sitting embalmed in light will spring to life and help. But no one lifts a finger.

"Ass put down roots over there guys? Waldo? Freddy? Edith, move your skinny butt!"

Freddy and a few others spring into action, but Waldo doesn't move. He's well past the familiar sadness of knowing you're among people who think you're ok when you're not even sure who you are. In a minute he'll be cradled in Penny's lap, sobbing that when he got out they promised him that things would get better, things would be *different*, but they're not. They're not!

"Yes," Penny says, stroking his stiff pine needles of hair as if they were the soft and curly hair of a child, "there's a depressing moment every day when we realize that the differences between one day and another that arrive like light through the window are just new ways the world finds to express the sameness of things."

The more he sobs and mutters the more his face loses its crisp furrow, like a skull that's been axed in half and clamped back together.

No matter what he does, he says, he ends up with nothing. *Nothing!* He could walk into any stranger's house and kill that fuck. Because the stranger has everything and he has nothing.

And there's no way to make the stranger understand why he has to share everything with the desperate fuck who has nothing....

This is what we all come to.

We gave up our dreams of being cosmonauts when the cosmonauts started coming back wandering the earth loony and depressed. They found out that there are other worlds out there but that they're just as dumb as this one....

"Is it a terrible thing to say?" Penny whispers soothingly, still stroking the hair she's managed to smooth down to a pleasing silkiness. "Is it an impossible burden to bear? What if it's true that you never will have anything? never have what you long for? Because *that isn't your destiny.* Is it too horrible to admit to ourselves that there are only so many leading roles — but that the one playing the leading role can't exist without the ones not playing the leading role — that the ones who sit at the background tables having inaudible conversations behind the leading one sitting audibly and visibly at the foreground table are also doing an important job. They have a destiny. What if our job, our destiny, is to talk but be inaudible, just so something else — something we don't necessarily know about — can take place that *is* audible. . . ? 'Neither visible nor invisible — but a kind of visible invisibility. . . .' Can we live with that or should we all kill ourselves?"

"But I really do have a destiny though, Penny? Tell the truth."

"Yes, you do, sweetheart," she murmurs. "And I think your destiny has something to do with Junior."

Waldo sits up, guilt-stricken.

"Where the fuck *is* Junior?"

Someone is dispatched to the maze-like basement, someone searches the house, someone ventures out into the windy pitch-blackness and it seems as if Junior's name is suddenly echoing through the universe.

13

TAMMY watches in disgust as her mom argues with the set, shouts advice and shakes her wobbly head, laughing with mock disapproval at the stupidity of it all.

"The idiot actually thinks that's his girlfriend!" her mom says to her, even though Tammy'd closed her eyes and stopped watching when the scene changed and they lost sight of the little boy who resembles Junior.

"It's not really your *girl*friend, dummy!" her mom says to the set. "It's just some ugly girl with look-alike hair and ass! God, they're all so *stupid*! What a nation of *morons* we've become!"

Her new head is getting more wobbly with every outburst.

Tammy closes her eyes again and dreams she's telling Junior what she discovered long ago: that even if you wake up one morning and realize that this is not— *this cannot be* — your family, what keeps us where we are is the fear of what happens to the integrity of our cell walls out there in the darkness where the wavelengths crackle unimpeded....

14

THE little boy begs two passing girls to take him with them. Take him with them exactly the way they take their dog. Their dog who loves them, needs no leash and runs on ahead, lags behind or circles beside them in wild loops across lawns and in quick dashes behind hedgerows. But they leave him behind and head home to the mother who pretends to be cross before she kisses them and strokes their dark and curly hair. So much tenderness that tears flow from the eyes of mother and daughters.

The little boy keeps running until there are no more houses or lights beyond the pale shadow of the light that hangs over everything as a weak, common glow.

Dark blue sky above the park where Junior falls asleep shades off into an ambiguous zone ragged and bright through dark evergreens, as if there the strange secondary radiance of the city is trapped in smoke.

He dreams that he's crying out to his lost sister. Crying and crying — an inconsolable grief that someone nevertheless does try to console — in language he doesn't understand and which doesn't console him at all.

"We returned the idea of her beauty to her," the consoling voice says, "and this returned beauty became the *self-conscious* beauty we can't stop looking at. The energy we gave her became hers and it's this lost energy we're drawn to. She looks at us as if we're the vacuum that we are and sometimes that makes her dizzy. We feel that she's falling into us, but she never arrives. The screen where she's visible is as real as every other thing, but it's a very *thin* reality — thin as the blade that cuts off a head...."

The strange sky grows dark as the grass grows wet and sounds of insects rise into one. The world hums like a network of transformers that help your cells mutate while you sleep. Later, when he wakes up, a shape runs by. He thinks it's a dog and runs after it.

15

NO matter how far away we get we continue to hear the surf of moronic laughter that sometimes degenerates into weeping or into the inconsolable gurgling of a stream eternally flowing past the same hidden point in the trees. We continue to think of it as the *same* stream, though a new body of particles is passing every instant. The remote surf of moronic laughter and the gurgle of concealed weeping are the static that crowd the universe.

16

SOMETIMES, walking alone in the city at night, we begin to run for no reason, then slow down to a walk and then start running again. From far away our movements look like those of someone dodging and stutter-stepping, trying to cross the empty length of the court and score a basket, while in fact we're getting lost on a path that only seems like a path to someone who knows what a path is.

17

JUNIOR is resting on a short flight of cracked green steps in his blue jacket and red cap, dozing off in the bluish light of an all-night video plaza and giving himself up to dreams that are like memories positioned at a different angle in the brain.

He's five years old and he's in the front seat of a car, next to a woman he thinks of as his mother. They're on US 630 out of Fort Wayne. His mother in the fast lane being passed slowly but steadily on the right by a small green car with a noisy engine.

The interior of each car fully in view in afternoon sunlight for the long length of the road.

A beautiful girl is brushing her dark hair in the back seat: brush follows the waves of her hair the way the car follows the sweeping groove of the road over a hill.

Brushes her hair with the peaceful smile of self-love — and her love of her own beauty adds to her beauty and to his desire to watch it.

Stares at her, memorizing because he's already forgetting.

Concentrates with the look of someone trying to remember her years later and feeling memory's fragility, thin as a glass Christmas ornament, little puff of forgetfulness sealed in the hollow sphere.

Concentrates with all his will — hard enough to transmit himself bodily from present to future or from future to past or from one car to the other. The beautiful girl turns and glances back toward the car losing ground so slowly she's able to look fully and carefully inside. When their eyes meet, she stops brushing her hair and turns away, leaving him confined in his own body — far away from the self that's traveled out and can never be retrieved.

.

Waldo Bunny pulls up in his van, says "hop in" and they're off, traveling away from the blue light of the video plaza at high speed, through wind and rain across ancient railroad overpasses above a broad river dried up into industrial islands and muddy tributaries.

At first they're alone on the dark bridge and then other cars are racing to and from the same obscure destination.

Waldo grows fidgety in traffic: nervously turns the steering wheel right and left though they're zipping straight ahead. Hands and arms keep shifting position. One hand drops limply to his lap and rests there lifeless as a leather glove, arm leans across steering wheel, elbow shifts to door frame, arm hangs out window, hands drop to bottom of steering wheel then jump to top, hand in lap scratches head, puts a finger in an ear, five fingers run through stiff hair as if combing it in furrows, rubs triply elongated jaw, testing its stubble, hangs by wrist over inner radius of steering wheel, feels giant Adam's apple thoughtfully and at length — all the while whizzing forward through traffic and looking hunched and nervous.

A low green sports car jumps to their right — as if sheer acceleration can tunnel it between Waldo's van and the rusty railing before the universe has time to notice that there isn't room.

Waldo is forced to his left, into the path of an oncoming truck, with a spark of a second to react. His hands give a tiny, surprised jump off the wheel as if reflexively giving him a chance to smile and ponder and scratch his head or even to escape into a dream of being somewhere else.

Junior looks out from the whizzing hub of the slowly revolving universe: the truck is coming straight at him — powerful headlights blazing — as if what's about to happen has already happened, waiting for events to catch up and explode.

From a perspective slightly behind himself, Junior can see the comical bobbing of their two dark blob-heads against the glare of the explosion rejoining itself in-progress.

Waldo's hands regain their grip on the wheel, giving it a sharp twist that sends them skidding across the road and effortlessly through the rotten guardrail with just a momentary view of the flickering red and blue neon sign of the CHINA CLIPPER restaurant where Waldo's eaten many a huge greasy and delicious bowl of roast duck chow fun.

Out over and down into the ravine Waldo'd driven over a thousand times without discovering what broken rocks, what purple-brown run-off, what race of unknown creatures lay at the bottom.

18

JUNIOR asks the nurse if this is death and, even though she's lost her voice, she laughs, holding her throat, and looks surprised. His friend has already been sent home, she says, and all he has to do is not disturb his bandaged crown or the bandages protecting the repair to his severed neck.

Hair pale blonde, voice whisper-sweet and childish, face kind and open.

She wants him to think about how lucky he is, not how unlucky he was to have had the accident or to find himself in this between-world. All of us are born into a between-world — our destiny broken and scattered as if on purpose. We all end up cursing the mess we're born into — but if we're lucky enough to be handed a nice new head — that should be enough to give us hope.

19

HIS mom & dad's house is suddenly before him, lemon-white and isolated in total darkness — as if on the face of a giant TV screen wheeled up in the middle of the night to the foot of the bed by the kindly nurse.

Above the house — above the hospital and above the world too — the trees are black clouds that sponge up every particle of escaping light. Far away in the dull, charcoal glow of the sky something is woofing in a muffled way. Muffled and regular.

Junior strains to listen.

The woof-woof-woofing at regular intervals, far away, behind houses layered as if each were in its own valley, strikes a deep chord. He knows this dog as well as if it were his own dog-like self running after someone who no longer wants to know he exists.

The longer he listens, the more the woofing sounds like hooting, the kind that draws you out into the forest, then makes you run back to the safety of the house and quickly close your window.

A powerful little meter begins to tune its clicks in the black tree-mass and then other, tiny meters follow suit — as if the dark streets were covered with grass. Much further away than the little meters in the grass, powerful meter clicking in the trees and the woofing that may be hooting, he can just about hear the hungry barking of crows from the hidden fields and forests that can't possibly exist near this ordinary neighborhood of cross-hatched streets and houses looked at so often they're invisible.

.

No one notices anything. You dream of a cloak of invisibility and find out you don't need one. They're always looking at something else. Distance looks at them and they look back. Space is the busy middle ground between this exchange of empty gazes. Easiest thing in the world to slip past them and peer at their idiotic goings-on through the warm, pumpkin glow of their windows.

.

He's looking into the little bedroom that's a flimsy add-on to the west wall of the house, the one where his mom has a secret shrine to Barbara Eden and the bed is barely wide enough for one bony person. His dad's in there with a woman who's not a spiny lobster like his mom. He's sure this is the woman called "Ethel" who's supposed to be a moron. She has a long, pleasant body and a pleasant face and her pleasantness is making the ordinary room pleasingly sunny. The sandstone bedspread has a pattern of turquoise and ruby hieroglyphics and the sun is making the pink walls look like the orange fruit punch your brain sees when it's out in the heat too long.

There's so much light on their skin that their bodies are little screens that cast a blue glow that may also be a red shadow on Junior's face.

His dad is propped up on one elbow and it gives his short body an unexpected muscular torsion. Looks strong instead of squat and the powerful stirring of his arm is able to make Ethel levitate three feet above the bed. The more he stirs, the more she levitates and the more their screens glow, her warm face rotating and long neck straining to get a look round the back of experience.

Likes what she sees, laughs and subsides back onto the bed.

His dad nestles down alongside her, her pale arm draped limply over his dark leg, his watch blazing tranquilly on his wrist like a space craft that's been zooming around the universe for years, searching for an abandoned child, and at last has come to rest on the red sand of a friendly desert. He looks like another, younger and happier man.

Junior feels that he's looking at his real parents. But. if that's so, then who are the others and why was he sent there? Why is his mom a different mom and why does his dad resemble himself yet seem like another person? Why are we shown these images if it's impossible to find our way into them? And why does looking at something so rarely fulfill its promise of *becoming* something?

His mom looks up, thrilled and flushed, scanning whatever horizon is hers.

Can't see him through the dark window, yet his presence is making the dazzling happiness of her eyes cloud over with memory or regret.

She turns away from the window and Junior follows her gaze toward a shaded inner doorway. The man who's just entered could be Waldo, but only if he's had his head changed again: considerably bigger and as if it had been to the beauty parlor, the mass of hair an ashblond dome of bubbles, the broken profile of someone whose ugliness is his livelihood.

His dad gets out of bed to confront the intruder and then the light of the house dies down to a distant pinpoint and the hospital room is dark again.

20

THE mind dozes as if all programming has been canceled. Nothing to do but watch the one program that's on — one tightly wound loop going round and round on its two freely spinning spindles.

.

Tammy, the paper girl, is at his bedside, a book facedown in her lap, pressing and pressing the buttons of the remote, trying without success to find something new for him to watch.

Opens his mouth to pour out his gratitude, as if she were trying to save his life, but the pain in his throat keeps the words from forming.

He makes room for her on the bed and they snuggle up together and watch whatever's on.

21

"LET me ask you something, Waldo," his so-called mom is saying to someone in a bloodstained shirt — someone who doesn't even look like the third or fourth replacement Waldo, but who must be Waldo because he can't be anyone else.

"Yup."

"Sometimes when you're in the middle of *this* life...."

"Uh-huh."

"Sometimes when I'm in the middle of this life I think to myself that I've blanked out before — at least once and most likely four or *five* times. I get a little inkling of having been alive a few years ago in the middle of another life."

"Yup, I've done that, I've had that," Waldo's un-Waldo-like head goes bobbing too easily in agreement. "Done something one day, forgotten it the next or vice versa. And then, jesus, when you find out what you did...!"

"But there are whole periods of my *life* I don't remember, Waldo. There was this period when I was living in Los Alamos. I was living in Los Alamos, but I took a trip to Cape Canaveral to see a friend go up on one of those ridiculous excursions and while I was visiting the Cape I stayed in a motel in Cocoa Beach and I met these two beautiful cowboys. And the next thing I knew I was in Mexico City. It was spring when I left Los Alamos, but now it's autumn and I'm sitting on a park bench in Mexico City, I look like hell and I don't know where the fuck I've been!

"I remember having thoughts and not knowing whose they were. I never thought them, but now I had them and they were mine.

"I remember wondering if the days of a life are continuous or if one day is absolutely separate from another.

"'If the days of a life *are* continuous,' I thought, 'then why don't I feel it was me living the life I remember? Same core of self from childhood to present should provide all the coherence we need. Shouldn't it? Yet this doesn't feel true. Why is that? Same self, different lives, or the other way around?

"'Maybe we're just the last ones to be able to see the thread of continuity in our own lives,' I thought.

"I look around and realize that it's sunny. Takes me a while to figure out that the sun comes as a shock because I've been buried somewhere where there is no sun — I've been buried in my black box again — under twenty tons of earth and rock — in a vault behind steel doors too thick for any drill — and now suddenly it's all sun and cabbage palms and pastel adobe!

"Where am I? Am I in Lee *County* again? Everyone says it's Mexico, but to me it looks exactly like Lee County. I start remembering the time my dad's network bought up some stations in Florida and they sent him down there to check things out. For a while they put us up in a cottage on General Sarnoff's old estate on Gasparilla Island and then I think we spent a month or two in the gatekeeper's bungalow on the grounds of Peter Goldmark's old place, not far from the Edison Museum on the Caloosahatchee. Daddy was always out playing golf and mom and I were left on our own. That made mom miserable and she used to drag me around from one theme park to the next.

"I remember being yanked up a long flight of stone steps: struggling and falling and getting up and falling again and then trying to crawl up on my hands and knees and starting to cry when I scraped myself and my mom getting mad and yanking me up a couple of steps by my little arm and then seeing some onlookers — nothing but the usual roving band of morons hoping to slip into the background of the shot or to voice an opinion — and changing her tune and cooing, 'Oh! You're a little shy about that *step*. *Aren't* you? Yes, you *aaarre*! But you're a *big* girl and you're going to *make* it! Of *course* you are! Here we go now! Wheeeeh!!' And she swings me all the way up to the top step with one hand. My little arm twists in its socket, like a chicken wing when the chicken's not fully cooked and you're having trouble tearing it off the carcass. I remember the pain in my shoulder and the weird little smile tucked under her big nose, in the shadow between the red-purple of her cheeks. And I remember how I laughed like an idiot when I landed because all the onlookers looked so happy — and when I saw them, lit up by the sun, far away but looking at me the same way I was looking at them, I got excited because I knew that my mom and I had a second, happy existence far away from ourselves — one that was only real because other people saw it.

"A thousand terrible memories of being a miserable little girl in Lee County come back to me. I remember how my father, who was a god when they sent him to Florida (my mother would have cut my head off if he told her to), would be a has-been six months later. I start crying and can't stop. Go scrounging in my pocketbook for some tissues. Feel something wet and look into my bag: it's all red and sticky. Can't use the tissues, because they're soaked with fresh blood!

"Reach in. A tiny hand. A little girl's *hand* is in my pocketbook!

"Now I remember having my little girl with me in Cocoa Beach and being told to hide under a blanket with her in the back of the van when we crossed the border. The two cowboys up front, high on something. The next thing I know I'm on a park bench somewhere in the tropics thinking someone else's thoughts and the next thing I know I'm in a hospital!"

"Let's face it, Penny," Waldo says reassuringly, "that door is never too far away. We've all gone through that door and sometimes we're kept waiting forever in a little reception area with comfortable chairs — sometimes we're in the little green room so long we forget why we came. But whenever we go through the door we never know if we'll come out the other side."

"And if we didn't come out, how would we know?"

That strikes her funny and the familiar skidding sound of her laugh gives her the comfortable feeling we get knowing just by listening that we're tuned to the right channel even when we're in the kitchen fixing something to eat.

It wakes up Junior's dad. And when he sees Waldo and Penny laughing together he knows they're the cackling voice of the terror in his nightmare. Again he's had the dream where the dead wife is staring up from under dark pines at the murderer staring back paralyzed through the curtains. Now he sees blood on Waldo's sleeve and on his hands, touches his head and feels a sticky, painful spot under his hair and bolts for the window.

·

The head outside in the cool night air stops to listen to a dog barking unhappily on a wooded mountain slope it had no idea existed anywhere within earshot of this low and invisible neighborhood, then wriggles its thick shoulders and stubby arms, confident that one more twist will spring it free from under the partially raised window stuck in its rusted tracks.

The noise of his far-away grunting can be heard echoing off the slopes by a thin white dog, starved and nervous, who pauses in his useless foraging to listen to the miserable human whining coming from a cross-hatched and populated valley he didn't know existed.

Junior's dad is stuck and wriggling like a fly who's stupidly crawled up between two panes of window glass, thinking the second pane is the transparency of the world.

In another instant the cry that comes from him will be the mysterious cry at the instant of mutation, from a fly's desperate ZZZ-ZZZ-ing to the terrified wailing of a newborn infant.

22

TAMMY'S sharing Junior's broiled scrod and mashed potatoes and eating most of it because he's having trouble swallowing. They're watching TV together and she's chattering
happily, asking him questions that he can't answer.

She wonders if watching tv brings up the same memories for
him as for her. Sometimes the sound of the television gets her
depressed. Sound of human conversation interrupted by laughter. Alternating rhythm of laughter and speech. Familiar theme
songs. The shaded masses of music, voice and laughter, meant
to be reassuring, for her = anxiety. Or depression. Or both.
The real, sickening nub of childhood is the so-called nostalgia
of our time in front of the set — the anxiety-depression of that
bored absence from the self — the nostalgia-comedy of television life mixed up with your own childhood misery.... Does he
have that too?

Junior doesn't answer. He's hovering above Waldo and
Penny — looking out the window with them — unseen and
behind them — hovering but having a little trouble holding
still — with a view down into the dark outer world.

Scaffolds of lights are trained on a lumpy square of dark
ground where police are digging with shovels. Something
about the scene is agitating Junior's mom. She's gripping Waldo's shoulder with two hands and chewing on the sour cloth of
his shirtsleeve. Waldo's got his arm around her, but he's also up
on tippy-toe, trying to get a better look.

"Isn't that Matt Dillon out there? Yup. I'm sure it is! Wait! Do I
mean 'Matt Dillon'? You know who I mean, don't you, Penny?"

His mom's starting to break down. She's sobbing and pounding with her bony fists on Waldo's arm and chest.

"That's a *head*, you idiot! That's a human *head* they're digging up! Don't you see who it is?"

Out in the yard they're unearthing a number of heads and bodies.

Feels himself receding from this place.

Back to the hospital, above the bed, then down into it, hiding under the covers.

There they are in the distance, covered with blood and screaming.

The image is held together by the dark room that couldn't exist without its internally glowing square.

Dark world around its red dance and blue spasm.

From afar: the irregular, difficult breathing of light through blowing curtains across the way.

Far away from his mom and dad, deep into total darkness.

How many times can we remember who we were?

A fresh universe around us like a broken egg.

When he's gone he wonders what happened back inside the little lighted window that long ago collapsed inside a twinkling pinpoint. Aside from the killers, he's the only one who knows who murdered his dad. But by tomorrow no one will remember who his dad was.

23

THE car stalls on a road through a birch forest high in the mountains. Air turns cold, snow begins to fall as fast as the rain that was falling down below. There are so many snowflakes striking so many leaves that the quiet sound of snow on leaves is the sound of the torrent that's always rushing inside him.

His only thought in the cold interior of the car is that experience takes place outside just so it can get inside us again. We watch it from a distance — allow ourselves to watch it because it *is* at a distance — but we're sensitive to the exterior screen as if it were a remote skin where a touch we can't feel replays itself obsessively in the mind as a sinewy little hologram of the world.

The outside life is now the inside life — or is it the other way around?

Listening follows the path of seeing.

Tune it carefully. Snow makes a little ticking sound on one leaf. Multiplies laterally through the forest and in tiers of varying intensity. Multiplication of leaf sounds rushes toward him as if he himself were out there, able to disperse again and again in an infinite way. As if the universe were living for him while he listened.

He thought his sister Valeria was hidden at the summit, where stunted trees are pressed down under snow and the rutted, looping road follows the mountain's knotted spine all the way to a fortress-like lodge, pylon and directional antenna visible to a cosmic distance. But the atmosphere is void, signals aren't returning, and he knows what it feels like to be a starved little blue jay sitting on wires, branches, roof drains and aerials on and off for thirty-four hours, squawking every code it can think of with no reply.

24

THIS dad's teeth spread out across his lower lip, pointy and a little yellow. His curly brown hair's getting wispy in the middle, but he compensates by letting it grow straight down the sides into a thick, reddish and bruiny beard. The wispy spot's only visible when he takes off his denim blue-and-brown suede Mohawk Trail cap, so the stupid cap's usually on. His eyes go cheerful and crinkly when he smiles, a little too much for Junior's taste. With his spread-out teeth and weathered face, the smile gives him the look of someone who's made kindness his profession. A yellow quilted vest and the sleeves of a green plaid shirt round off his perpetual look. Never without his narrow-ruled, three-subject notebook, he's forever stealing a guilty minute to scribble something with a sort of shy compulsion, staring at a stranger or looking out a window as if he were an artist sketching.

A friendly but decisive jerk of his dad's chin tells Junior to slide into the window-side of the booth. Dad slides in after him and, facing Dad, Junior's little sister, one he's never seen before and who Dad calls "honey" so often it must be her name.

Junior looks out the window. A couple of crappy centuries are crowded into the view.

While it's true that through every window we look through distance is an odd paste carved against the glass and it's also true that in every town we gaze out through the narrow band of wood-fired pizza tavern windows and see ancient, resurrected factories, weary mini-malls and boarded donut shops, governors' mansions and courthouses that are now antique shops or restaurants, here and there an inexplicable stairway, a shabby rooftop patio or picnic table and umbrella set out festively in the midst of a tract of rusted auto bodies — here, at the base of a lofty mountain where sixteen looping miles of road plunge from a region of true earthly unearthliness to a terminal of life at its most human and most exhausted, the falsely receding horizon line of distance reconstitutes itself toward the center of town as a virtual billboard of discarded sites and time zones.

Junior turns to ask his dad if these are the factories that once-upon-a-time were *paper* factories and later were revived as *television* factories, the ones where they manufactured the famous Nipkow disk and then after that the components of the iconoscope, and after that one of the early, failed digital television systems, but his dad is scribbling, lifting his cap to scratch his head and talking to himself.

He looks up at Junior as if he's really stymied by the insoluble difficulty of the problem he's set himself.

"What does a window resemble?" he asks good-naturedly. "Is what we see through a window the same as being outside the window and looking around? And if not, why not? When we see life through a window, is it life any longer? If it doesn't resemble life, does it resemble a film? a painting? television? What do we really mean when we talk about 'virtual reality'? For the mind, is there any other kind? Is the view through a window virtual reality or something else? And where exactly does the reality of the mind reside? What exactly is a thought? What substance is a thought made of? Is there such a thing as a physics of thinking?"

He's put his cap back on and he's shaking his head, shuffling through the pages of his drawing tablet as if marveling at the stuff that's come oozing out of his pen.

Gives the waitress a friendly greeting. *Overly* friendly as far as Junior's concerned. "My dad's full of shit," he might think if he weren't already beginning to like this dad. If this dad weren't friendly Junior never would have met him and never would have had him as a dad. Remembers the moment of meeting: looking out a train window when there was nothing to see; looking in order not to talk to anyone. And then a pleasant voice asking, "How're you doing, hombre?" Turned to see the pleasant, bearded face of one more guy in cap, plaid shirt and jeans.

Because there's a possibility of happiness, Junior begins to feel depressed. It's the familiar depression that begins with the knowledge that your parents aren't going to let you get what you want because it costs too much and that ends in the dark lake where you have a memory of having drowned.

But this dad says festively, "Bring my son a pizza! And make it a big one! One with *everything*! Put on sausage and peppers and pepperoni and extra cheese and extra sauce and onions and garlic!"

"And meatballs and anchovies?" Junior says tentatively.

"And meatballs and anchovies!" his dad echoes and everyone laughs.

Cheese ravioli with marinara sauce for little Honey and a salad for his dad.

Now Junior is happy, but this happiness feels like an even deeper sadness.

The pretty young waitress, whose eyes are as overbright as an anchorwoman's at the odd instant of feeling her own thrilling emission of electrons, wants to know what they'll have to drink. She cheerfully recites the long list of possible sodas, Junior takes an age to settle on root beer, his dad says beer for him and milk for Honey and then Junior remembers something from another lifetime and changes his drink to a root beer *float*. Honey has an inspiration too and wants fried mozzarella sticks.

"Fried mozzarella sticks for everyone!"

For once it feels natural to find himself among the distant, laughing ones instead of feeling a depressing kinship with the ones bent over the burgers that seem to have arrived in their plates already eaten, like clots of space disposal falling from a thousand miles up into the ketchup.

A little later they're dipping fried mozzarella sticks into spicy marinara sauce and the waitress slips in next to Honey just before his dad starts telling parts of the same story he told on the train — about the peculiar path he followed from Beaver City to Provo to Los Angeles to San Francisco to Philadelphia to Wyndmore, Pennsylvania, to Fort Wayne to Nyack to North Adams — all to try and track down an old buddy from the signal corps who was in the salvage business — and how that didn't work out and he ended up in Wellfleet, stranded and alone, but not at all unhappy — because when you're alone in a strange town you're not yourself and we only know we're alive when we're not ourselves. He ended up getting married there and living peacefully on the Cape for years, until the day his wife and child disappeared. Two years later she returned without the child, claiming that they'd been abducted by aliens. The way she looked it might have been true, but the child never turned up. He couldn't stay there and started traveling again until he found his way here.

The waitress, who's been listening to the peaceful smoothness of his coagulated tenor so raptly she could easily become Junior's new mom, suddenly seems to realize how long she's been sitting and gets up to get their food.

The steaming plates are delivered, but his dad isn't paying attention. He's listening to a conversation in the booth behind him and feverishly taking notes.

25

THE little house is cozy and warm. The wood-burning stove in the basement sends up abundant heat that's peculiarly friendly. Not quite aromatic, but with the feeling that a woodsmoke aroma is being translated into properties pleasing to the skin, radiating up through a system of floor grilles installed in every room for that purpose. Junior's never lived in such a cozy house. Even the tiny glowing coal of sadness he feels deep in his dad, sadness about what he has no idea, adds to the sense of coziness.

Junior's doing the dishes, the sink right below a broad, three-part window that looks out at a dark evergreen forest. Honey is asleep and Dad's at his old slope-faced school desk, writing a mile-a-minute in his drawing tablet. Junior loves when his dad gets so carried away by something he's written that he has to share it, like now, when he calls out *this* is weird! I don't know where this came from!," and Junior turns off the water to listen.

"'It's wonderful to be free of the feeling of being on display, but the price of this freedom is being outside everything — outside the bright, unnatural light of society — like a settler on one of the space stations no longer visited by any private vehicle or public ferry.

"'Someone talks about the light we carry with us from childhood and likewise the darkness. With this one a luminous glow as if dipped in some phosphorescent substance, with that one a dark stain visible as a dismal atmosphere, like a November day when it can't quite rain.

"'This glow or this stain is bound to find corresponding zones — here on Earth and throughout the universe — harmonic vibrations — so that there are moments when we feel a deep chord being struck.'

"'A bit too much of this glow can turn you into an electronic pickup tube — and this hungry radiance is what we call fame. A bit too little: well that's nothing but the tarnished netherworld of the everyday.'"

Junior wants to know if that's where they are. Are they outside the light of society? *Is* there a place outside the light of society? Wouldn't that be the same as finding a place outside *time*? And even a moron sometimes feels that wherever there's human life there's time: that time is a problem introduced into the universe with every birth. So, if time is a human problem, how can we get away from it? And the same with the light of society.

His dad's not listening. He's following his own line of thought and says that when he began writing in his tired hours after work all he really wanted was to turn out a decent mystery. But he couldn't control what he wrote and these are the strange things that have always filled his sketchbooks. He's shaking his head and smiling.

Junior calls his dad over to listen to the sound he's been hearing on and off for an hour or more.

They listen intently together, waiting for the faint hoo-hoo-hooing in the woods.

The longer they listen the longer the intervals. More silence, fainter and fainter cries, to the point where hearing it is the same as remembering it.

Dad says that now the owl has retreated deep into the woods and soon they're not going to hear it at all. But Junior argues that what they're hearing is a creature that carries darkness and invisibility with it — the voice that darkness, invisibility and distance would have if they had a voice — and therefore the more distant the creature sounds, the nearer it is.

Well, his dad says, the only way Junior's going to find out is to go out alone. Go out alone, because if the truth is going to approach it always approaches one alone, never two together.

He gives Junior a sack of stale bread to scatter for the eternal foraging of the crows and returns to his writing.

26

THERE he is, alone at the edge of the forest.

From a distance (if his dad is, in fact, keeping an eye on him from the kitchen window) he's a small figure in a white t-shirt and jeans — long, mowed field of grass behind him in a rippling plane, tall weeds and wild underbrush before him like the surging basin of an ocean he's about to wade into.

Beyond rippling plane and surging ocean, a soaring lattice of green clouds and dark verticals — an oddly flaming light embedded exactly in the spaces where darkness will be most fathomless.

As darkness flows into the ragged evergreen lattice, a second light appears, harsh and silvery as the escaping electrons of an unassigned TV channel.

It's the strange moment before nightfall, with all its rising earth fragrance and biting insects.

He finds it pleasurable to heave chunks of stale bread, left-over donuts and half-eaten blueberry muffins up high and wait for the distant thud at the foot of the evergreens, imagining the forest animals that will sneak out to nibble them at night, when everyone's asleep.

Silvery leaves are beginning to turn their dark face toward him. Once the wind turns them over they can't turn back, like the darkness that's turned over above you and that you don't have the strength to turn again.

Because he's listening he hears something.

The unknown species of bird that gives off its little unmusical cry when night starts blowing through the forest.

The sound of wind in trees that may also be the sound of a solitary car traveling down a wet highway.

A woman's voice, calling "Daaa-viiddd" from far away, carries all the way to the forest's edge. Makes him turn and turning brings a house into view that isn't his dad's warm and cozy one. Seems to him that he's looking out across the road that bisects the valley at the house high up on the wooded slope that mirrors their cleared one — where the blue light of an old TV set is always blowing on and off like a candle in the orange glow of one of the bedroom windows. Bedroom window of a little girl who never wants to go to sleep. Wants to keep watching forever. Calls out to her mom & dad in the livingroom that she's not *sleeping* yet and her voice blows across the grass and the valley like a puffy seed cloud on an uprooted green stem.

27

J UNIOR loses track of time following the path of wind that comes around the corner of the house, passing off into the trees to his right. Listens to wind in trees with his right ear only. Sound of wind in trees, even with one ear, describes a universe. One blended sound until ear does its fine tuning. Path of wind in each tree is different. Sound of wind in one tree not the same as sound of wind in another. Listen long enough and you can tell tree from tree by the particular swirling path or violent shaking path of wind through branches — and then the individual tree sounds group together and add up in clusters — and these groups of clustered individually different wind-in-tree sounds are also distinctly different from one another — and all this surrounds you in a swirling, massive way at this dark hour.

He walks away from the forest toward the house, but having his back to the dark forest makes him turn again and again to face it. Turning, he inhales the startling aroma and coldness of the earth-and-root wind sweeping down toward him through the surging basin of grass, a living chance to smell what a corpse smells for the split second it's alive. Drawing close to the house, he sees a beautiful turquoise-and-sandstone coverlet lit up through a bedroom window.

His dad's not in the kitchen, watching over him from the lighted window that isn't as wide as it used to be and isn't divided into three parts. He goes from room to room. His dad's not in the house and neither is his little sister. But there is a lot of blood in one of the bedrooms, a strange red already turning

black where the pillows make a hump under the beautiful turquoise-and-sandstone coverlet. The television is on and when
its blue light washes against the walls their terrible pink turns
an even more terrible orange.

28

I T isn't until they're in another state that they untie Junior and take off his blindfold.

The woman who claims to be his mom says she doesn't look like his mom because she's been through so much. When Junior ran away everyone said that she aged overnight, but what they didn't say is that she looks like shit. She's going to look like shit for the rest of her life because of him.

Junior tries to get a look at her from the back of the van. If it is her, her hair's gone from an ugly blonde to an ugly brown. Before, there were a lot of dark roots showing, darker than what a shovel throws away, and now there's a harsh, rusted red. Face is more convex, a couple of bites missing from its blade. Smaller, firmer chin keeps the jaw from waggling.

The guy she's with — Len, Leonard or Lenny — looks like a microphone at the end of its fully extended adjustable stand, with a receding chin that has a habit of tucking right into the folds of the neck as if the unit's designed that way, a baritone that rumbles like a wooden radio and big glasses with dark frames.

Leonard picks up where his mom left off.

Someone cut his dad's head off and planted it out in the yard. What did he think would happen when he ran away from that? Did it ever occur to him that the police might assume he did it? And that he had accomplices. That his mom might be implicated? That by running away like that he was putting his mom in jeopardy? Did he ever wonder how she was doing? Think of coming forward to clear her name? Wonder why someone killed his dad? Why they cut off his head? Wonder about the meaning of that? Why the head? The head in particular. And why bury it out in the yard, where the police would be sure to find it. Find it in the family's front yard and leap to the obvious, stupid conclusion. Arrest his mom. Figure she had Junior mesmerized. One of those weird mother-son cases of hypnosis. The son like a living corpse out on the lawn — mom looking down and hypnotizing him from the upstairs window while the son axes his dad's head off. Did he ever think about his mom for one little second…?

His voice is droning and monotonous. Even though it's deliberately insincere, it sounds like a deeper lie than it's meant to. The droning and lying put Junior to sleep and while he's sleeping he's aware that they're still talking and that there's no way to defend his dreams from their conversation. In his dreams he knows as surely as if he were seeing it on TV that they cut his latest, best dad's head off. For a while they just let it lie there on the bed, looking for all the world as if it were smiling a stupid, toothy smile of contentment through its reddish nest of beard. Then they buried it in the woods behind the house. "Bury it deep!" the woman kept saying. "Deep! Deeper!" How many times did she say it? It seemed like nothing would satisfy her. "Why? What's wrong with you?" the tall man complained, digging hard through a sinewy network of roots. "I thought the idea was *not* to bury it too deep. Otherwise, what's the point, honey? Am I missing something, or what?" "We live in an age," the woman said, "when you can never bury a man's head deep enough." The tall man gave her an uncomprehending look but went on with his digging. Other small, tidy packages were buried too and what wakes Junior up is the guilty memory that this is the first time he's wondered about his sister.

29

IT was just summer and now it's autumn; just autumn, now winter; just winter. . . . Without moving from one place to another, you're somewhere else.

30

EVEN though his head's still his, Junior sometimes has the pleasant sensation of looking in the mirror and seeing someone else. And he has to admit to himself that the reason for the change is his new dad, Len: black t-shirt with sawed-off armholes and a silkscreen of RCA Model TRK-12 front and back, black leather motorcycle cap and a charcoal denim vest with ripped-off sleeve-stumps are his perpetual outfit.

Len carries with him at all times two complete sets of tools capable of fixing any piece of broadcast equipment ever invented, each in its own enormous metal box. His van is equipped for life on the move and just about any time he'll say to Junior and Junior's mom "let's go! let's hit the road!" and they throw their stuff in and take off. They drive all over the map, doing a little business along the way. Len has an incredible knack for finding antique sets with just enough wrong with them that their owners are eager to unload them, but not so much wrong that he can't get them running in an afternoon. He makes his living buying and selling these broken down/fixed up antique television sets along the secondary highways of the United States.

No matter how far they go, they always return to their secluded campsite at the end of a muddy pretzel loop winding down through a remote private campground called Kinyon's Kaverns to an isolated evergreen promontory directly over the whitewater surge of the creek.

The forest is beautiful — or *would* be beautiful if only people like Junior's mom & dad weren't hiding in it.

Their so-called mobile home's squashed and rusted as if

something unimaginable's stepped on it, with more bluegreen patina than a Roman bronze. And they've got the front yard all done up with the crappy doodads real people go in for when they're putting down roots. His dad's hammered together a rustic pavilion between the mobile home and the creek — a family-size redwood picnic table and attached picnic benches under a lopsided pyramid roof for barbecuing with a shaded water view.

Sitting on a rock one day, eating a turkey, bacon, lettuce, to-mato and mayonnaise club sandwich with a mug of hot coffee and enjoying the deep rotten-leaf smell of the green and golden forest on either side of the creek, Junior comes to the conclusion that it's impossible to know another person's pleasure. Nothing could be more outside us or inside another. The pleasure an-other person takes in his or her own mess, for example. Dirty dishes, goo on the table, underwear on the floor, objects strewn and papers stock-piled, unswept floors and tacky shower stall: who can know the pleasure Len and his mom get out of it? Or out of their endless barbecue dinners and arguments over what to watch. With no dinner hour and no breakfast hour, no bed-time and no morning, each person follows his or her own time-path through the day — and after a while the days combine into a pleasant and glutinous tangle, like a heap of overcooked spaghetti.

One night, when Len is sulking and tinkering with a hope-lessly corroded receiver because every set is tuned to a differ-ent one of Junior's mom's favorite news channels and not one to the sitcoms of long ago (whose regressive stupidity Len is addicted to), his mom lets out a strange cry and they go over to look at the imperceptibly variable images of dark fields shad-ing up to the edge of a forest. Dozens of troopers are digging in ground so tightly woven it's as if there's a wire web strung through it. Some of them are bent over their shovels and others are looking up toward the night sky with one forearm shielding their eyes from the helicopter beams, the other hand trying to keep their broad-brimmed hats from blowing away.

Below the woods and the sloping meadow where the troopers are digging for skulls and torsos, it's just possible to make out the dark shape of a little house and the rutted furrow that becomes an impassable mountain road running the ragged length of a knotted ridge of mountains and looping down the other side to an abandoned industrial town whose last electronics factory closed half-a-century ago — leaving the famous donut shop as the only reason anyone ever passes that way.

What they've found so far is a delicate little skeleton, fragile as a model sailing ship, and the oversized skull of a middle-aged man.

A reporter's hand, gesturing from inside the helicopter and looking enormous in the lower righthand foreground of the screen, points downward with one stubby finger. No matter how loud he shouts, the pilot can't hear him over the explosive throbbing of the blades and he has to point over and over to get the pilot to drop down closer — then closer still — to the skull smiling optimistically on the ground.

Junior's mom turns right where she's standing and starts banging her narrow head hard against the thin, beer can wall of the trailer. Len goes over and takes her around, but his embrace makes her start sobbing and screaming unintelligible things into his chest.

.

A little later Junior hears his mom sobbing again and Len trying to comfort her, promising that things will change this way and that way, as if choosing from a take-out menu of possible better lives.

Late that same night Len knocks on Junior's door and tells him to get his stuff together for a trip. He warns him to take more stuff than usual and not to leave behind anything he's attached to, because it may be a long trip and they may not even come back.

Len is mutating into another Len before Junior's eyes and may not notice how Junior doesn't flinch away when he stretches his arms out for an embrace.

31

THEY drive all day and half the night before Len admits he miscalculated and there's no way they're going to make it without stopping. They pull off into a graveled picnic area and curl up under jackets and blankets as best they can.

Junior dreams that they've driven too far — to the outside of any conceivable inside. His mom's smashed her head so hard against the trailer wall that it's split open. There are seeds inside, something like the mush and seeds at the center of a cantaloupe, and each of these seeds is a potential new head. He and Len barbecue some steaks together and Junior tosses a salad. It's comforting to be eating at the old picnic table, but after a while, when it's too late, he realizes that some of the melon seeds have fallen into the salad and that he and Len have eaten them.

Junior's head is thrown back, eyes closed, mouth open: the face of a murder victim fifteen seconds after the murder, terror just disappearing into the tunnel of not-being-alive and, just below the surface of the face that barely has time to grieve for its lost body, a weird snapshot of the murderer's crazy rapture is still floating like the reflection of three people on a motel balcony staring down at something strange in the swimming pool.

In this horrible sleep there's a terror that feels like waking up suddenly, not quite alive but still breathing, struggling for breath, and then being forced down toward death again where the mind already knows there's no air — and then coming out the other side so suddenly that waking up is like speeding across the last bridge into a city, the lights and shabbiness that

are the unmistakable signs of civilization's collective inwardness headed straight for your windshield.

At about six a.m. they reach a sloping crossroad. Church
bells are chiming out an unfamiliar melody, simple and impossible to remember as a bird's fluidly changing code.

They slow down, put their heads out the windows, smell the
hidden fields and think of things they've never experienced and
never will.

32

JUNIOR and Leonard are reading their breakfast menus. The
diner window looks out from one end of the ancient horse-
shoe-shaped mini-mall in a shallow depression at the base of
a hill, giving Junior a view upward toward a gated fence and
masses of trees at the top of the hill, above them the tall chim-
neys of a brick manor house whose age is impossible to calcu-
late now that centuries are going by faster than they used to.

"I know what you're thinking," Leonard says. "You're
thinking it's ugly out here. And that we live in an ugly, stupid
way, one experience more senseless than the last. You're thinking that the only reality we ever know is the one that lags far
behind a remote future, which is always made out to be cold
and unlivable — while our little shithole in time is supposed
to be cozy and superior. But what if the ugliness that we live
with is the last vestige of a vanishing disorder? And if the most
interesting thing we can do is navigate the disorder? And if we
even go so far as to say that we're *lucky* to be navigating that
disorder...?"

Junior says that all he was doing was daydreaming about
home. Just before they left he'd picked out a grove by the creek
where he wants to build his own little cabin. And he'd like to
begin to learn the mysteries of television repair.

He's afraid they may not make it back to the campsite, Len
says. But this is not the time to be getting sentimental. Senti-
mentality is what always cooks your goose.

The waitress is there to take their orders and while Len is ordering a three-egg, five-ingredient omelette, home fries, wheat

toast, coffee, sausage links and marmalade and a tall stack of five wild blueberry buttermilk griddlecakes with lots of butter and maple syrup for them to share, Junior's staring with fascination at a mismatched back-of-head-and-neck-unit in the next booth.

Between two pink and delicate ears a matted ducktail forms an arrow that points down the median of the lightbulb-shaped head to a neck that's red and angry. The hidden gaze of the delicate-and-angry lightbulb-head is aligned with Junior's — staring forward at a set of narrow eyes staring back under a bar of solidly woven eyebrows — nose and mouth of a devilish fleshiness. Dark hair as this-way-and-that-way as the fibers of a machine-washed bathmat.

Junior can tell that he's staring at a face that hates being stared at.

Food arrives at the next table: a huge, green-banded oval ironstone platter in the waitress's left hand held out level with the angry furrows of the forehead while she clears a space on the cluttered table with a sweep of her right forearm. Face comes up before she can lower the plate. Eyes up above plate level, shining and cocked at a devouring, dog-like angle an inch away from a steaming heap of meat, mashed potatoes, mixed vegetables — all glazed in blond gravy. As the plate hits the formica, before the face gets a chance to dip down between knife and fork and knife-fork-and-face have a chance to col-laborate in carving and scooping-in a burning mound of meat-potato-and-vegetable, the mouth is already going through a reflexive spasm of licking and chewing.

The faculty of teleportation, even when it's faded with all the other faculties of childhood, never deserts us entirely.

Stare at something in the distance, there you are.

Stare at a face devouring its meal in the next booth and you're inside it, regretting that, instead of the normal breakfast you're about to eat, you aren't burying nose and chin in hot gravied meat.

It's the dog's feverish appetite that gives dogfood its mouth-watering aroma.

It's a relief for Junior when their waitress approaches and cuts off the view.

Len attacks his puffy, overstuffed omelette and Junior falls eagerly to carving up his steaming stack of blueberry griddle-cakes, buttery and glistening with syrup, shiny, bursting sausage links on the side, crisp and salty.

Suddenly Len stops eating and seems to have developed a keen interest in the dark parking lot and the distant mountains that, when the sun was out, had the tight and nubbly brown-gold weave of a handknit sweater — or to be following the miniaturized window reflection of the man who's just entered — choosing to follow his fly-like progress across the window glass rather than look at him openly.

A simpleton's face, round and spud-like with a round and spud-like nose; small, bushy brown moustache; hair nothing but reeds growing up straight and wild at the muddy edge of a pond.

Stands there looking for somewhere to sit though the place is empty, finds himself a stool at the counter and pretzels his legs around the stool post as if he planned to sit there forever.

Leonard whispers that he knows this man. His name is Holloway and the last time he saw him he was dead!

Once-upon-a-time Holloway was married to Junior's mom. Holloway was a musician at that time. The whole family was musical and the world eagerly followed the adventures of their musical family. When Junior was tiny he sang and was famous for being so tiny and playing the drums. Does he remember any of that? Does he remember — at the height of his popularity — being suddenly stricken with a fatal disease and taken to the hospital? Gone so long that when he came back he was in the wrong family. He and the family really had mutated while he was away and not one thing matched properly the way everything did before he went in. Does any of that sound familiar?

Then he came along and he and Holloway became partners. Why Holloway gave up a successful career as a do-nothing TV personality and became a hard-working technician is a long story. . . .

Leonard clams up while Holloway swivels on his stool, the thin-skinned, baby-potato face under its wild pond-growth of hair squinting puzzled at the loopy scrawl on the handwritten menuboard off to the side.

When Junior's mom was married to Holloway, Leonard continues in an even lower whisper, she was a medical doctor. Yes! His mom once was a doctor on the staff of a big urban hospital! She was the head of the trauma unit and she was the first one to establish a halfway house for those suffering from post-head-replacement crisis. It was an important *medical* position and it was an important *political* position. The pressure got to her and she began to go a little nutty. Began to tell people she was a goat farmer and then went out and actually bought some goats and began to do some goat farming. But, even with the goat farming, she couldn't shake the feeling that everyone knew she was a doctor — the famous *trauma* doctor, Dr. Quatermaine — and the fact that she was a famous doctor — a star at the height of her power and popularity — made her want to escape to another state. Hide out there, lose herself completely. The capacity for deliberate amnesia is a talent not many people have. Junior's mom's always had it, but no matter how many times you forget yourself or how many times you mutate into someone else, there always seems to be a stubborn residue of identity. Even half a dozen head replacements don't erase it. An irreducible pellet that stays with you — that *is* you — through all your recycling. Each one of us likes to think he's something fresh and new on the face of the earth, but the truth is that the principle of recycling works better on us than on our trash. Try to escape from yourself and your little pellet will always track you down. Add to this another, more serious problem. Not only was she being pursued by the irreducible pellet of her self, but there were whole regions of the States that had to be avoided: a patchwork of territories along the interstates where she'd abandoned her children and someone might still be on the lookout.

When she decided to go into hiding they installed a deep freeze in the trailer, slaughtered the goats and made up zillions of tiny packets of frozen goat meat.

He helped them load up, watched them pull away, then followed at a distance, as planned.

When he caught up with them, camping at the edge of an ugly little swamp, she'd already struck Holloway one good blow. He was lying there like an infant and sobbing. A horrible sound that brought no pity. The sobbing of an idiot. The boo-hoo-hooing of a self-pitying idiot watering himself for the millionth and last stupid time. A self-pitying idiot sobbing to reassure himself that he was human enough to be sobbing. He never hated anyone as much as he hated Holloway lying there in the mud, lit up by his flashlight, a little blood leaking out from under his weedy hair, with an expression on his face like a little boy who's just been told that he can never-ever-ever-again watch his favorite program.

He had no trouble using the hammer he'd taken from his tool box, but it was ugly. You never know how much screaming and blood are inside a creature until you try to kill it. After he'd finally cracked the skull he cut up the body. Cut off the head, of course — wrapped up the head in clear plastic — and the little steaks and chops in freezer paper, labeling them with marker just like Holloway'd done with the goat meat — and mixed the goat meat packets in with the Holloway packets and re-stacked them all neatly in the deepfreeze.

Holloway was the last link to their old identities.

With that murder they'd unknowingly begun a new career, ugly but socially useful.

There have been many times over the years he's dreamed about Holloway — and sometimes he's carving him up again and sometimes he's digging a sloppy grave for him out under a tangle of dead branches in the swamp. But there he is now — the living corpse of Holloway — the hungry ghost wandering in for a hearty diner meal — ordering dinner and looking no worse for wear than if he were his own hand-picked replacement.

.

The man who once was and may still be Holloway turns, eyes blinking as if his vision is impaired, and stares at Junior as if he knows him. About to get off his stool and come toward him with a simpleton's smile hello. But it doesn't happen. The moment with its single narrow certainty and its infinite possibilities passes and Junior thinks to himself that he's familiar with the moment-too-full, overloaded with an about-to-be that never happens, the disappointing evaporation that doesn't even have the meaningless residue of memory.

Holloway continues scanning until the severe torsion of the neck forces the body to turn on its stool, eyes coming to rest on the two faces taking a breather from their cooling mounds of meat-potatoes-gravy-and-vegetables, eyes closed and heads back against the vegetable green vinyl.

Sense Holloway's gaze, straighten up and immediately break into smiles of recognition. Holloway starts to sing and they sing along with him a tune that's hauntingly repetitive and familiar.

"Tah-*tee*-tah—tah-ta-ta-ta-*tah*. Tah-ta-tah-ta-tah-ta—tah-tah-tah-*tee*. Hmm-*hmm*-hmm. . . ."

The piercing nostalgia of the almost-forgotten theme song of a series not from your own lost childhood, but from the lost childhood of parents, grandparents and beyond.

The three men laugh ruefully and shake their heads over the shared half-memory.

That was always his grandmother's favorite program, potato-head says. He used to love to watch the re-runs with her. He would sit on the floor by her chair and sometimes she would rub his head and he would fall asleep with his face against her knee. But when the familiar sign-off melody came on — it meant up to bed and school the next morning. It meant the end of bliss: the fall back into daily anxiety.

Holloway makes a gesture of tooting a toy horn, devil face

goes TOOT-TOOT and they all laugh — remembering the hours they spent together playing a band of happy children on early morning TV.

They sing one more song from their shared TV childhood and turn back to their lunches.

Now it's Holloway's turn to eat as if trying to get to the other side of something hidden in his lunch, taking huge bites of his hot and soggy whitebread meatloaf sandwich with gravy over it, cottage fries and ketchup on the side.

Holloway finishes eating while his childhood friends are still working on coffee and big wedges of peanut butter pie with chocolate graham cracker crust. Swings off his stool and comes straight over to Leonard, slides in next to Junior and takes out his wallet. Introduces himself as Buck Singleton, shakes Leonard's hand and shows proof that he's the one Leonard came to meet.

Leonard is examining his documents and trying to figure out how Singleton could be Holloway after all.

Holloway/Singleton is already standing and zipping up his hooded yellow rain slicker.

Leonard puts a rubber-band packet of bills in Junior's hand and he and Holloway/Singleton go out into the rain where Junior's mom is already waiting decapitated in the back of Holloway/Singleton's van.

33

JUNIOR looks out the window: as dark as if someone's pulled the plug.

Time goes by with nothing to measure it.

Rain is falling steadily and here and there a puddle makes a lighted little hole in the ground.

The moon appears suddenly and briefly over low mountains to the east. Under the black sky's blue light the evergreen forest stands high and isolated, clouds swirling like wind-blown ground vapors.

Rain lets up, but the air remains charged with the storm that's already arrived and departed.

Later, an ambulance with a noisy motor pulls in, its roof flasher flashing the same colors as an old TV set, colors as unstable as the moon's when the moon is a screen for rogue transmissions.

The two attendants wile away the time by sending what may be a soccer ball bouncing and splashing through the puddles, making a makeshift goal out of a small green dumpster.

Junior falls asleep and when he wakes up the parking lot is dark and empty, even the lightning flares behind the mountains having died down to a dull phosphorescence.

34

THE kindly motorist is on his way to the famous donut shop to get a dozen donuts for his wife. Since they dug up all those skulls on the old logging road that runs in a rugged loop below Ray D. Kell State Park the dying town's revived and the famous donut shop runs out of raspberry-jelly-filled donuts by noon.

The kindly motorist buys six raspberry-jelly-filled, two plain fried, two cinnamon-sugar-crusted and two coconut-glazed and starts on his long trip home.

35

THE two beautiful, dark-haired little sisters want their donuts. The older sister's face is fatter, rosier, yet more oddly
adult. They run together toward the donut counter. Granpa's
indulgent but tired. Lanky in a hunter's red wool plaid jac-shirt,
squashed tweed hat and forest green corduroys. The face that
once was smooth and friendly has grown weathered and sour
instead of aging.

"Come *on*, Granpa!"

Another forgotten memory in the making.

Granpa follows slowly to the counter, walking as if he's having trouble with his hip. The young waitress knows him.

"Hi, Mr. Strelkoff, feeling any better today?"

Instead of answering, granpa asks the waitress sharply if she
thinks that time and age have anything to do with one another.
The fact that the body keeps deteriorating — does that have
anything to do with *time*? Are genetic predestination and time
one and the same?

Without waiting for the answer he knows can never come,
he says that when she's old and useless like him, she'll discover that age comes to everyone in the same way. At first we're
honest and greet the obvious signs of physical deterioration
with anguish, but then we do the human, predictable thing and
blame our deterioration on *time*. One day, thirty years ago,
when his opinion still meant something at Channel 343 (or was
it still only 34?), lifting the marble ashtray on his desk with his
right hand, he experienced a sharp pain in his wrist. So sharp
that for the rest of the afternoon he couldn't lift or even *grip*

anything without an agonizing knot shooting from a point below the base of the thumb all the way up through the elbow, as if forcing its way through a constricted artery. Two days later, when the pain hadn't subsided and he'd catalogued and rejected every possible disease, he came to the conclusion that this is how age arrives. The arrival of the inner affliction that spins the outer look of age that others wear. Others, not you, until now. By the end of the week he was beginning to congratulate himself on the agility with which his left hand was taking up the tasks that used to be assigned to the right hand. Age lodged in his right wrist first and spread out from there. The world always divines our secrets a few seconds after we do and acts accordingly. The week that age attached itself permanently to him, the station had one of its cyclical purges. He was out and that awful woman and her honor guard of zealots was back in. His career has never been the same. It deteriorated along with his body and along with the world. His only satisfaction is in living long enough to have seen the wheel turn one more time. Turned and rolled right over her infernal head. . . .

"But isn't she the one who first said 'What if there *is* no time?' Mr. Strelkoff? Isn't it really her idea that if time existed it would have to be the most powerful force in the universe — yet it has absolutely no effect on a broken pencil lying at the bottom of a drawer or a plastic sandwich bag in a vacant lot. 'Is time really weaker than a kitchen match? less destructive than a hungry mouth?' Didn't you translate those ideas into your own commercial language and make money off them, Mr. Strelkoff? And isn't that why you still hate her?"

Granpa Strelkoff snatches up his big, string-tied box of two dozen assorted donuts and, despite his bad hip and bad knee, hurries away from the waitress so fast that his beautiful granddaughters have to take hundreds of skipping steps to keep up with his hobbled strides. On his way out, he roughly brushes aside a man with a frightened expression and clownish stocking cap, fleeing indoors as if from the inhuman cold of another medium.

The frightened man takes a seat at the counter with an odd little hop and pulls off his cap, as if to set his peculiarly flattened, rather squared-off head free to swivel and pick up random signals.

When the waitress comes over to take his order he gets out "I'll have" and pauses, as if trying to figure out what to say next.

"Coffee?" she suggests.

"Coffee!" he agrees.

The waitress brings it.

"Thank you kindly," he says and drinks the hot coffee down in three gulps while he corkscrews both legs around the stool post.

The flattened head with its unblinking, childish stare stops at Junior — drinking coffee, eating a perfectly browned and tender stack of wild blueberry pancakes, maple syrup on his lips.

Junior looks away.

The distant mountains now have the brown-in-yellow, orange-in-brown woven look of autumn.

Just summer, now autumn, and already winter on the most lofty and distant peak — a crunchy, forbidding dome of white, a sort of visually edible Mt. Fuji without the volcanic cone-top.

"Without moving from one place to another, life revolves. It revolves like a broad round tray on a spindle. And now you reach out toward what you assume is the same bowl in the same position and taste something entirely different."

Junior can tell that the other guy's adjusted his head like a radar detector so that his gaze is aligned with Junior's — out the window and up toward the mountains. And he wonders if Radar-head still has the full power of teleportation that he himself once had: the power to travel straight through the glass and into the evergreens below the peak.

The hot coffee in his hand makes him shiver as his eye travels easily through the transparent leaves, across the cold iodine and heather of the forest floor.

Thinks to himself that we call it beautiful but when we use

the word "beauty" we're looking for language to express our pathetic desire for what's far away and untouchable. Reality flows under the bridge of the gaze that connects two nowheres. While we're lazily admiring the far-away beauty of the world, the true, bitter dampness of reality is entering someone else's body through the nose — so that the mind can chew on its aroma like the narcotic leaves of South American rainforests.

Radar-head calls out abruptly, "nuther cup of *coffee* please!" and Junior's concentration is broken.

Gets his coffee, drinks half the boiling stuff off, bolts to the donut counter and asks how much he owes.

"A dollar forty-four."

"Dolla fawty-faw?"

"Dollar forty-four."

Rushes back to his stool, corkscrews his legs back in place and drains off his coffee.

"DOLLA FAWTY-FAW!" he calls out, slaps a couple of bills on the counter and stares out the window again.

Junior aligns his gaze, hoping to recover his lost powers. What was involuntary then now takes a horrible effort of concentration. What was an uncontrollable fire can now barely be fanned into life. And yet the thing we're most afraid of losing is also what we couldn't wait to be free of. Free of it, we're haunted by its loss. Now, through the radar-headed man's eyes, we're able to see that something black is looming up and swaying a bit over the evergreen tips, the way a bear stands up on its hind legs and waves its paws. Lower down there's a bright and crackling object in the leaves, a dancing fire of blues and reds within a wavering frame that's mirror-like and absorbent, a tiny upright lake with its reflective surface and fathomless bottom silty with the slime of decaying images.

Radar-head pulls on his blue parka and clownish red stocking cap and bolts out the door.

A waitress whose face has had all its expressions recycled too many times over the centuries exchanges looks with a skinny griddle cook loafing in the kitchen doorway and they laugh but shut up abruptly when Radar-head flies back in, looks around and says "dolla fawty-faw?"

"You paid already," the waitress who served him coffee says kindly.

"I paid already?"

"Uh-huh, it's taken care of. You don't owe any more."

"Oh," he says in a clear and sensible voice. "My mother was supposed to meet me here. But that was two months ago."

They watch him cross the two lane highway, dodging traffic speeding to and from a neighboring state on the other side of a low mountain.

36

JUNIOR is in the small but tidy apartment the waitress rents from a farmer eight minutes from the donut shop (calculated on the faulty speedometer of an old blue stationwagon traveling a slow and bumpy sixty miles an hour). They pop some popcorn and watch TV and now his face is in the brown-and-orange fiber of the sweater her mom knit for her five years ago. Both the sweater and her hair smell like pine needles. Why is that? Have they taken on the aroma of the couch cushions, which are hard and heavy and rustle stiffly when you move? His head burrows into the sweater, which has burning creases hidden between its hills and valleys.

The pressure against his mouth brings his body and its lifetime rising up with force behind the back of his face.

A warm body pressing against the human mouth can feel the softness yielding before the core of bone, but it can never know what it's pressing against.

Leads swiftly beyond tenderness.

Instant has a thin shell that explodes easily.

And inside it?

Thin shell of love itself at all times a gate into what will explode it.

Mouth holds passion and agony and doesn't know the difference.

The mouth that kisses is folded softly over the one that bites.

37

I T'S the waitress's day off and she decides to go shopping at the
mall. While she's shopping Junior sits deep in a booth of the
giant pasta and pizza restaurant and finds himself eating more
of a sixteen inch pizza with sausage, peppers, pepperoni, extra cheese, extra sauce, onions, garlic, meatballs and anchovies
than he wanted to and drinking his second "mile high" root
beer float while he tries to make life's incessant mutation slow
down by writing in a narrow-ruled spiral bound notebook. He
keeps re-reading his tomato-stained scrawl and making changes.

"I'm beginning to not know who I was.

"The farthest back I can remember is our campsite — and
there is no path that leads toward it, only away from it.

"What does it mean to say: 'our daily amnesia'?

"Where do the expressions that spring to mind fully formed
come from?

"Does anyone ever actually 'know' himself/herself? Aren't
we known only by those who know us? Known by strangers or
not at all?"

He doesn't completely understand what he's written and
looks out from his vantage point deep in the restaurant's interior toward the tables that line the window-wall looking up
into multiple shopping levels. His eye falls on a young couple
talking. The girl is standing, her body at a 45° angle to one
corner of the table, facing the seated young man who's looking up at her — so that Junior is seeing the distant and sharply
cut-out profile of what the young man is seeing close, round
and complete.

She's wearing a white shirt with long sleeves and jeans worn to a texture whose velvet smoothness the eye can feel as if with the girl's own hand. She's slender and her movements are quick. Skin is a dark, toasted brown, also very smooth to the eye. Slips into the seat facing the thin young man with a moody and convex face, short chin, dark eyes and eyebrows, unhappy-looking in a way the beautiful young woman finds attractive.

She slouches under the table, straightens up, slouches, sits bolt upright, slides hands over velvety jeans-surface of her legs or sketches looping diagrams in the air, all the while talking and laughing.

Can't keep still. Her self-love, flowing over itself and shining like water, is impossible not to watch.

Now big groups of students ordering fresh rounds of beer and flirting loudly with their waitresses over pizza toppings and grinder fillings make it hard to tune into the young couple's frequency traveling along a helpful curve of glass wall and ceiling.

Thinks he hears the unhappy young man ask, "Do you remember if she said, 'the automobile invented the movies,' or is it the other way around?"

"Is that on the same page where she talks about the opening of *Voyage in Italy*? — where she says that there is no distinction between the fact that a film is beginning — an audience is beginning to *watch* a film beginning — and the forward propulsion of the through-the-windshield gaze of someone driving into the approaching distance along a little highway in Italy. It's then that she talks about the equation between the perspective of the automobile windshield and the movie screen — the triad of viewer, screen and implied depth of reality — and makes a remark about the mutual invention of driving and movie-going and the beginning of a new journey of speed and perception. . . ."

"When does she talk about the invention of time? 'The apparent plunge into the bottomless depth of the screen — the plunge into the distance of the highway, which may or may not be infinite — are for each person the absolute first moment of

the invention of time.' And where does she talk about the para-
doxical invention of time and eradication of time in the forward
plunge of driving and viewing. . . ?"

They're both leafing through copies of the same fat manual
whose cover is a storm of red and blue particles like the one the
brain sees at the moment of impact.

"All I can find is this paragraph where she talks about how
speed was the most important thing the last century invented.
'The last century added velocity to everything, which ultimate-
ly resulted in two parallel, self-contained systems for the re-
production of reality.' "

Junior's brow furrows with the young woman's while she
leafs through the manual.

The young man says that he has to admit that it has more of
an impact on him when it's less theoretical.

"'Parents are another name for the distance we're born
with. Some of us have a feeling of being separated at birth —
others feel it more as time goes on, as if it were a separation
from the self — but in any case we're never sure from whom
or from what.'

"'True or false: a) the world is always becoming another
world (each new thing re-invents everything before it) or b)
reality has only been significantly re-invented an absurdly tiny
number of times.'"

That reminds the beautiful young woman of something and
she starts acting out scenes from a film they've seen together.
The unhappy young man looks at her with undisguised delight
while she playacts and laughs to the point of coughing. A harsh
note that travels across the squared-off cathedral dome of the
restaurant and that makes Junior see the cigarette in her hand.
"It doesn't suit her, yet it's hers."

Wants to cross over to them — sit at their table — rather
than stay in his booth with the remains of his pizza and dregs of
rootbeer float — and ask if they agree that human identity exists like this: each helped into existence by the gaze of the other.
No existence at all, for anyone, without a perpetual exchange

of gazes. Don't they agree? Isn't that how everything exists in the world? A conspiracy of looking, for which we've invented engines that manufacture things to see. There's no end to the machinery of visibility...."

When the couple exits, reappearing momentarily on an escalator leading to one of the upper shopping tiers, Junior feels so alone his reality thins out to the point where he needs to nibble on his cold pizza and sip the warm, syrupy dregs of his float just to feel that his body is alive and breathing. The young and kindly waitress is waiting for him at an appointed spot somewhere in the shopping mall, but Junior's face is already asleep on the map he's taken from his back pocket and flattened on the table.

38

JUNIOR is walking down the local highway, dragging his blue duffel bag.

It's barely daylight, the sky an icy pond with an unlikely slice of lemon squashed at the bottom of it.

An old and enormous baby blue convertible stops and idles. The driver, a pleasant-looking woman with fluffy grey-blonde hair, round cheeks, beaver teeth and lively eyes, offers him a lift. He tries to describe the location of the campsite he left behind in another lifetime years (or is it months?) ago. The driver turns her head and says to her companions that the campsite he's describing reminds her of the place where they once filmed an episode — a truly stupid and funny one — the famous "Fly Fishing" episode, in fact.

Someone in the depths of the car growls an answer and the fluffy-haired driver's somewhat drawling voice and the growling passenger's voice, taken together, have the sentimental ring of a familiar but forgotten theme song.

•

The old convertible runs smoothly on its fuel of nostalgia.

Junior is in the back, wedged between an old woman with white clown face and a man who looks like a hideously aged version of a handsome singing bandleader, hair on the shrunken and speckled head trimmed to a black fin, a livid surgical scar across a bulging forehead that hasn't finished healing.

The convertible quickly drives into twilight and, when it turns dark, they exit and stop for gas in a small town.

Junior leans against the car. Breathes deeply: the air of a local eternity, tranquil and depressed, a fragrant, deeply-anchored nowhere, as if a meteor shower had deposited it in the landscape along with a thousand towns no-one-knows-how-many aeons ago.

The clown-faced Lucy-look-alike (less Lucy-like in the open air) comes loping back from the gas station gift shop, her loose mouth munching on a big wedge of fudge.

Wants to know if anyone here would be able to identify Claudia Schiffer even if she'd aged badly and been through some awful throat surgery that mangled the pleasant voice and German accent.

The fluffy-haired driver says that once the electronic stocking mask is removed it all starts oozing out every which way like pancake batter. Must-must-must stay inside it no matter what!

Someone else doesn't see how it can be Claudia Schiffer because he remembers Claudia Schiffer vanishing off the face of the earth and someone else isn't at all sure who Claudia Schiffer is or was or why anyone *should* recognize Claudia Schiffer, the worm of oblivion programmed in from the beginning.

Well, the un-Lucy-like Lucy-lookalike says, she wishes someone would just go in and take one look. Because, as far as she's concerned, Claudia Schiffer, who'd disappeared in that weird way and was given up for dead so many years ago, is in there now, fat and happy and selling tons of her famous maple walnut fudge made with real Vermont maple syrup....

·

The bluff, bald-headed man with the growling voice gets behind the wheel and in a minute they're back on the road, the clown-faced lookalike falling even more silent and sulky than the hideously aged bandleader in his dark corner.

·

The black intervals between the houses gradually grow longer and eventually eat the town. One second you're driving past scattered houses and businesses, then you're in town, and then you're zipping along through pure blackness at an incredible rate, frustrating the eye's innate desire to look, even at nothing, and keeping it from lingering on the hidden yellow light of the house in the woods or the orange sparkle of an eye that's just loped across the road and turned to have a look at what tried to kill it.

"The essence of driving is to keep on driving with no end in sight," Junior thinks, "feeding discs into the dashboard slot as if that's the fuel that makes it endless."

·

A long avenue runs along the edge of a cemetery for miles straight ahead. Makes him feel alone in the midst of large sheets of space. The hand that holds the sheets is not apparent, but when they're shaken out what falls to earth are the long avenue, the cemetery, the black gate and a fence dividing the world unequally. Now it can be seen that the sheets are one continuous sheet and that that sheet is a plane of snow that cuts across all other planes, particularly the plane of air. To get to the other side of the cemetery is urgent, if only to escape from the endless continuity of perspective. Fence and gate are a simple obstacle. Cemetery itself is a park and no discernible order to the pathways among the uneven rows of ancient trees and headstones. One could easily get lost here like an abandoned child, the cemetery's job.

The path around the cemetery goes on forever, wide enough for a solitary person on foot.

He sets off along the path that runs beside the fence, snow on either side.

He hasn't gone far when he stops to listen to a cry somewhere on the other side of the cemetery, where the sun seems warm and yellow on the snow. Two tall women, moving slowly and beautifully as giraffes, meet and kiss under plumed hats floating broadly above them like parasols. Plumed hats, dresses that could just as easily be puffed and shimmering coats, are the hazy rose and frozen blue of pond reflections.

One of them (the one with a full upper lip pulling up a bit

118

from gleaming incisors that are touchingly girlish) cries out as
if about to weep.

"*Clowd*ia! Oh, Clowd-*ee!*"

As if one of the women has come back from the dead.

The woman who has fawn-like skin and large eyes that are
sad but not stupid smiles and dips her body in the opening ripple of ecstasy. She presses her two long hands to either side of
her face, framing her plaintive eyes in a gesture that's senseless
but magnetic.

It's all senseless, but not as senseless as the first haunting cry.

"*Clowd*ia! Oh, Clowd-*ee!*"

What can it mean? He wonders in what lifetime he's heard
this cry before. And if it's true that it's always the senseless
thing that haunts us.

·

When Junior wakes up Lucy-not-Lucy is driving and suddenly there's gravel under the tires and they've arrived.

Arrive before you know you've arrived, as always.

Things go on just long enough to make you forget that
they're not going to go on forever.

39

AT night, in the cheaper inns and motels, everyone who turns on the TV follows the path of the same murderer, the adventure of the same lost child, while in the exclusive ones there are a dizzying number of sites and events to tune in on.

.

Junior wakes up to the distant sound of voices that could be live human voices or TV voices that have gotten trapped in the plaster and wiring. Rotates his head as if trying to recover a lost faculty. Voices die away in the carpeted peacefulness of the room: traveling from any point in the hotel, down at least one long corridor, around a bend and then to the end of another corridor, to this remote, windowed corner where no sound reaches.

Lies down and, from the horizontal, can tell that the voices are behind him in the wall, a little louder than the buzzing of a fly trapped between two windows, crawling upward to a point somewhere above his head, as if sensitive to the magnetic field surrounding the human brain and trying to creep out of range.

He gets into a kneeling position and presses his ear against the wall above the headboard. The wall is cold and alive with the hum of trapped electrons. The edge of the headboard digs into the neck, so that the head, numbing itself against the neck's discomfort, loses its body and is suspended in the thin realm that mirrors the thin realm on the other side of the wall where a man's voice is vibrating deep and clear.

"The weirdest thing to me is how they keep coming after you. They just keep coming back!"

Someone else says like flies you think you've killed with a swatter and bug spray, but who start zzz-zzz-ing again every time the temperature rises. . . .

"It's like you have to go through the same thing one-hundred-and-twenty-one times!"

"Till we get it right?"

"Till we get it right!"

"And if we *never* get it right?"

They laugh at themselves, but the mystery of their laugh, sharp and stupid, will never be solved — lost in the surge of the television, where the blended and amplified voice of the arena crowd lifts off and can never be reunited with its human origin.

"*There* goes a hundred bucks!" one of the men says.

"A fuckn three pointa! A fuckn three pointa! He hadda make a fuckn three pointa now?!"

"*This* game is fucked. Shut the fuckn thing off."

"No, let's watch the news for a second, honey," a woman's far sweeter voice says from the thicker atmosphere away from the wall.

"Could that be them?"

A minute passes. Sound of the TV is lowered and almost inaudible.

"Doesn't look like them."

A toilet flushes in the distance, and a man yells, "Somebody call me?"

"Amigo, come and have a look!"

Junior scrambles across the bed, searching in the bedclothes for the remote.

The screen is small, the image reduced and precisely observed: lenses that correct the vision of all the eyes in the world.

Two bodies are hanging from a tree: strung up by their ankles, heads missing, arms and fingers pointing stiffly toward something hidden in the white brilliance of the blue water surging behind them between green promontory and brown slope.

A ladder has been laid against the tree and someone in uniform is climbing it.

The noise of rushing water is loud enough to give the sensation of being there, catching a damp whiff of forest floor.

Now he thinks he hears one of the men say that it's always the same: the beauty of nature is and always has been nothing but the background for the ugliest of human adventures. And the woman says with a clear, sweet and bell-like vibration through the wall, "Shut it off. Tomorrow is another long, filthy day."

After that there's nothing to be heard and Junior stretches out again on the big bed and falls into a fearful sleep.

40

DAYLIGHT cuts a short way into the room through slightly parted drapes. Beds are unmade, remains of food and drink on a low table, towels and newspapers on the floor. Junior sits up. Finds his watch inside a tissue box. It's two in the afternoon, lamp on though it's light outside. Knows that there's a reason he's sitting on the edge of the bed in striped pajamas, hair uncombed, feeling as if he could sleep all day, but doesn't remember what it is.

He crosses to the window, opens the drapes and the extraordinary volume of the day fits exactly into the dimensions of the room. The volume of the day and the beauty of the day: blue and white as far as the eye can see. Edge of what's blue has been scraped white and what's rough and white sails out across what's blue, which becomes smooth again only because a white sail is ironing out its creases.

Takes one step closer to the window, looks down. Mind goes over the brink like a springy metal coil able to send one end down through one-hundred-and-twenty-three stories of air and sunlight all the way to the sidewalk while the other end remains stuck to the hotel-room floor.

Springs back up and dizzily regards the massive garage wall, sunlit from edge to edge without a shadow and tilted up as a plateau it could walk straight out on. Mind remembers another, contradictory truth, equally true, and springs back again to its rooted spot on the floor.

Gazing to the right, out over the wall, the medium is impossibly blue: a little thing, boat or plane in sky or water, shining and crawling forward in it.

A darker region in the deep distance, oddly furrowed, wind forever brushing across the residual basins that never succeed in evaporating entirely.

Wind also brushes across the surface of a distant hotel pool deck: green awning and solitary swimmer, who seems to be looking Junior's way.

Zigzag pedestrian routes, encountered from above, with the human subtracted from the human, take on a meaningless clarity and an electronic economy of purpose.

"If we see the extraordinary clarity of the day straight out under sky and clouds and are also perfectly sealed off from it, are the clarity of the day and our distance from it one and the same?"

Gets back into bed, turns on the TV and is comforted to pick up the thread of a pleasure whose familiarity and stupidity can't be disentangled.

·

When he wakes up the bright day looks like the same day, maybe brighter, but it feels more like a day that's gone by. Wind is still blowing clouds and blue air around the tower. Tiny bursts of remotest voice tone, explosive clips of static, the noise-universe always available between assigned frequencies. Dashes of music, bird cries, a voice trying to reach other voices through a microphone, droning of airplane engines, all going in and out of transmission, very faintly and remotely, barely enough to add up to a stable boundary. To hear anything he has to struggle toward it. Doesn't come toward him, whether for lack of strength or for some other reason. Turn the head, retune the ear, and the mind breaks up and travels out toward the sound-horizon's thin and scattered bands and clouds. The more thin and scattered the sound-horizon, the more dazzling the visible world that gives rise to it.

The wide and sunny outer world only makes him more alone.

Turns on the TV and immediately feels restored to an impersonal lifetime of experience that ought to belong to everyone but belongs only to him, like a mirror where you can always go to see something familiar, a gesture as instinctive and repetitive as the hand combing the hair. The unruly pretzel loops and spaghetti tangles are combed out precisely so that the breezes of the world can restore their tangled loops so that the combing or brushing gesture will be repeated over and over with the dullest of pleasure.

Feels itself laughing at the fact that nothing will be seen but the thing that can't help being seen because it exists only to be seen, like the microwavable plastic sac of spinach in butter sauce that exists for no other reason than the obvious, circular one.

Slumped between window and television, Junior wonders how he arrived at the age of twenty. *How it began* is hard to remember and also the dodging path of steps that followed. Your very own life disappears from you as you're living it. Your very own life, yet it isn't available to you. Everything puts you at a distance from it. You're living it — there's no denying that — but as if for someone else. There you are, lying on the coarse hotel bedspread, remote button under your spastic thumb, leapfrogging through distant images, some of them familiar, like someone confined to bed with a mysterious and debilitating ailment, the remote perpetually in his grip — at the other end, scrambling electrons pretending to be a living person leading the life that should have been yours.

·

It's night again and Junior is lifelessly watching an old movie about scientists trapped on a space station. A long time ago they made an important discovery, one that has to do with the invention of Time, but they've forgotten what it was.

"There are forms of life that flourish here like viruses. They're *not* viruses, but they *act* like viruses."

"I think that what we did was to annihilate the human up here and then find a way to *preserve* that annihilated humanity and ship it back to earth."

"Like a pill of immortality that must be swallowed daily."

"The less alive we are, the more immortal."

"This is what it would be like to be dead-alive: not seeing, not feeling, not hearing: but *knowing: the mind permanently embalmed in the delusion that it knows the world directly through its remote contact.*"

"Each new self makes another self disappear," the eldest scientist concludes sadly, lighting up his pipe and taking a reflective swivel in his chair. "Memory is worthless and may not even exist. The truth of experience is real but replaced easily by the *next* truth. And to the extent that experience depends on memory it comes into question too. I worry constantly about the instability of the instant, but I've never been able to come up with the equation to express it."

"But," someone else says, "if the instant is constantly crawling into the next instant, what does that do to the stability of the self? Which one is it?: that the self can barely remember itself from one day to the next or that nothing, neither styrofoam nor tungsten, is more stubborn and unchangeable."

"Little blob spins until it takes on shape and identity. For a second we belong to ourselves. Feel the whishing of our little blob and the emptiness around it. But this is the part that I'll never understand! it flies off its axis and twirls away from us. There it is in the distance: what used to be us: now we need a telescope to see it. Our identity — what we experienced, what we knew as our selves —is now grooved into the twirling spindle of infinity. . . ."

"Right now for example: I can feel where the thickness of my self ends and something else that's thinner and isn't my self begins."

"And when you leave this room you'll just be another figure walking along the base perimeter of a sunny garage wall massive as an Aztec pyramid."

"Known by everyone while I myself know nothing. . . ."

"Less immortal down there or up here?"

"Our only idea of the afterlife is the remoteness we already feel from ourselves as living beings...."

.

Hours later, when it's dark and the only lights are the lights of other hotels and the colorful lights of road and flightpath traffic, there's a quiet tapping at the connecting door and the gruff-voiced man, bald and bluff, comes in to say that he's sorry that they were gone so long, but the plan is to get an early start. He seems downcast, like a boy who's been scolded. The others also poke their heads in to say goodnight and not one of them seems like the same person.

41

THEY drive silently all morning. The woman who used to have fluffy yellow-white hair and a pleasant, puffy face is driving and the one who never really looked like Lucy, wearing a towering black wig that makes her big nose even bigger, has the job of reading off complex directions from the map. They're looking for an interstate and the only time they use their voices is to argue bitterly over directions.

They find themselves on a small country road and Junior can't tell from their bickering if this is where they want to be or if they've missed the entrance loop to the interstate. The road grows smaller as it dips below the white ribbon fencing and smooth, rising meadows of horse farms and then climbs toward a rounded crest where, from its low elevation, there's a blue and sketchy view of distant mountains, very high and with irregular, drooping cone-tips and jigsaw scallops, but with little sense of solid mass.

Road and car continue on, as always.

A distant valley and its wooded upslope appear over a nearby hill. The green hill in the foreground is like a shoulder over which you cast your look. The hill is your own green shoulder and for that reason the bluish lavender of the layered mountains is soft and intimate. Mountains stay where they are while their distance approaches.

Inevitably the road turns — turns and turns again — so that what was on one side is now on the other. Across a low meadow and through an opening in the forest the mountains recover their distance. No measuring how many wafers of distance are compressed in the sloping blue camelback that extends to the left in one wavy line, the heathery color of pure far-awayness.

The many turns of the road and the fleeting perspectives that were yours are suddenly lost to you, as always.

What was the object of a sidelong glance now rises dead ahead as if it were your destination.

Someone is hungry, someone else hears the sound of migrating geese and they decide to stop and have a picnic on the shore of a long pond that bends in twisted figure eights around grassy islands, rippling against a far shore that's also a sloping hill like the side of a pitched green roof. Up and down the green roof-slope of the hill cows have arranged themselves singly and in clusters, sitting folded or standing and staring, with the random order that always seems impossible to improve on.

They break out sandwiches and coffee. One set of aged lookalikes leans against the hood of the car, the other set remaining in the relative comfort of the interior and Junior taking his lunch down to the shore, where he can stretch out on the uneven ground, listen to the rustling of tiny animals in the tangled shore growth and smell the wild brown smell of roots, the reassuring green smell of slime.

If the surface of the pond records the surface of the sky, Junior thinks in a horizontal way, hands under head, not really thinking, then what does the surface of the sky record? And the bottom of the pond? How are we supposed to get to know that? Bottom of pond and bottom of sky certainly have nothing to do with one another. Each seems to entirely reject the nature of the other — finding a common ground only in a transparent exchange of looks somewhere above the level of the human head....

Cows live with it all calmly. Is it knowledge? Is it indifference? Always folded in their meadows....

Junior has only to lift his head a little to see a dark wave of geese arrive over the far hill — dropping down over the rim with wings pulled back and legs extended — while other, more massive waves circle at a greater altitude over the tree line. The rise-and-fall of their massed calls sounds like the overlapping bays and cries, yipping and full-throated, the persistent seesawing of depth and hysteria, the faraway hammering on wood and its ringing echo, of hunting dogs, their cries uncannily reaching this spot from the hidden distance of the mountains. Their wild cries, collecting in this basin and sliding too easily from domestic contentment to a wanderer's anguish, guide those still distant or circling.

As it continues into dusk and the baying grows more desperate and strange, Junior realizes that it's been a long time since he's heard a sound from the others.

Lying on his back, with his jacket bunched up under his head, he tries to twist his neck around to have a look but finds the effort too great and falls back to daydreaming.

"The great horizontality of evening," he recites to himself from memory something that was read to him a long time ago in a quiet livingroom by someone who died an ugly death.

"The weight of the day.

"Everything that's light has already risen into the thinner air of the sky. At the instant of dusk, the number of bird cries multiplies. Below the light and in front of the woods where you can already feel the solid compression of the dark bottom of the world under the weight of the day, space is a suspended little sky dome whose only boundary is the broad interval between cry and answer of the peculiar birds of twilight."

He hears a car door open and close and he's happy that someone is coming down to join him. He wants to ask if this is what they mean when they talk about being outside the bright, unnatural light of society. Is this it? Are they there? And was that their destination? The long moments feel important to *him*. They feel extraordinary. Is it possible they don't feel it too? He turns his head just enough to see the distorted fraction of his face reflected in the blade sailing toward his neck.

42

OOH la la", a little girl's voice sings way down below the window. Far from room and bed, an unimaginable distance.

"This is how you do it: 'LA la la'."

Singing to other children.

Lying in bed, feeling feverish. When the illness began a woman was looking into his crib. The woman didn't say she was his mother and in his own mind she wasn't his mother. Family'd gone out and left this woman to watch him. Auburn hair cut as if with the strict boundaries of the television screen in mind, heart-shaped face not so much kind as inquisitive, eyeglasses with a bluish pearlized rim, and mouth with a disarming over-bite all bend themselves into a single unified image and bend down deep into the crib, close to the child's face. Mouth wide open in the act of laughing or calling out to someone who's entered the room deep in the concealed background could also be the mouth screaming because the car is headed for the guard rail spliced open as if the car's already gone through it.

His earliest memory of another human being is of this oddly familiar stranger — and it coincides with the beginning of his illness.

At the beginning the family isn't there, but no one ever remembers the beginning.

•

What we actually experience is very small. And what's called reality is the territory that lies outside the tiny province of experience and presses it into shape.

Since there's so little of it, the mind rehearses its memories of experience over and over to give itself a certain repetitive pleasure. This is our only actual life, while the reality we live in every day is an alien sphere outside us that doesn't have one day's immortality in the mind. The self and its little store of experience learn to negotiate the alien sphere in order to be able to tear loose the little bits it wants to play with obsessively.

Secretly live in this tiny, repetitive sphere. Travels with us always, within the orbiting debris of all the rest.

With illness the context of experience disappears, just as in childhood.

43

H E'S standing on the uneven lawn below his grandmother's house, eating from a bag of lime-flavored jelly candies crusted with granulated sugar. A wide porch with logs cut and stacked high at one end for the wood-burning stove in the parlor. Snow on the ground. A river shining here and there, audible in a discontinuous way that doesn't seem to match the shining points of visibility through a golden stand of larches. On the other shore, hidden and scattered, campsites with their fragrant smoke.

Wide porch elevated over lawn and broad, fast-moving river. Woodsmoke aroma.

Sun through golden larch needles.

River whose noise and light come and go like the damp earth-and-root smell he catches only when the wind blows his way.

Nothing here matches another cherished memory he'd always believed was real: small apartment above the shop where she once sold candy and toys, on a rough street as warm and comfortable as if carpeted and furnished, but only because his grandmother lived there.

Remembers standing on the sidewalk in front of his grandmother's toy-and-candy shop, a red box of raisins in his fist.

Filled mouth begins to chew its raisins automatically and compulsively.

Taste and smell of raisins and of sticky, raisin-stained cardboard.

Covers the instant, like a bag over the head. As if the head is entirely inside the raisin box. Replaced by the raisin box and its smell. Replaced then and always will be.

Two years old, yet he's on the sidewalk alone. Waiting in a broad and sunlit space for a car to arrive, no one waiting with him. Waiting for his uncle, only what uncle would that be? His uncle is coming to drive him to the hospital. Knows he's going to the hospital, but does he know why? A second illness comes later. Seems like a different illness but may be the same one. And the child may know the future of all its illnesses on the sidewalk, chewing blindly on a hundred raisins.

•

Sometimes a corpse enters a hospital and is told to lie down. And sometimes the touch of a kindly nurse revives it.

•

"That's it! *Ah* la la!"

The child's sweet voice is further away. Wind blows through it and between voice and building. Whole rim of the hospital trembles with little noises. Wind rushes around and around as if bound to it. Metal spikes squeal like little forest animals.

•

"In general," the grandmotherly nurse says, stroking his hair, "we depend on the kindness of others."

"But I learned very early, before my earliest memories," he says in a hoarse voice he doesn't recognize as his own, "not to depend on anyone. And I also learned early that others aren't kind."

"Not to be told the truth about ourselves is often more kindness than we can expect. And if others weren't kind wouldn't every day end in blood?"

•

The doctor, already out the door, pokes his head back in and says to the nurse that it might just be the right medicine to have the television turned back on.

They switch it on and stand watching idly with the comatose patient whose body doesn't seem eager to accept the fact that the newly grafted head resembles one of the joking and mugging television heads bobbing yes to everything that's said.

44

JUNIE is in the kitchen, beginning to mix her wet ingredients into her dry ingredients in a big blue-banded mixing bowl. This is her popover batter and when it's done she sets it aside and washes a few dishes and starts to get her smothered chicken with mushroom gravy going and all the little side dishes that go along with it.

The doorbell rings, a little too early for Waldo to be back from his job on the distant islands.

The kitchen door comes off its hinges, as always — triggering an expression that might be one of lowgrade despair (having to fix for the ten thousandth time the stupid thing you had to fix an hour before) if it didn't also reflect consciousness of the surf of distant laughter.

Gets the door open, crosses the blue, threadbare carpet to the front door, opens that and exclaims, "Oh, Elinore, it's *you*!"

"Yeah, Mrs. Anderson, it's me. Who'd you think it was? The famous *Head*-monster who's come to cut off your head? They say he was sighted not too far from our neighborhood, Mrs. Anderson."

"My head? Are you saying I forgot to put my head on, Elinore?"

A smaller girl steps out from behind Elinore. She's got one eye closed, her thumb is in her mouth and she's hanging onto her sister's sleeve.

"I only stopped by because Lauren wanted to say hello to Junior."

"Ok girls, come on in."

135

Junie has to make three attempts to jerk the weight of the kitchen door upward and simultaneously shoulder it sideways to get it to fit back into its groove and close.

"Making supper?"

Elinore takes a couple of sniffs with an expression that says that something stinks.

"Well, yes, getting started, sweetheart."

She's beginning to feel anxious and to hate this awful twelve-year-old who's making her anxious.

"Where's David?"

"David? Oh, he's not feeling all that great, honey. He's sitting in the other room, watching TV with Junior. They're eating super-crunchy peanut butter and doing a frame-by-frame analysis of the Alga Hessler episode of *You Asked For It*, so you can imagine what kind of shape they're in."

"Is there anything for us to munch on, Mrs. Anderson?"

"Gee, no, honey, there isn't. Nothing to munch on in this house but that one tub of super-crunchy peanut butter David and Junior are sharing in there. Unless you'd like some pop-over batter or some raw chicken."

"Did you ever have any of those toasted almonds that come in a jar with a little salt and spicy powder on them, Mrs. Anderson?"

"No, I'm sorry, honey, I don't think we have any little toasted almonds with spicy powder."

"No, I said did you *ever* have."

"Oh I'm sure I must have tasted them, Elinore. We all have other lifetimes where we get to taste things. That's how we acquire our pleasant memories. But right now, in *this* lifetime, we can't afford any spicy almonds."

"*My* dad's pretty much a deadbeat, Mrs. Anderson, and we always have spicy almonds in *our* house. How come we have stuff to munch on and you don't?"

"Well, honey, in our house we just seem to prefer peanut butter."

"Do you think I could see David and Junior for a teentsy

second, Mrs. Anderson? They haven't been in school for ages and my mom's a little worried."

"Well, honey, just explain to your mom that since I got back from the hospital — or you can tell her that it started way before I got back from the hospital — probably when David came back from the dead — between David's ordeal and then my ordeal — and Junior being such an all-round-pain-in-the-ass and Waldo being the headless wonder he's always been — life in our house isn't exactly the same as life in your house. Could you tell your mom that?"

"Well, I think she'd feel a whole lot better if I could tell her that I saw David and Junior and that they're ok, Mrs. Anderson."

The doorbell rings.

On their way out the girls pass Waldo coming in. When the kitchen door slams firmly for the third time, the younger sister whispers to the older, "Was that *him*?"

"Yes."

"He doesn't look like anything to *me*."

"That's because you're too young. Mom says that when she was a little girl Waldo Anderson did something that made him famous. Only his name wasn't Anderson then and she can't remember what it was he did."

•

Waldo's eating and watching TV as if that's his assignment. The scene he's watching takes place in a livingroom not altogether different from the one he's in, except that the image of that one is sharper and more colorful than the image of the one he's in. In the last scene, the children struck poses, wrinkled their noses and traded insults. Then Dad appeared with the look of someone making tracks from kitchen to toilet, stopped for a second as if the squabbling children needed his advice, said something so stupid it had a tranquilizing effect on everyone on-and-off-screen, leaving each one to the individual pursuit of boredom.

Now the doorbell's rung.

Not bored, only waiting for something to react to.

Important, always, to get in close. Focus on nothing but the facial reactions of the children and you're in the presence of a special theater. The stage of this special theater is the adolescent and pre-adolescent face and the mystical X-space of the looks passing between one face and another. What is the reality of a look while it's in the act of traveling? No longer on one face and not yet on the other. There the viewer is — in the space between one face and another — feeling in herself or himself the mild agitation of the particle that isn't quite happiness but isn't unhappiness either.

More it resembles happiness, the more an anti-particle of unhappiness is bound to appear in it.

Every emotion includes its own mocking negation.

With the mocking negation of happiness we secretly pursue happiness.

The "pursuit of happiness" now has an ingredient added that extends its shelf life indefinitely.

The joke line always follows the emotion line and is its preservative.

At least ten ingredients added to the bottle to keep it from spoiling.

The next character bursts on the scene, saying the things already pleasantly anticipated in the facial preparations of those waiting.

The beautiful arms and legs hanging awkwardly from pre-adolescent faces as smooth as kneecaps are what Waldo finds himself staring at as he polishes off his third huge helping of smothered chicken, gravy, popovers, applesauce, sweet potato pie and salad.

45

A T 4:30 in the afternoon a boy in an old blue parka runs out onto the porch of his house, howling. A thin woman, cursing and breathless, manages to outrun the boy with long strides, grab a fistful of nylon and wrestle him to the ground.

Boy is spinning around on the cold porch boards, trying to get in a position to kick her leg.

Thin woman kneels on one knee, reaches under the parka with an expression on her face like she's trying to twist off a non-twist bottle cap.

Howling again, he breaks loose, runs down the steps to the street and stands wiping his eyes as if, given the slightest encouragement, he'd apologize and slink back up.

"Get the hell away!" the thin woman screams. "Get away from the house! Run as far as you can! Disappear from the face of the earth!"

46

DON'T you ever tell me that you don't love me any more, Jimmy, cause that makes me all insecure an' I go off the deep end. As you well know!"

It's time for the bronchial laugh with blood in it, the laugh that makes Jimmy honk like a goose shot down over a dark lake.

"You've gotta leave it in another hour, James. Then the bacon comes out, you baste it a little with its own juices and give it another ten minutes or so."

Junie and Jimmy are cooking together. They've baked a blueberry pie and now there's a big meat casserole in the oven. Junie's got an ancient green cookbook spread out and wants to run through the recipe again to make sure they've followed all the steps.

"We melted the butter in the casserole, we drained the meat and reserved the meat *and* half the marinade with the seasonings."

"Right."

"Placed the meat in the casserole and added the reserved liquid and seasonings?"

"Salted it to taste. Uh-huh, we did those both."

"Placed the casserole — *uncovered* — in the center of the oven. Cooked it about one hour...."

"Then reduced the heat to about three hundred. Yup."

"So right now the point we're at — we just turned the meat in the liquid and then covered each piece of meat with bacon. Continue cooking about one hour...."

"Or until the meat is tender?"

"Until the meat is tender, then remove the bacon and discard it."

"Not only *remove* it, but *discard* it."

"Cook the meat about ten minutes longer, transfer to a warm platter and strain the liquid. Discard the solids. Then there's some more stuff, but we don't need to know that yet."

"Don't we have to get some noodles up?"

"Uh-huh. Yep. 'Serve hot with noodles, dumplings or potatoes'."

The kitchen door opens noisily on its loose hinges. It's Junior.

"Come on in! We made a blueberry pie!"

The pie, still warm but cooling on the counter, gives off a tiny, pleasant vapor-cloud dwarfed by the dark, animal smell of whatever's simmering in the oven.

·

After dinner Junior goes out to play. And two hours later, getting on towards ten, the door chimes go off in the nine tone sequence of xylophone notes that reminds every visitor of the theme song of a beloved but forgotten TV show. It's Junior's friend Ollie. Narrow bean face and a drooping wave of sandy hair. A plaintive expression that inspires sympathy and punches.

He was on his way back from the cleaner's with his cowboy hat, because he has to have it for the school play tomorrow. They've put together a few *Time Tunnel* and *Gunsmoke* episodes and in one of them time gets all pretzelled up and we travel back to Matt Dillon's horrible childhood. He plays the young Matt Dillon and that's why he needs his cowboy hat, but Junior grabbed it and took it down to the marsh with Elinore and Lauren and they're all down there now smashing *crabs* against the rocks and filling up his hat with slime and goo!

Junie sits the sobbing boy down with a big wedge of blueberry pie and a tall glass of cold milk and sends Jimmy out to find Junior while she nervously tries to follow the rest of the recipe on her own.

•

Later, Junie's bending into the oven, gingerly pulling out a giant roasting pan and flinching back from the escaping steam, while Jimmy's chasing Junior around the house and Junior is laughing and howling with bloodcurdling pleasure.

47

TEN a.m. the next morning Jimmy's got the ancient Mr. Coffee *zzz-zzz*-ing and chugging and his laundry going in Junie's half-size machine.

"I could eat some scrambled eggs."

"I guess I could make some eggs."

"Don't like eggs?"

"I could try'n mix'm'up without looking at them. If you really have to have an egg."

"I have to admit that I really am in the mood for an egg."

"Okeedoke then."

Junie slams a pan down on the stove and in a second a couple of eggs are sizzling as if being deep-fried.

Waldo hasn't been home for days, but no one thinks about it until the phone rings and it's Waldo calling to explain why he hasn't been home.

"Hi, honey," she says. "Oh, yeah? *Really?* Well, gee, I think it was David who noticed the picture was out, but it never occurred to *me* — and I don't think it occurred to Jimmy or Junior or David or even little Ollie or Elinore or Lauren — that the whole northeastern seaboard was without a picture because you fucked up again, honey. Huh? I SAID, BOY, I BET YOU COULD GO FOR A PIECE OF MY HOMEMADE *PIE* RIGHT NOW, HUH? *PIE.* YUP. COMIN' HOME TONIGHT, HONEY? WELL I'LL HAVE JIMMY'N'JUNIOR HELP ME GET SOME *PIES* UP THEN! Bye, honey."

Hangs up and says, "The truth is, last time he was home he ate about *half* the pie."

"Two *thirds* of the pie!" Junior says.

"Five or *six* pies," Jimmy says, honking.

This is one of those moments when, for no reason at all, everyone's suddenly in high spirits and the high spirits lend each one an exaggerated visual magnetism that immediately attracts viewers like a light in the window.

"He sure loves his pie, I guess," Elinore says.

"I was afraid to take a piece," Junie says.

"Me too!"

Jittery and honking, coughing and giggling, their laughter is reaching a crescendo.

"Well, let's face it. He's famous for his appetite."

"True. Without his appetite, what is he?"

"That must be his job then."

"Does everyone have a job to do? And is every job we have to do a *stupid* job? The stupid job we have to do the way we're known and remembered?"

"What's *my* stupid job?"

"Haven't found anything stupid enough to *be* your job!"

·

"Just stir that. Stir that *vigorously*."

"I'm stirrin'! I'm stirrin'!"

They laugh together.

"Hey, how come you never make *strawberry* pie? Whyz't always *blue*berry?"

"*Strawberry?*"

"A strawberry pie. Ah lahk strawberry pah!"

"Sure. Whyznt everyone make out lists of the stuff they like!"

"All's I said is I like strawberry pie. I like strawberry's all."

"Well, I'd like my own program. Just me myself alone. Not one other living human. And I'd like to exist only when I'm on. I'd like my entire waking existence to take place when I'm alone on the TV screen. And the rest of the time I'd be suspended in orbit in another universe."

48

NO one's seen David for days and no one's knocked at his door. As if, when he'd returned, they'd signed a contract guaranteeing his invisibility.

·

Every morning is like this: before getting out of bed you take an extra minute, longing for something to begin that never does — reluctantly begin to move, afraid to disturb the miserable thing that wakes up no matter what.

For example. One morning he's told that his grandmother is coming for dinner and he curls up under the covers, daydreaming of the one he loved and at the same time cringing with dread, waiting for the one he hated. But, when she arrives, he doesn't remember her at all. Thin and taciturn, his grandmother only because they say so, she sits at the kitchen table and drinks until they have to carry her into one of the bedrooms.

·

The hand goes instinctively to the throat and finds the smooth red line of memory. It itself is real — the fingers are always able to go there and feel its smoothness and its warmth — yet it separates the self's two fictions of itself.

"The self has its selves," David thinks, lying on his back with his hand unconsciously fingering his throat. "'We' have the self: the inner other one we talk to as proof of the reality of our inner life. But all other inner realities belong to *it*, not to us. Memory is one of the self's inner realities that has reality for *it* but not for us. (*It* likes to rummage through its filing cabinets, while we're preoccupied with the heat of the heavy ironstone coffee mug in our hands and the idiotic overload of doubtful information on every screen. And then, when we commune with it, it's like a book that keeps flipping open to the same familiar page."

·

When David goes into his room and locks the door, no one calls him and he calls no one.

Already one of his favorite things is to go to his console and watch the longest running comedy in the history of any medium.

·

Junie hasn't left her bedroom since Waldo came back from the outer islands.

Her voice is a harsh quaver.

"Yes, Waldo," "No, Waldo," "Ok, Waldo," like a sick little girl.

The first time she hears herself say, "Yes, Waldo, honey," the pathos in her weak croaking makes her cry. And the sound of her own quiet crying even more than of her pathetic croaking gives her the feeling that she must have been abandoned in infancy. She can almost feel her memories adjusting to the modulations of her voice and when Waldo looks in he's affected deeply by the image of the sad child curled up in bed.

For a while it's strangely quiet in the house and then Junie wants her girlfriends around her bedside, as if to say good-by. Her little bedroom is crowded with well-wishers, but after a while a general depression sets in and someone turns on the set.

On screen a beautiful twelve-year-old is wrinkling her nose and saying "Ooh! I think Mom's made *fish* sticks again!"

The little brother gets a louder, crisper laugh by asking, "How far below the national poverty line does that mean we *are*, Sis?"

"It doesn't mean we're *poor*, son," Dad says. "It's just our way of reminding ourselves that a day doesn't go by without our having to swallow something that stinks."

49

JIMMY'S cursing, keys are jingling, can't get the fuckn thing in the lock. As soon as he's in, thumps the grocery bag on the red formica table top, races through the kitchen to Junie's bedroom door.

"Hope I don't fuck this one up too," he says, his voice pinched with anxiety.

"*Can't* fuck this one up, Jim. Can *not!* They only give you so many fuckups per reincarnation. Understand that, James?"

He starts banging pans around on the stove, frying something, running water in the sink, washing some of the filthy dishes that are always piled up there.

Junie's lounging in bed in her country home, waking to the sound of the gushing brook down below the back porch and sloping garden. The water continues to splash and gurgle pleasantly, running over stones, down into the dark and mossy drain at the bottom of everything, until the gurgling water starts to spatter strangely and the spattering becomes an unpleasant sizzle, the sizzle giving off the savory stench of pan-fried meat.

She gets up, closes the door, gets back into bed and covers her head with a pillow.

The front door chimes sound.

It's Junior and bean-faced Ollie.

"Gotta be real *quiet* t'day, kids," Jimmy says. "Cause your mother's in there and she's very sick. Understand?"

"She's in there?" Ollie says, jerking his long head toward the kitchen.

"She's in her bedroom. She's sick and she's in bed, Ollie.

147

She may even be dying, for all we know. At first we thought it was just a terrible head cold, but it's something much worse. It may be that new virus they've isolated in the rotten housing of old TV sets. But we don't want to jump to conclusions. If it does turn out to be the new TV virus, we're sunk — because we can't afford a new TV and without her TV she's as good as dead. The important thing is that we have to act normal for once and keep it down, ok?"

•

Half-an-hour later Junior's running across the kitchen, screaming, "Fuck you, fuck *you*, you fuckn asshole!" and Jimmy catches him and hits him hard just as he's trying to dive under the table. Gets tangled in the chrome chair legs, panics, gets up too fast and bangs his head hard on the solid wood table bottom.

•

"Fish sticks."

"How many?"

"About eighteen. Enough?"

"*Should* be enough."

"I dunno. Your dad sure likes his fish sticks."

"Eighteen — twenty-two — twenty-five — how about Ollie? How many fish sticks can you eat, Ollie?"

"I'd rather go home an' eat my mom's tuna melt."

"Junior? Do me a favor and open a window."

50

I T'S late in the afternoon and David's in his room monitoring Junior with the blinds half-drawn and a depressingly deep and warm orange light on the green vines of his fragrant vinyl wall-covering. Junior's in the kitchen with his hand cupped around the telephone mouthpiece, talking low enough not to be overheard and loud enough to draw attention to the fact that he doesn't want to be overheard, taking a look every once in a while at the door leading to the livingroom and satellite bedrooms, listening for a telltale creak in case his gramma (who's supposedly there to look after his mom) suddenly drags herself up from her drunken sleep or his mom crawls in from her so-called deathbed. When Junior's gramma wakes up suddenly like that she sometimes forgets who she is and starts pulling out kitchen drawers looking for a knife sharp enough to cut through cartilage, sinew and bone without too much mess.

"I'll be gettn five thousand dolliz from Tammy, right? I give two thousand dolliz to you. No, *two* thousand! Two thousand to *you*! Right. An then you talk to Jeff — Jeff comes down, right, an you see him first cause you know him — I don't know Jeff, right, so you talk to him an then I come along. What's wrong? No, no, what's the *matter* with you? I've got five thousand dolliz, right? I start with five thousand — no, I don't *spend* it all — I hold out — I give *you* two thousand — two thousand out of the original *five* thousand — so I'm still holdin most of it, right? Two thousand's for you to give to Jeff! An he gives you the plans. An we divide them up. I want everyone to get their fair share. You like this plan? Why not? Jesus, you're worse

149

than my grandmother! You've got an argument for everything!
Five thousand dolliz from Tammy, take two thousand away for
Jeff — I give it to *you* — to *you*! Right! An you give it to Jeff
— talk a little bullshit — then we get the plans — but we better divide them up right away cause if you get caught with that
money — oh boy I'd be in a lot of trouble! I'd be in trouble
with the police, of course, an I'd be in trouble with my *dad* —
an *Tammy* would be in trouble — oh god, Tammy! — she'd
be an *accomplice* — jesus, an 'accessory' — cause she gave me
the money!

"I'm so excited, I can't wait! I can feel it in my stomach.
Thinkin about the money. What else? If I get the money I can
get *out*, dummy.

"My brother David got out. But he came back. How the fuck
should *I* know? Cause he's stupid, that's how come. Actually,
honestly, I have no idea. I was too young to know anything. I
don't remember *anything*. I don't actually remember him leaving and I don't remember him coming back. I don't remember
him *existing*. It's like suddenly I have this older brother David
who's living in this bedroom they added on and who you never
see. This is a sick house, this is a weird house — I keep telling
you that, but you don't believe me!

"I have no childhood memories, do you?

"David tells me that when I was two-and-a-half I was in the
hospital. I was there for a long time — and I died there and
came back to life. It was considered a miracle and I was famous
for a little while as the Miracle Child who died and was resurrected.

"He says that we're not exactly test tube babies — we may
or may not be children of the tube — but we're not exactly
human either.

"I said, 'but at least I'm *alive*, right?' An' he said, 'give me
your definition of "alive".'

"He says that the only proof we have that we were alive
comes when we're dead.

"I told Ollie that my brother told me I was never really born, that I'm alive in some other strange way an all this other shit. He couldn't tell if it was true. His brain couldn't process it. I thought I'd shorted out his whole system! Cause it's bullshit but it's true, right? And it's always the true bullshit that drives us crazy!"

There's his gramma in the doorway, looking strange, her hair completely black and piled straight up on her head like some infernal ice cream cone.

51

THE sound of voices through closed windows restores David to childhood.

Remote, in a thin tinsel snowflake drifting far away, sleigh bell drifting far away from the remote tinkling of the nearby street, as if childhood itself were an illness.

.

When he looks out the window he's looking down into the blue wading pool that just about fills a neighbor's small back yard or toward the shimmering green image that may be a reflection or a memory.

Dive into the ambiguous shimmer between water and image.

Sit stubbornly on the bottom and open your mouth.

An inwardly glowing green light gurgles in while the eyes wide open in their goggles stare straight up at the thin blue matrix of the world.

.

This has always been one of his favorite things: to look out the window straight down at the eternal talkshow in his neighbor's kitchen. Or at the evening's odd programming from window to window. Or toward the intersection suspended in the distance between one roof and another.

Now he's found a better way.

There, crawling across the interior surface of the screen, black and tiny, following the curve of a little band of sidewalk visible over the low roofs, skirting a dirty automotive plaza and almost eclipsed by the thrusting roof trimmed with pink-and-green neon of the diner isolated on its local highway island, Junior and Jimmy are on their way to the market.

Junior hugs Jimmy around the waist, then gives him a hard shove and tries to run away. Jimmy catches him easily and pounds him to the ground.

.

The supermarket manager looks up at his monitor and sees Junior walking like a robot through the bakery section, spraying all the fresh and packaged breads and pastries with thick doodles of pressurized orange cheese spread.

.

Now they're in the supermarket parking lot and Jimmy's got Junior by the hair. Junior manages to break loose and throw something heavy through the window. Now Jimmy's strangling him and the harder Jimmy strangles him the more he cackles and the harder he cackles the more Jimmy strangles him.

52

A BLONDE woman arrives by bicycle in a back yard, jumping off while the bicycle is still in motion. Her mouth is forming words, but only the woman's mother hears her, opening the screen door to greet her. As they approach one another they laugh because they're embarrassed to discover that they're wearing identical grey sweatshirts embossed with the shiny blue lettering of their favorite website. Together they lift the infant son-and-grandson from his blue bicycle basket, hold him up high and exclaim over him while he wriggles and gurgles.

.

He activates another site: an ancient grandfather weeding; vigorous grandmother helping with the weeding; sourpuss aunt; handsome young father in work clothes; young mother looking older than her years, with long arms and a patient expression on her long face; many small children playing, some in earth, some in grass, some in a green wading pool.

Without knowing what's happening everyone makes life happen. The hot day with its weak breezes is either the neutral background for whatever tiny needle happens to be pricking consciousness or it's there as the clearest and most specific boundary that defines what you're not, the perpetually receding target of your whole being.

A child splashing in a green wading pool suddenly sees the clear fractions of light in the tree-like hedges. A little boy has to be snatched up by his mother because he's banged his head hard on the metal frame and plunged in face down and lifeless. Memories are being formed whose nature it is not to be remembered.

.

David is thinking about the unconscious sweetness of life. The unconscious and mysterious sweetness of the moment for the children being watched-over in their pool like new-hatched goslings. Mother with soft face cradling infant in blue blanket: tender kiss of beautiful lips on baby's arm, cheek and shoulder: kindness and love are one and the same for the happy infant and his tiny quacking gurgle is the sound he'll later make unhappily in dreams, drooling over an impossible tenderness. If every life has its store of unconscious sweetness, its memories-without-memory made unknowingly with loving kindness, and this un-remembered reservoir of unconscious sweetness is what makes us human, why is there so little sweetness or human kindness in his nature?

53

ONE summer afternoon David is monitoring one of his favorite neighborhood sites and sees the blonde daughter lounging in the sun in a turquoise summer dress, her blue bicycle propped against the sagging redwood fence. The child is passing its time on the hot earth of the grassless yard shoveling dirt into a green plastic pail with a yellow plastic shovel and throwing gravel at the family dog, worn-out from a decade or more of yapping and dozing.

Toward evening he sees Waldo cross the yard, climb the back steps, look both ways and duck his elongated head inside under the low header. A few minutes later a light goes on in a small upstairs window and a dark rectangle appears inside the lighted one, as if someone, deep in the lighted recess, has opened a door into an unlit passage. Window's been raised 2/3, so that the bottom edge of the framed pane of frosted glass cuts off neck and head above the turquoise summer dress that suddenly flares up in the bright foreground.

Bright bolt of turquoise disappears — reappears — from side to side — in and out of view from left or right — into lighted rectangle and then out again through dark inner rectangle.

Bolt of turquoise returns, rushes into the bright foreground, luminous as a paper lantern.

Balloons out and up like a parachute: bare skin, oddly reflective: dark inner, pen-and-ink line of skin, knee, thigh: delicate stem of shadow does not form a slender cocktail glass, but rises into a startlingly black and furry thistle.

Turquoise dress flies up and out of view.

Dark skin of Waldo's forearm against pale skin of hip and belly. (David recognizes Waldo's wristwatch, its crystal big and glittering as a flying saucer.)

A child's face appears in the dark inner rectangle — red, no longer sobbing, distorted by something inconsolable.

Light as a styrofoam container, child is easy for Waldo to lift up high with one hand. Up near the ceiling light, therefore only visible to David as a shadowy blob through the glass.

Woman's hand reaches up toward floating shadow-blob but in a second it whips away from her like a towel. Back and forth across the lighted frame, and in and out through the dark recess, beautiful human skin is tangled in spaghetti loops and stained with blood.

Drop down out of view and bob back up, wet and vigorously toweling off with thin towels that seems to have absorbed blood more easily than water.

Ambiguity of sobbing and shrieking lead David to believe that he needs to refine his process.

54

THE blonde daughter is bicycling wildly across the dangerous Karolus Overpass. It's raining, she's pedaling hard and
she keeps glancing at the dark street arching behind her — its
random gleaming highlights unaccountably ordered and repetitive. Skids to a stop, dismounts, goes to the blue plastic infant
carrier and retrieves two parcels wrapped and secured in white
freezer wrap and paper tape, as if against leakage and freezer
burn. Sails them out into the scenic ugliness of the rocky cul-
vert and for a minute stands sniffing the addictive foulness of
the black water gushing out toward the suburbs between centuries-old layers of fallen leaves.

55

WALDO, dead asleep, head way back as if a seam had opened at the odd juncture of head and neck, is awakened by loud noises. Looks out the window and sees squad cars at his neighbors'.

TV's already on. Switches from channel to channel: the same story of child murder.

Starts to lace up his boots, panics, stands up, sits back down, watches another channel, hears a name that sounds like a senseless, unforgettable version of his, hears it again and again till he has to accept the fact that it *is* senseless and it is his name, sees an image of David and hears him described as an elusive Television Genius, the originator of a new form of life-like television narrative, gets up again, opens the door and is surprised to find that the bright, unnatural light of visibility is a reality that can be felt on the skin.

56

THE notorious child-murderer's mother is having a cigarette on the short flight of cement steps leading from backyard to screen door.

Her head is like a cracked walnut, scalp showing darkly through thin hair, forehead wrinkled, shrunken body folded still smaller inside a pale blue raincoat, smoking taking more concentration than the withered being can muster.

Hears a noise and stands up. A nurse with a plump and kindly face opens the screen door and guides a frail, ailing man out into the yard.

Nurse on one side, wife on the other, the terribly thin man unrecognizable as father or husband is led down to a rusted iron garden chair on tinted flagging within a close boundary of basketweave pseudo-redwood fence.

Head down under grey wool fedora that has an almost invisible green thread running through it, like the most miserable life's unacknowledged thread of hopefulness. A little wistful blue also in the grey of the slippers that are really a heavy wool slipper-sock cut out like a sandal to accommodate the twisted toes. Arms, in an old wool-tweed jacket, rest lifelessly on the rusted armrests.

Too weak to lift his head, he's staring at the rusted vinework of the iron garden bench and at the glowing amber of the cane-head of the cane resting at an angle from chair to ground and thinking-without-thinking about the peculiarities of autumn sunlight (weak on the skin, profoundly saturated to the eye) and the daylit netherworld of the everyday.

The far-away world remains where it is and has no way of approaching the one as weak as wax inside his baggy clothing.

Between cold light on the skin of bare hands and the sun radiant in its bluewhite lake of virtual sky penned in remotely overhead, there used to be a region of warmth hovering over but never touching Earth or its inhabitants, like a UFO.

This is the region that's been cut away.

He wonders if he's right in feeling that a world already weak is growing weaker. And that his own illness is responsible for the weakness of the world.

"Now we're like noisy horseflies making noise between two panes of reality and able to do nothing but interrogate what we see in every direction. The result of our interrogation is not an answer, but the invention of still one more reality that attracts more flies.

"To live out our life under a sky whose light resembles the light of afternoon television doesn't grant us immunity against disease and death, but it does grant immunity against their tragedy.

"If I can get up and make it to the screen door, then time can start up again."

57

ONE day Junior wakes up, smells an unfamiliar breakfast aroma, the aroma of charred red spices, and senses with alarm that he's awakened in the wrong reality. Goes out into the empty livingroom and then into the empty kitchen and stands there a long time absorbing the fact that he's alone before getting dressed and leaving.

.

Jimmy's got the TV on and he's shaking his head over the shameless reduction of life to absurdity. He's watching with one angry eye, trying to fry up some onions, mushrooms, bacon and a few burgers and wondering why it is that in order for life to become entertaining what has to be left out is the reality of reality: all we see is the abstraction of the self, but never the self: all the things you do that make you know you're you are the things that no one wants to watch. But his reverie is interrupted by the door chimes sounding their ridiculous theme song.

Junior's down below the front porch steps, ready to throw a handful of broken rock.

"I want you to get in the house," Jimmy says. "Your mom's in the hospital and I'm all you've got. That means I'm your fuckn *dad* now. Get it?"

"It means fuck you is what it means," Junior says.

Junior's friend Ollie, further back on the sidewalk, has become tall and mean. His long face, no longer bean-like, is exhausted and cruel, as if its former invitation to cruelty, its sponge-like absorption, has mutated into its own poisoned inversion. He's wearing a black ski cap and has something in his hand that looks like a gun.

Jimmy gets mad and starts down the steps. The two boys back away despite Ollie's weapon. They trade fuck yous. Jimmy goes back up. Ollie shoots but misses, shattering entry glass, and Jimmy goes in.

58

JUNIOR sets out with the vague intention of finding his now-famous brother, but doesn't get any further than the first big city and its video arcades.

One night he's picked up there by a man whose commanding head, with its sagging, houndish jaws, could be the twin of the world's most long-running anchorman, a lion with droopy eyes and an odd mane of hair whose see-through hollowness has suddenly become embarrassingly apparent.

·

What flees along the road beyond their headlights seems to Junior a strange substance that resembles darkness but is actually living, a black deer bounding down the road — only steps ahead of them and unable to get out of the path of the speeding mass pursuing it.

Wants to ask the famous anchorman if he knows the name of the substance just out of reach of their headlight beams, but sees that the impressive head has dozed off and is falling forward. Grabs hold of the wheel and manages to steer the car up a steep pretzel-loop driveway to a motel, an endless horseshoe of attached units dwarfed by the monumental red letters anchored on its roof — high on a rocky slope with a panoramic view of four important thruway loops.

·

The famous anchorman stretches out and doesn't object when Junior doesn't want to lie down next to him. While Junior watches TV, circumnavigating a globe incandescent with the pure visibility of channels no one is watching, the revered anchorman lies there grumbling that they have another thing coming if they think they can put him out to pasture on some giant goat farm in the mountains! When History rejects you, why do they always think Nature will console you?

Nothing gets more beautiful with age. On the contrary. Only ugliness improves. We're engineered for our ugliness and exhaustion to bloom so that death will become acceptable. What starts out ugly only perfects its ugliness and what's beautiful ends up ugly too. So ugliness not beauty is the dominant force. Exhaustion ripens with time as well. When we look at the world with exhausted eyes we can see how our tiredness has ripped beauty out of it. (As if beauty were an additive, an impurity, and tiredness filtered it out.) Struck him while they were driving tonight that, because he was exhausted, driving through the world was like being tuned to a channel devoted to ugliness and that that might be the kernel of a great idea. Find a way to make ugliness entertaining and create a *craving* for ugliness. Is that what the new young genius is already doing? Did this new young genius steal the idea a few weeks before it was about to come to him? Did he have his destiny stolen from him *again*? And by a distant member of the same *family*?

Drive fast through the ugly world.

The ugliness of the world flies past us.

The spindles of the trees twirl through us like the burred edges of soup cans. Memory has a little blood on it for once, but even so we won't remember what we saw in the next life that's already spinning toward us.

Given a name and then it's supposed to be the name for all we've experienced. But all we are are the things that keep ballooning through the little keyhole of the head. The part of us that's alive in the world has nothing to do with what they mean when they call our name. And the part of us that answers to its name has nothing to do with being alive.

They expected to turn him into a depressed old man in his backyard — with or without his cane or walker — or out on some stupid golf course that looks like a goat farm, bending over a golf ball with all the concentration of an idiot stirring a sugar cube into his coffee — or crawling on all fours in old clothes in his flower beds with his little toy shovel. . . .

"But I'll live to have them all killed. And when I have them killed I'll tell them to bury the heads deep — so deep the animals can't sniff them out while they're grazing and nuzzle them up to the surface. So deep they can't end up smiling at me on the Six O'clock News."

In another second he's sleeping, his Adam's apple like a weird erection bobbing in his throat and his sleeping face collapsing into a smaller, less commanding model of the waking one.

Junior goes over and watches him snore. He feels as if it's the first time he understands the hatred he's always felt. They win just by snoring — because others are bound to fail. And if others don't fail, or don't fail fast enough, then they win by murder.

He takes a lumpy motel pillow from the bed, places it over the fallen bigshot's face and presses down hard. Keeps pressing, as if he wants the face to take a fresh look at the world through the back of its head, and only lets go when he feels something pop like bubble wrap.

On the long, fast drive home he squashes every living thing that comes near his wheels. Arrives at the house ready to kill more, but only falls asleep in the bedroom that Jimmy's tidied up pleasantly in his absence.

59

JUNIE returns from the hospital aged and flabby. It's really a different face entirely unless you catch a glimpse of the old face in the new face when the day is fading in the living room or when she's in the kitchen and you come through the door at a strange angle. Looks like someone, but who? Are there times when the face isn't its own face but a *memory*-face? Times when the face is a *future*-face? The other day Junior walked into the kitchen and thought Junie was one of his grammas: not the first one, probably the most horrible one — unless he's forgotten and the first and most horrible one are one and the same. Memory-face or future-face may replace the everyday face through shock or sudden loss. And seeing the beloved face the-way-it-once-was or the-way-it-will-become taints reality with the mixture of sadness and desire-for-what-never-was-or-can-be we call nostalgia.

•

Jimmy and Junie like nothing better than to crawl into bed and lie there side by side having low, serious conversations that rumble through the wall and only rarely break out into coughing and braying. They talk for a long time in a way that's touchingly human, then it gets completely quiet, as if they'd fallen asleep.

Junior spends four solid months in front of the TV set, as if he's come to the conclusion that it's the only place he'll find David, but finds nothing but a mirror that's also a camera buried so deep inside house-and-family that it's like a nose hovering over a casserole of meat, noodles, onions and dark gravy just out of the oven, lid lifted for a little scalding taste.

60

SEATED alone at a table in the dining car, using a dull butter-knife to carve his tempting slice of charred and fatty ribeye steak with dark gravy and mushrooms, he feels crushed by the wave of attention that's also giving him the energy to exist. The familiar stream of photons tickling the back of the neck is enough to make it ripple tightly into the hard grey-pink blob of the shaved head.

He's asked to put out his cigarette and limps to the waste-disposal unit near the door. Walks as if his left leg is crumpled inside the baggy green fatigues. A loose green shirt hangs on a damaged torso. As he returns to his seat he can sense how many are staring, surprised that this stump has a face. Smiles at the one who isn't staring (a tall woman with beautifully reflective black skin sternly carving a block of chicken baked inside a red and spicy crust, a once-famous-and-fashionable designer's name stitched in gold across her black sweater), but she doesn't return his look. Only looks his way when he turns to refold his body between fixed table and padded banquette. Now she glances sideways and sees the strange, wounded dent in the crown of his skull and the scar running in a zigzag path along his throat.

·

Conversation builds up to the point that he can't help over-hearing it, as always.

Two beautiful sisters, dark-haired and thirtyish in childish twin plaid jumpers, are babbling un-self-consciously to a man with a worm-like moustache and tongue, drinking vodka and staring at them without talking.

One of them says a sudden heart attack.

The other says maybe a stroke.

Much better than something slow.

The autopsy results will be in by the time they reach Orlando.

They say asphyxiation. But that makes no sense.

May have choked on something. That's possible. But the way they're putting it, it sounds suspicious. You'd think he was strangled.

Seventy-eight but seemed like sixty.

Forty!

Forty? That's going too far.

Kind of man who could live forever! No longer went to the office, but still pretty much ran the network from his bedroom.

When the call came in, the slightly more beautiful sister says, she heard her husband say, oh, that's terrible! that's *awful*! Oh no! She knew it was something bad, but she never imagined that it could be her *grandad*!

Just the last person in the world you would ever think of dying. He had no *reason* to die, if that makes any sense.

If not this conversation, then another. They come toward him like smoke under the low ceiling. Thinks to himself that the world is filled with conversation. All its channels overloaded, air waves and bandwidths, cable filaments and signals packed with static that sometimes but not always clusters into words. And sometimes he feels all the world's static and conversation pass through him and he doesn't know how to escape.

•

The tall woman in the black sweater has to bend her knees and then her long neck to make out what the damaged young man had written and left behind on paper napkins, pressing hard to form childish block letters with an inky, fine-point pen.

A BEAUTIFUL CHILD PASSES AND LATER YOU SEE HER PLAYING CARDS WITH HER EQUALLY BEAUTIFUL AUNT, EYES STUBBORNLY CLOSED AS IF ASLEEP FOR 1690 MILES UNDER HEADPHONES. LATER THE CHILD CHOOSES YOU AND YOU

PLAY CARDS ALL AFTERNOON, FEELING THAT SHE LOVES YOU ONLY SO LONG AS YOU ALLOW HER TO WIN. REMINDS YOU OF ANOTHER KIND OF LOVE, FAMILIAR AND JUST AS ABSURD. LOVE OF A BEAUTIFUL FACE AND VOICE FOR HALF AN HOUR — FOR AN HOUR — FOR THE SAME HOUR AGAIN — SAME HOUR THAT IS AND ISN'T THE SAME HOUR. SECOND CHILDHOOD BOUND IN PARALLEL WITH THE FIRST. FACES WE REMEMBER BETTER THAN FACES OF THE FIRST CHILDHOOD. LOVE THEM AS IF THEY WERE TOYS WE COULD BEND AND FONDLE AND OUR LOVE IS MIXED UP WITH ODD, POWERFUL FEELINGS OF REGRET AND ANTICIPATION.

AM I THE ONLY ONE WHO FINDS LOOKING OUT A TRAIN WINDOW AT NIGHT — INTO A TOWN WITH ITS CLOSED SHOPS, LIGHTED WINDOWS, DARK STREETS, ITS BLUE AND RED SPLASHES LIKE EVERY IDIOT'S MOMENT OF GENIUS — MORE COMPELLING THAN ANY IDEA? AS LONG AS IT'S PASSING QUICKLY. EYE HAS TO CHASE AFTER IT. NO MATTER HOW EYES FIX ON IT, STILL CAN'T SEE IT. THEREFORE ABSTRACT AN IMAGE THAT MEMORY CAN'T HOLD.

ONE WAY OF VISITING THE REGION THAT'S LOST DAILY?

LIGHT THAT HAS NO SOURCE SHINES ON THE FLAT SLOPES OF ROOFS AND CAN BE FOUND SHINING ON ABSOLUTELY NOT ONE OTHER SURFACE.

NOTHING BUT LIGHT, BUT THE MIND DEMANDS ITS IMAGES.

DEMANDS ITS IMAGES AND BUILDS UP THE INVISIBLE INTO VISIBLE AGGREGATES.

WHILE WE'RE LOOKING SOMETHING IS PASSING THAT WE ASSUME IS TIME. MIGHT USE OUR TRAVELS TO CONDUCT AN EXPERIMENT.

FOR EXAMPLE: WHAT OCCURS INSIDE THE TRAIN COULD BE LAID OUT AGAINST WHAT THE TRAIN PASSES THROUGH AND EACH SET OF OCCURRENCES LAID OUT ALONGSIDE THE CONVENTIONAL TIME MARKINGS ON A WATCH FACE. CIRCLING WATCH FACE LAID OUT PRECISELY AGAINST 1650

MILES OF FLEEING VISUAL EVENT AND CIRCLING WATCH FACE LAID OUT PRECISELY AGAINST HUMAN ACTIVITY IN-SIDE THE TRAIN. IN THIS WAY WOULDN'T WE HAVE THREE SIMULTANEOUS MEASURES OF TIME? SIMULTANEOUS AND MEASURING EACH OTHER — AS THREE WAYS THAT TIME EXISTS: WHAT HAPPENS, WHAT DISAPPEARS, WHAT TICKS LIKE A METER MEASURING NOTHING — THE EMPTINESS OF TIME WHEN DESCRIBING A CIRCLE AROUND ITSELF BY COUNTING.

HOWEVER: THIS IS AN IDEA OF TIME THAT LEAVES OUT TIME'S CENTER. THE HUMAN BEING AT THE CENTER WHO RADIATES TIME LIKE A LIGHTHOUSE INTO ALL THE OBJECTS OF THE UNIVERSE, THE HUMAN BEING WHO IS TIME AND HAS NOTHING TO DO WITH WATCH OR FLEEING LAND-SCAPE.

WHICH IS THE MORE POWERFUL FORCE IN HUMAN LIFE: IGNORANCE OR KNOWLEDGE? AND SIMILARLY: MEMORY OR FORGETFULNESS? STUPIDITY OR WHATEVER THE OP-POSITE OF STUPIDITY IS. EXPERIENCE HELD TOGETHER BY KNOWLEDGE OR IGNORANCE? FORGETFULNESS OR MEM-ORY? STUPIDITY OR ITS OPPOSITE? BORN AT THE DEEP END, SWIM TOWARD THE SHALLOW.

The bald young man stops at a table in the almost-empty lounge car. A beautiful young woman is playing cards with a little girl and every inch of the surface of the table is covered with colorful playing cards from a child's TV character deck. The young woman's dark hair is spread out on either side of her intelligent face and so is the little girl's, who might be her sister or her daughter.

For a second it seems as if the bald young man is about to in-troduce himself and go through the difficult maneuver of bend-ing and sliding his damaged torso under the edge of the table and onto one of the narrow banquettes. But when the young woman looks up, he continues on his way.

•

He falls asleep with his naked head against the window and dreams that a young woman, small and dark, has just left his side. Sat beside him, sharing tropical candies from a big, crinkly bag. She reminded him achingly of someone else. The resemblance was slight, but made his heart race, like an encounter with the ghost of a child loved in childhood and then forgotten.

Now he's awake and looking out the window. The houses are dark. No one home. A long length of wet road runs alongside the track. The outer world goes by quickly yet is pulled to great length inside you. Stare out and feel that the fleeing world is willing to come no closer than wet road and curtained window. And that the irreducible distance of the world coincides oddly with the fact that the self extends no further than it sees: exists entirely at the point of contact between its furthest look and the nearest approach of the world.

"Time — always inside us, born at the second we are, like a virus that's sometimes benign and sometimes isn't — stares out at a world that ages because we're looking."

•

In his new dream morning is a strangely tinted form of night. The horizon is a shell with a pearly inner lining that casts an orange glow upward and a vast white light downward. The white light of Earth outlines the curved edges of autos and the square roofs of trailers.

Sits up, unaware of the little shudder of electricity the body gives when signaling to itself that a dream needs to be abandoned if it's going to live till morning.

•

The beautiful child is curled up on the seat directly across the aisle, her body covered with a small coverlet of sandstone and turquoise, her head in the lap of her beautiful older double drinking coffee and frowning over narrowly ruled sheets of musical notation, digging at them with her pen as if trying to clean something out of the dark lines and blots with its sharp point.

The desire to approach her is overwhelming, but he feels

172

annihilated. And even though it's true that on the days when annihilation rises up in us and does its job (days when we wake up, having been annihilated in our sleep) no one seems to see our look of annihilation, he's sure she'll recognize it and turn away.

The impossibility of approaching her makes him fall asleep.

·

A horse is in its meadow, rolling happily in the grass. Kicking its legs for pleasure. Suddenly it stops and listens — still on its side, legs straight out in the air — hears the roar of a train just as it explodes out of its little pouch of distance — and struggles to get to its feet. Struggles, makes a wrong movement, can't get upright. Pulls its rubbery lips back and makes a sound that lets the world know that with such terrible difficulty all pleasure in living is gone. The young man staring blindly out the train window at the reciprocal blindness of the world thinks he sees a horse struggling in a meadow as it spins away and feels in what's folded up in himself the painful folds in the horse's body.

In another instant he's looking into the middle distance where a thin man with unusually long arms is climbing a shallow hill under tall trees and a woman in a pink sweater on a different path is also climbing into the same dark grove.

·

He and the beautiful young woman are having lunch together in the dining car. He's feeling peculiarly light and happy but nevertheless asks what are we remembering when we have memories? We assume: "first life, then memory." As if every memory is a memory of what we've lived. But is that true? Don't we sometimes remember something we haven't lived? Some memories, for example, may be memories of other memories.

She says that the only purpose of memory (but then is it memory any longer?) is to chronicle the world as it evaporates — in such ridiculous detail and over such a long span of time it may not look like the world. But we're not up to it — and, even if we were, we don't live long enough. ...

Man put on earth to cure the illness of time? Time a virus that long ago infected essential codes. . . .

.

The black-and-gold scarf wrapped around the throat of the woman with beautiful, reflective black skin, black-and-gold sweater and a stern demeanor slips down as she's reading the notes scribbled on cocktail napkins, exposing the rubbery ridges of a long-ago-healed wound.

.

Outside another town, deep into evening, they see a river and a tiny highway, dark but precise. Red lights fleeing and yellow lights approaching.

Always-always-always the concealed fiber-optics terminal at the edge of town! he says, becoming unaccountably agitated. At the edges of every highway the next century is always quietly being planted, as if new sewer pipe were being laid. Then the giant billboard with its lenses and sensors, then the dark tract, then the weird orange glow above the town! Here it is again! Another town that's *not* a town! But if it's not a town what is it? A town that's not a town that *is* a town only because a population reduced to idiocy *thinks* it's a town!

Can't stop talking, though he's now hovering at a distance from himself and observing how absurd and repellent his face has become during its bitter ranting.

"What morons! What a nation of *morons*! Asleep in their houses in the middle of nowhere! They think that because they close their eyes they can't be seen!"

Yes, she answers matter-of-factly, it's as if these towns were places in a world that's neither there nor here, absolutely real, but only while we're traveling through it, like the world we see when we're nearing death, mercifully given a remote control to carry with us.

.

Later they find an empty sleeper, undress and curl up together.

In the morning the world outside is flat and brilliant, here and there a starved white cow or blinding plane of water looking odd in the sunbaked landscape, the final destination only minutes away. He sees in the window glass that during the night he's turned into someone else. There's nothing wrong with his leg, he has dark, receding hair and a small beard and he's wearing jeans and an old grey herringbone sports jacket, as hard to look at as an ancient, quivering test pattern.

1

THE ailing Television Genius opens his eyes just a little under the long bill of his multi-colored pie-wedge baseball cap and looks around the sunny terrace. A baby is sitting at the round table, banging his chartreuse plastic cup against the textured lucite that's clear but has a subtle and watery aqua tint to it. Plastic on plastic makes a hollow tok-tok noise. A little too weak to give pleasure. Again, but harder. *Tok-Tok! TOK-TOK!* Satisfied, the baby burbles *"Bo!"* Next comes something like a sentence dripping from a faucet, then "Bo! Bo! Bo!" — *TOK-TOKING!* of chartreuse cup on table — longish dribble of speech — then *"Eep!* Peep! Peep!" — *"Oh!* Bo!" — and a bit more *TOK-TOK-TOKING!*

The baby passes its own afternoon and passes the ailing man's afternoon for him pleasantly in this way — as clouds cover the tropical sun and cut off the surge and sparkle of the ocean through the tall Australian pines.

The ailing man dozes off, wakes up, dozes off, wakes up, doesn't see the baby at its table and wonders how many times we die in a lifetime.

·

A bright and tiny plane is rumbling noisily across the sky like a trunk being pulled along a concrete platform. Powerful saws and the heavy motors of cement mixers are grinding and churning, hidden in the distant pines across the treacherous Plumbicon. Heat and tropical breezes are funneling down through the universal cone of light.

Half asleep on the sunny terrace the genius in us slumbers.

177

As if the self starts dying at the same instant it stops mutating uncontrollably.

Now we're free to live the life of our image-self — and no one dares to question our identity.

The world really does exist because we're looking at it. Now we think. Now we look. Now we lift our hands and move our fingers. We hear ourselves saying forcefully, no! like this!, and our little image-self leaps spinning and kicking over all opponents and before long concrete is being poured across the inlet.

·

While the genius in us slumbers, the sun shooting straight over the villa roof toward the horizon misfires and strikes the blue-black plastic of the wraparound sunglasses on the wicker stool next to the beach chair. Light along that curve is so intense the self feels small and sleepy next to it and is only awakened by the steady TOK-TOK-TOKING that comes and goes.

All the half-closed eye can see are five brilliant palm fronds waving with heat, a heavy green syrup running down the center of what's orange and fiery — like the jam the mind spreads on its tongue but can't get the taste of.

Force the eye to see a little further — to the black pine trunks marking off blue blocks of sunlit Gulf — green cabbage palms stuck like burrs to the horizon.

The ailing Television Genius dozes off again, wondering which is the graver mistake: the mistake of assuming that what we feel is unique or the mistake of assuming it's universal.

2

SOMETHING'S wrong, as it is every morning: the dull alert-ness others say they find lively.

June, on the other hand, has long since returned from her walk on the sand path under the pines. She's spent hours at her desk, talked on the phone, had her swim with the girls.

She's eaten a drop and doesn't want to eat more. The guest, her dad, is hungry as always and makes breakfast for himself and the girls. Nothing for her, but she sits at the table next to her dad, nibbling at his bacon, eggs-over-easy and home fries and talking shop — while Flora brings a tray of tea, toast, his favorite wild palmetto honey and cherry jam to her ailing father's lounger.

After breakfast he changes into an unattractive green bathing suit, faded and baggy, and an old white shirt that's grown several sizes too big. June passes by the bedroom door, sees what he's doing and sings something out from the passage as if he were a little boy who needs to be encouraged to go out and play.

•

Now he's on the steps that lead into the pool's shallow end, wiggling a foot in water.

June and her father are on the terrace, clearly visible over cropped palms, drinking coffee, sharing a fluffy wedge of key lime pie and going over proposals that have accumulated during his long illness.

Sounds carry easily here and distant things look close enough to eat.

At the same instant his foot is feeling completely the absolute sensation of cold, her voice reaches him, asking, "Cold?" And she can feel by reaching out her hand the coldness of the water surrounding his foot, isolating it from his body, and of the breeze grazing the back of his neck.

They hear with equal clarity and at the same instant the cries of human children calling from a larger pool cut out of the tufty green of the distant foreground.

Takes a step down. The cold water at his ankles is already growing less absolutely cold. A red-haired woman who'd been sunning herself face down, trim but flabby in a small black suit, turns over and proves to be a young actress on one of their shows. Smiles at him warmly, as if human warmth were a gift that should never be questioned, its attractive giftwrap already torn open as you're handed the little puzzle that returns to being a puzzle no matter how many times you solve it.

A little behind the red-haired actress a silver-haired woman with flushed cheeks and green bikini is writing rapidly in a tiny pad: ideas he'll hear tomorrow — not from her, but from a stranger who'll give no clue where they came from.

An elderly man with bloated white belly and red swimsuit even more worn and baggy than his own is asleep and horizontal in an armless lounger, fingertips of both hands touching cold paving, mouth open — the stupid face of someone who long ago was able to stop thinking for a living, giant shuttle of the Adam's apple going frantically up and down as if the slate's wiped clean and the sleeping brain is desperately trying to remember the secret of human speech.

•

All our efforts are bent toward improving the precision of our instruments of perception, the ailing Television Genius memorizes what he'll later write into his secret journal. And then we feel it's precisely our super-clarity of perception that holds us at arm's length from the world. As if all the things that help us know we're here also crystallize the moment as a too-clearly-observed one: the perceived moment perceptible only because it's already been perceived. If the clarity of the look of the world precedes our look at the world then our look now only documents what's already been looked at. We dived into the adjusted image long ago and now that we've arrived we have a yearning for the mess we left behind.

·

Returning along the sand path under the pines, he runs into his father-in-law on his way to the pool with Flora and little Valeria. His father-in-law wastes no time and begins to sketch in the backgrounds of the baby geniuses flying in from China and the conceited puppies coming in later from Seattle and Mumbai, but the ailing man's only pleasure is in the never-ending mental ping-pong he plays with little Valeria.

"What do we see when we gaze out and see the world the sun makes?" he hears himself say.

She answers without hesitating that in the first place we see how hard the sun is trying to *make* a world: we can see its energy as it sheds it.

"Yes, but *where* can I see it?"

Just to the left, she says, the water is glittering so hard you can see the word "glittering" and also that the word "glittering" is only a word that can't get below its own hard surface — and that what's really happening in the world is that dents are being hammered in by the end points of the distant robot-rays the sun sends down to do its work.

"Digging into whatever medium gets in their way?"

Yes, she laughs and they laugh together, digging into whatever medium gets in their way! Can't he see? — can't he really see that the brilliant patch off to the left behind the sea grapes is full of dents? Dents and scratches it's hard for the eye to look at.

"It's strange how visible the world is in our shiny basin."

They gaze together toward a point where a boat is crossing the brilliant patch, coming from the invisible zone, off screen to the left.

"The arc of the horizon, visible from end to end, shoots things toward us."

Visibility itself is shot toward us, the beautiful child says.

The visible world displaying its visibility.

"Should we be proud of ourselves?" he asks. "Is our perfect visibility an achievement?"

She frowns and shrugs. This is a question she doesn't like. She doesn't say it's a *stupid* question, but he can tell that's what she's thinking.

Tiny particle jets are shooting up everywhere, she says. Minute but blinding geysers where the sun strikes. And only the living knows how to defend itself.

He raises a curious eyebrow. This is an idea he'd never thought of.

Some forms are lifeless because they don't know how to take in the blows of the sun and make use of them. To turn the world into yourself equals life. Whatever isn't life propels the world away from itself in brilliant geysers. Out there on the beautiful green billiard table the balls that are always shooting away aren't life....

They watch the boat crossing to the right and carrying a trail of brilliance out of the patch it passed through. It disappears behind the little concrete poolhouse where a motor is humming quietly, happy to be allowed to do its work without human intervention. Boat never comes back into view, but they can still hear it slapping its way toward islands beyond this island's most distant point.

"The desire to be there doesn't get us there and that hurts," she says. "We can't actually feel the separation of the water under the prow...."

"Everything seen, everything heard, yet we're still pathetic...?"

His father-in-law shakes his head and laughs with proud bewilderment.

"When you two get together...!"

It always comes as a surprise to the ailing Television Genius that any part of their conversation has leaked out into the sphere of human hearing.

He picks little Valeria up high and gives her fat cheek a kiss, and then he watches Granpa lead the two girls toward the pool.

3

THE villa is empty when he returns and there's a note from June saying that she'd had to handle three or four unpleasant calls that were meant for him — that she'd had enough and gone down to the pool to be with Daddy and the girls.

There are messages on the machine and a written list of calls to make.

Sits down at the desk, picks up the telephone, replaces it in the cradle, sits back in his chair and falls asleep at once, as if rejoining a program already in progress. The dream is not unfamiliar. He knows this unpleasant woman with longish yellow-white hair combed straight down on either side of a slightly pouchy face with drooping mouth and bulging eyes. She knows him too and locates him immediately (waiting irritably for him to fall asleep), stares at him with boiled eyes, jaw working, then looks down and opens her bag. Reaches in, rummages around. Rifles and rifles through it. Hand goes in, paws around, comes out empty, goes back in, paws and paws and paws, pushes stuff around, pulls stuff out, examines it as if she's never seen it before, paws again for something else and at last comes up with the thick, bound copy of this week's summary of the show's eternal tangle of themes and plot lines — neatly typed, but blotted with messy cross-outs and scribbled add-ins.

Stares hard at it.

Staring at what's printed there twists her jaw as if two hands have grabbed hold of her head and are trying to wring out whatever's wrong with it.

Seems to him that her bulging eyes are looking straight into his while she tries to tear up the thick, book-like mass of pages, grimacing as if shredding it with her teeth.

Opens her mouth wide to swallow all the shredded pages, but a scream forces its way out: face red, fists clenched, body folded in half at the waist as if throwing up.

Now she's pulled herself together sufficiently to stop screaming. Her face is terribly close to his. She's straightened up and is only muttering and drooling a little.

"At what age does this become the iron rule of life: 'What can happen already *has* happened. Whatever hasn't happened can *never* happen.' Unfulfilled = unfulfillable."

Her steps are strange and her face is monstrous but calm. As if with her few sentences she's expelled all her misery and lodged it in him.

"I dozed off while I was writing," she says, "in the white leather chair under my desk — so low and wide and comfortable, more like a cradle than anything else, it encourages dozing more than writing. And for once I didn't have a nightmare. I wasn't locked inside my little black box. I wasn't buried somewhere, waiting for someone to shovel off thirty-three centuries of dirt.

"I was in the hill towns — in the season when leaves are falling. Sometimes whole stems fall, eight or ten leaves to a stem, and then the tree seems to be surrounded by its leaves in the way that a day sometimes breaks down and you can see the random swirl of hours, minutes, glowing particles of seconds in the air around the dark trunk of the day. One leaf doesn't fall like the others. It twists and flutters in the air for a long time and then it begins to fly — wafts up, dodges, hops, skips, takes a slow step this way, three fast steps that way and makes a dash for the woods, as if for a hoop far away and out of view. Stare after it, but can't really follow it in the failing light — feeling in your heart that it's fallen short and is lying miserably in the grass.

"That's when you discover that you're alone. Alone and neglected, like everyone else. Think about the children you've had and wonder where they are. Try *not* to think about what you may have done to them. They never knew that you were murdered, they only know their own murder and probably think of you as their murderer. I don't know what the rules are for who gets to survive their own murder, be reborn and go on to have a happy and successful life. The ones who do are happy, have a family of their own and don't even know their mother existed. Now I'm nothing but a bad dream to them — but sometimes we have our revenge and get to come back and attach ourselves fatally to a vital organ...."

He wakes up with a fierce desire to be with people and hurries back down toward the pool.

4

JUNE and her dad are head to head, talking German, as usual. Valeria's little yellow bathing cap is bobbing pleasurably like a toy boat, the beautiful round head of a little girl who, for once, isn't talking.

The moment is sweet, but doesn't feel like his. If not his, then who is it that's feeling its sweetness?

The sentences of experience makes sense if we read them quickly, but not if we think too much about the space between the sentences and between the words.

He starts down the steps into the shallow end where Valeria is paddling with other children. Sun is high, babies wading under the watchful gaze of their mothers. How to describe, even to oneself, the sounds these infants are making! The guttural slurpiness of their *eh-yehs*!; their whooping *aigh*s and whining *nyeh-ehh*s!; ambiguously happy or melancholy *mmm*s and *ahh*s; cranky self-solacing *ah-ahh* singsong; burbling spigot of near-words and murmurs flowing out: the unique and random universe begins again, the soul set afloat forever on its unformed goo of speech and memory-without-memory. The sticky little ball begins to roll and stuff sticks to it, some of it stuff that will never stick to another....

Stares down into the pool, where light and shadows are boiling together as if there were a flame under the greenish floor. The sunlight of a wonderful green aquarium where the same ruffled washes we see as light are the ones we see as shadow. The transparent thing that casts a shadow as it wriggles like a wave without its matter. Stare down into it and think as you stare. As if staring could improve your thinking and then thinking become a new way of staring and then this staring/thinking make the moment your own.

Wiggles a foot in warm water. The foot itself — the foot alone — is surprised by the water's warmth.

Valeria calls "Daaa—ddyyy!" from the deepest corner of the pool. There's her round face in its puckered yellow cap.

"When I've lived one-hundred-and-eighty-seven lifetimes and I'm the most brilliant woman alive — a beautiful old woman who's still a little girl with a messy room — will you come and find me even if I'm walking down a big hill on a tiny road where only turtles live in their pond with its grassy islands and the wind is blowing through the marsh grass and the aspens… will you be able to tell my voice apart from all the frogs and geese calling from the other end of the universe, Daddy…?"

The weakness of his voice makes the pool long.

He wants to say that she's brilliant now — and he feels that he has found her from the other end of the universe, but she's already not listening — up on the ledge playing a loud jumping-diving-and-splashing game with Flora and an unfamiliar boy who reminds him — not altogether pleasantly — of himself.

Stands wiggling his feet on the lowest step, feeling the lightest tickle of a breeze in the curly wisps of hair at the back of his neck and wondering if the reflections of pines in the water have any weight — and if the weight of reflections, if there is any, give them any actual depth in the water? If no weight, then what is it? Tries to chart similarities and differences between reflections of pine tree in water, idea of pine tree in the mind, the words pine tree written or spoken, image of pine tree on a television screen. Weight, depth and charge of an idea in the mind…?

June paddles near and says that he looks like a ghost. He should either get out and wrap himself up or come all the way in where it's heated….

Immediately reverses direction and heads with long strokes back toward deep water, scooping Valeria up onto her shoulders, where she splashes happily from her lookout position above the heads of the adults.

He follows slowly after them and rests in a sunny corner of the pool's deep end, elbows on the run-off ledge. Dark images of trees have come up from the bottom and the few swimmers that are left are crowded into one narrow lane of sunlight.

Eyes closed see the green and orange shadows of the pool's brilliance.

What if we were to think of the mind as a swimming pool?

Thinking might equal swimming and swimming might reinvent existence by stretching out an arm.

Dive down to the bottom: sky a wavering lattice too bright to look at.

Top and bottom of the pool look freely at one another, filled completely with the image of what they're looking at.

Is that the same as or different from the fact that to think about something is always, at all times, to change places with something. And are both exactly the same as the fact that every look into the world becomes completely and absolutely the self at that moment? The more real a look the more memory is squeezed out of it.

The adult on the surface of the water is always thinking with anger and nostalgia of the child at the bottom or the other way around. But there's no way to know how often the child is thinking with dread of the adult that's beginning to accumulate as the sticky ball rolls forward.

Children's voices continue calling, joyously or miserably, from a pool somewhere far away, where sunlight is still full and warm. Mothers have their children there and are cooing over them and making sure that they don't drown.

Far-away voices in their little capsules are like sleighs jingling from valley over hill to valley — and the loud but tiny voices of the children in the jingling sleighs are like the faraway television voices you hear when you wake up from illness or surgery in your too-dark bedroom — the ones buried in the third dense wall beyond the thin near wall — living a strange life unto themselves, the happiness of their remote laughter signaling unhappiness for you.

Time itself has a voice that finds a way to speak, if only through the television audible through someone else's window.

Open the three pound tin of stewed fruit, lift it with difficulty in your small hands and drain off the heavy syrup. Pears or peaches. Is this memory…?

A swimmer splashes up next to him, lays one heavy hand on the ledge inches away from where his head is resting.

The heavy hand belongs to an older man with a broad forehead gazing adoringly up at a handsome woman in a black bathing suit. As she bends down, lovingly guarding the child teetering on the slippery perimeter, her white breasts begin to flow out like milk from a pitcher, but the milk is too thick and creamy to pass through the narrow spout. Milk that makes you thirsty as you drink it.

"Aye! Aye-aye-aye, *Florinda!*" the older man calls up joyously at the tiny girl, wrapped warmly in a thick persimmon towel, a lemon long-billed terry-cloth cap pulled down firmly on her head.

"Ab heindernichts," the mother murmurs. "*Hein*dernichts, Florr-aaa."

The child might be little Flora — as she was twelve years ago, before June was quite so tan and slender (the pleasant bounty of soft shoulders and breasts now visible through the body's new tightness only occasionally and from a distance, when she's approaching along the sand path that skirts the perimeter of the villa, but never when she's sunbathing by the pool).

And the heavyset man cooing grandfatherly gibberish could be his father-in-law, Ernst, but only if Ernst had shed a few significant degrees of his body's gross contour.

"Oob-anderens?"

"*Hein*dernichts. Zis der ober!"

189

The little girl is laughing and straining toward her granpa, who responds by trying to hoist himself up and climb over the pool rim. He can't manage it and plops back in, shrugging good-naturedly at the ballast of time's gravity.

The ailing Television Genius flies up easily out of the water, landing perfectly on two feet, torso cold and glittering in the double shade where shadow from above finds its congruent shadow rising, and kisses the laughing child who once again is his daughter.

5

THE young man is eating his enormous mesquite-grilled grouper sandwich with lettuce, tomato, thinly sliced Bermuda onion and spicy remoulade on the sunny terrace of his rented villa. Anxiously watches his idol make his way with teetering difficulty down the few deeply terraced steps to the broad pool deck, then pick his way unsteadily between vacant chairs and outstretched loungers. The ailing Television Genius settles deep in a corner, hidden from view by a dense barrier of sea grapes, but minutes later he's changed position, in full view in the sunny space at the head of the pool, outstretched in an armless chaise lounge lowered to the maximum horizontal. Motionless, thin as a cadaver, surrounded by manicured jungle growth, staring through dark glasses at the pool's raw plane of electrons intercepted before they've become images.

The young man convinces himself that he can feel with the ailing man how time and distance draw close, stirring the hairs of the arm and giving the mind the feeling that it has a skin. Sun burrows through all with corrosive friendliness and we welcome its aggression because everything else is far away. Far-away world remains where it is and has no way of approaching the one as weak as wax melting inside its baggy clothing.

·

The young man keeps his distance. Does a few quick laps, then conceals himself among the sunbathers reclining under their swordfish bills and headsets.

The beautiful older daughter is lying face down, bikini top unhooked. After a while she hooks herself up, turns over and reads a novel whose dust jacket is a blizzard of red and blue particles, then turns on her stomach again and, spreading a small red-covered diary open on the hot tile, starts writing as if she can't write fast enough.

The prematurely-aged father makes his way to the pool, descends and walks slowly back and forth across the shallow end. Water a little above the waist impedes his progress and the bottom of the pool has the tangled siltiness of a lake.

His wife calls out with great tenderness and asks if the water is cold.

Now others are becoming interested in the spectacle of the ailing man.

He continues his peculiar form of exercise and, when he approaches the near edge of the pool, the younger daughter Valeria comes over and kneels at the tiled perimeter. Their heads lean close. The young man strains to listen, the preternatural acuteness of his hearing having grown a little dull.

"How do we end it?" he thinks he hears the ailing Television Genius say. "Whatever we'd like to end does *not* end and the other way around. We have no energy, but *it* does. Keeps surging no matter what. For example: our lifelong bout of grief (grieving for what we never knew but always knew it was real and would find its reason) does not abate, as they promised it would. Always haunted by grief and therefore always looking for ways to make others grieve for us?"

The little daughter says something that changes her father's mood entirely. And when it comes time to walk home, he seems invigorated, his gait almost lively — and they stroll together, laughing and chattering like children.

6

EARLY the next morning the young man is doing sluggish laps and watching the Television Genius's wife — glancing over between lazy strokes, staring openly when he lounges in the sun against the opposing wall. She's alone, her back is toward him and she seems to have no sense of being watched, giving him the opportunity to discover that she doesn't look like herself. He'd thought of her as tan and slender, hair dark, face relaxed and friendly. A tan and slender, dark-haired woman with a competent, friendly manner. But, from numerous angles and distances, the planes and cones of her body appear white and solid — a white solidity that at the same time is round and pliant. A leg that might in fact be slender, laid on its side, viewed from behind and below, becomes a monumental block — hip and thigh white as the novel, bleached wordless, balanced on her stomach with one hand. Now he wonders where he got his assumptions and, even more troubling, why he'd begun to think of her as a potential ally, even though he'd been warned otherwise.

Yesterday he sat on the terrace, hurriedly reading through the document it seems to him he's carried around since birth, dreaming of the moment the Television Genius would hold it in his hands. Now he finds himself wondering who the Television Genius really is! Can it be the barely-breathing invalid? Or is it really the beautiful daughter, Flora. Or father and daughter together. Or, not only father and daughter, but all of them — ailing Genius, competent, intelligent wife, even the brilliant little girl, Valeria. No one of them the "Genius" —

193

genius only in the spark that flies from one brain to the other. Genius never a permanent condition, but an accumulation of instants that die out as easily as the head is turned toward a fresh, random view....

Now he's climbing out of the pool by one of the side ladders and approaching the wife, just as Flora warned him not to.

Little Valeria is standing by her mother's chair, dripping. Her hair is far darker than her mother's and so is her skin. The hair heaped on top of her head in pretzel loops emphasizes the fatness of the cheeks. A sack of shortbread butter cookies, a baby bottle full of what looks like apple juice are fished out one-handed by the mother from a straw bag. The little girl stands before her, prattling unintelligibly, years younger than she was yesterday. Touches the wraparound curve of her mother's leg and the mother responds by stroking her daughter's fat cheek. The little girl pulls at the super-sweet juice, endlessly available through the tough rubber nipple, letting her hand rest on the warm hill of her mother's hip, enjoying her mother's light caress.

He comes close, sponging pool water out of his receding, wavy hair with a thick, blue towel someone's left behind, and sees that today the Television Genius's wife has blonde- blonde hair that's been cropped at an angle that slants parallel to the central angle of the sharp, unfriendly nose between prominent cheeks. It's a weak face that nevertheless sends a strong signal. Bored because her husband is forever asleep upstairs in the cool back bedroom, its weakness is already collapsing into a hard and radiant point that commands the space around it, a powerful lighthouse beam with no lighthouse to account for it.

When the child returns to the water, he sits down close enough to the sunlit block of the woman's hip to smell the lotion on it and starts talking. Can't remember, he says, at what absurdly early age he began to think about television and whether or not he did his thinking *electronically* like everyone else or if it began by scribbling his own ideas in notebooks instead of listening to his teachers and taking notes in class or it could even have been the ideas he thought of as stories that he spray-painted on sidewalks in cities all across the United States.... Wherever he was he tried to get her husband's attention any way he could, but never got an answer. Has a site of his own, naturally, and other so-called geniuses have responded to his ideas, but none of that matters.

Knows he's babbling and that Flora was right, but can't stop.

Periodically, he continues, History loses steam, as if Time itself had fallen asleep. These periods resemble a moron's smiling shrug, his *eh* while smiling at life and rubbing his eyes — the long, despairing *eh* of History — the depressed sloughs that *are* History — till there's a fresh eruption of Time and things speed up again.

In the not-too-distant past, when Time had rolled into the weeds like a golf ball and was sinking a little deeper into the mud every year, as lost as the skull of an unknown murder victim, her husband came along, took a majestic swing and drove it onto a sloping fairway in the next century. But that was a long time ago. And now Time is lost and dozing again because of his condition.

When we used to watch TV we'd always find the characters struggling in the over-bright wrapping of their world, like flies buzzing between two panes of glass. And sometimes we'd feel the crisp edge of that over-definition in ourselves. Her husband found a way to cut open the tight plastic wrap of the old television and liberate the human figure and, since to change television is to recondition the human gaze, that was a great accomplishment.

But now his great accomplishment is every dummy's way of looking at the world.

Her husband used to think about nothing but the future, but now he's lost in his "Memory Channel"....

He pauses for breath.

This is all wrong. This is *not* what he wanted to say. What he wanted to say is odd. He himself doesn't know the meaning of it.

Memory in any familiar sense has no place on television. Television's closed system of self-references should not be mistaken for memory. Memory, like television, belongs to the class of things that really do exist without having any real existence. Where is the television image? Where is its actual location? In each set? On the microscopically thin inner surface of each screen in each house? Or in the ether or cable filaments before the impulse is intercepted and channeled? Somewhere further back along the chain? In the studio or camera? Somewhere further out, where the wave-particles intersect the surface of the eye? Or only when the little coded clusters of information have been sent to the brain and back? In the same way, where is memory and what is it made of? Memory and television compete for the same ambiguous space in the mind and therefore they're incompatible....

Television should be the windshield of the house. When we turn on the set, a wall of the house should fall away and we should feel the rush of the engine that's about to launch us on our adventure. Her husband started down that path — but now he's like someone who's stopped under a tree to take a nap and whose head has rolled far off down the grassy slope....

He stops, feeling that his ideas haven't lived up to this moment he's dreamed of forever and then tries to reassure himself with the thought that it doesn't matter because she hadn't been paying the slightest attention.

Seeing the young man's expression of distress, she laughs and lays her two hands straight up against the sides of her face in a senseless but attractive gesture that stirs what in some is memory, in others nostalgia and in still others desire.

7

WITH his eyes closed he hears someone call "David!" from the far end.

"Da-vid!"

And then again, but more drawn out, "DAAA-VIID!"

Calls back, "YES!", but doesn't feel his voice resounding in his chest cavity.

Nearby, behind him, a tall pine is casting its shadow across a green and brown and sunny slope and then into the corner of the water just below the spot where he's resting.

"David! I found you!"

But no one comes near. Must be another David, one who's still alive.

The little striped awning on the speckled slope.

Little awning with red stripes.

Children playing quietly on the slope and a woman in a long dress going up the steps of the house: she's the one who called out to her David, waiting for him to come up from his swim.

"Always from the outside we feel life gather. Feel *how* life gathers. The completeness of life, but only from the outside."

It was all there from the second he put his foot in the water: the whole pool, the whole experience, already there around the foot.

This is the moment Flora arrives. Touches him on the arm, says "Daddy?" and makes him rejoin the living — just so that she can introduce him to an extraordinarily thin young man with a lick of fine brown hair over his forehead, strong eyebrows, almond-shaped eyes that might either be warm or hooded and a convex, tapering face whose weak point is strengthened by a brush of beard.

Almost-but-not-quite the face, elongated or pulled out sideways, cheeks sunken into a monkeyish old age or stretched flat into a demented youthfulness, he sees when he bends to test the water in his bathtub.

8

VALERIA is in the pool alone, amusing herself by diving and holding her breath underwater, a compact and shiny tadpole. Her self-sufficiency touches the thin young man huddled with Flora under a lime green towel in the far corner.

Her mother is sunbathing in a chair next to the father, who's having a bad day, his skin a terrible yellow-white.

She suddenly closes the novel she's been holding out as the sunlit target for her forward gaze, swings to a seated position with both feet on the cool tile — slips the husband's heavy book out of his rigid grip and stares hard at the sleeping face. The intensity of her gaze doesn't wake him, not even the touch of two fingertips on his thin forearm. It's only when she shakes the arm that he shows enough life for her to tell him that she's boating over to the mainland.

.

The Television Genius sleeps, keeping an eye on his daughter only when he wakes up fitfully. When he closes his eyes he never knows whose voice he's going to hear or whose face he's going to see. Sometimes it's a face he loves, kindly, round and smooth, with wrinkles that are less like wrinkles than like the smooth impressions a finger might make in cream that's been whisked and sweetened with vanilla sugar, and around the face waves of hair that are white and silky. As she's wheeling him down the hospital corridor she's bending low to whisper in his ear, telling him stories. Or they're sitting next to each other at the donut shop counter having coffee ice cream sodas and identical bacon-lettuce-and-tomato sandwiches with plenty of mayonnaise. But he never gets that one any more. Instead he gets the one with the aging face, convex and bitter, despite the false smile between age-reddened cheeks. Its wrinkles are real wrinkles, the kind that have sunk into the deep grooves that worry always eats into the bone.

The aging and miserable face is close to his, complaining, as usual.

It's another normal day, she says. Can't sleep and can't wake up. All day long you hear them running wild outside your bedroom door. You scream out for your husband to whack them and they get whacked and start cackling. Whack'm some more and they start coughing and begging. You lie there listening to them running and getting whomped. No telling why some things make them laugh and some things make them howl. Sooner or later they start spitting and cursing and you call a time out and the TV goes on. You can hear someone frying something up and then there's a cozy feeling when they all settle down together in front of the set.

But the cozy feeling doesn't last. One of them is bound to come in and tell you how much he loves the smell of your chili. They lift their noses and they sniff and go ahh! and rub their bellies. But when they think you're asleep again they sneak into your room and steal your pin money! First he says he doesn't know anything about it, then he says he found it on the floor. One lie stupider than the other! All he has left is one dollar. Grab him by the neck, shake him, suddenly he's got more! One-two-three-four! "Where's the rest of it?! Whad you *spend* it on? Give me back my money! Give me back my *pin* money!"

One day a friend comes over and you say, "I've got to get away!"

She says, "yup, we've got to get away from them periodically."

"Periodically?" you say. "I mean like every *day*! I mean *permanently*!"

She knows the name of some agency and you call and you say, "Hello, I need help! We're having terrible trouble with our seven-year-old! He's completely out of control. He's a thief, he's a little shit and I'm afraid for my life. He was always bad, but now he's worse. It's gotten to the point where if I wanna take a shower I've gotta tie his hands to a towel bar! That's pretty bad, wudn you say? Is there anything we can do? Uh-huh. Yup. Yep. Wait! Let me get this straight. If I cut off his head and bury it in the yard overnight, by morning I can screw it back on and he'll be a different kid? He'll be changed and he'll be real sweet? He'll be all curly-haired an' cuddly again? An' I'll kiss'm good night an' sing him 'Tura-lura-lura'? *That* makes sense! At his age it has a chance of growing back, right? Not like us...."

He opens his eyes. Valeria is sitting on the footrest of his lounger, drying herself with a fluffy green towel.

If we're asleep and we see something, he asks, does that automatically mean that we're dreaming? Is there such a thing as a sleep-memory that isn't a dream? Or are "dream" and "memory" two words for the same thing? Or: same substance, different states, like ice and vapor?

That's not what bothers *her*, Valeria answers, forehead above her little plum-face furrowed. What bothers her (and it should bother him too!) is that, free to invent any life we want, we're always re-inventing the *same* life. So most of what's called "life" isn't much more than the stubborn mutation of a handful of memories that may not even be memories. . . .

She puts on her favorite sun goggles with their red rubber straps and blue lenses and snuggles up next to him. He drapes a weak arm around her and they lie that way for a long time.

•

Now the Television Genius's head is all the way back, eyes closed, and little Valeria is stroking his hair, comforting him like a mother and reciting every tale she can think of.

The young man strains his weakened faculties to listen.

"Once there was a boy who, by the age of fifteen, had already traveled so far that no matter how warped or beautiful the scenery

he'd fall asleep as soon as he left the terminal. The more beautiful, in fact, the more impossible he found it to pay attention, as if Beauty is what gets in the way of seeing — the goo we have to plow through before we can see how one thing actually stands in relation to another....

"Always, always he wakes up, just outside a city and sees the golden light in the rushes that bristle everywhere in the brown waterways.

"Always the glowing orange of the sodden leaf beds.

"Heather purple of the metaphysical.

"Where once there were factories, something shining like the mineral-coated inner surface of the see-through outer surface.

"The turn of which century?

"Whole towns go by like the book you flip through in a bookstore — making up your own book by reading five random sentences.

"Later on it seemed to him that this is when he began to have a secret code that resurrected him. Only now he keeps forgetting the code and has to struggle to re-invent it before he can come back to life.

"We all have memories, but few return to life.

"Therefore, to have a secret code of resurrection is probably not the same as having memories.

"It seems to him that once upon-a-time there was a cure. A way to change your head. But it never seems to happen anymore. On the contrary. You find yourself longing for the thing that used to frighten you to death.

·

"What is it that goes around a bend as if about to disappear, but can't? Bends and keeps bending, you can see it and are drawn along with it as if your long gaze, attached at one end to the stupid craning of your neck, giving your head a dumb, awkward look in profile, were burrowing time into things that otherwise would be timeless and making them age.

·

"Once-upon-a-time, a little boy and his father were living

202

alone in a house by the woods. The father, upstairs in his bed-room, happened to glance out the window as he was dressing. The light that had been passing through the windows and the house was laid out against the evergreen slope in the middle distance. There the eye falls, as if by nature. Look toward the sun's target, as if it's a book that's been opened for you and which you're meant to read in all its superficial enormity but which you find as illeg-ible as the dust-novel that gathers on a train window.

"House of cedar in the shaded evergreen hollow, up the slope where the background darkness of the evergreens steps forward and walks down the slope into the foreground. Swing your gaze to the right, away from the man in the cherry red shirt on his noisy tractor, away from the darkening evergreen hollow — through one of the (west) windows that look out behind your house. Sun going down outlines the dark matter of the forest's density. Light shines down the glossy leaves at a steep angle and dark poles shoot up across what's shining. Channels are cut and light can only travel along these channels through the back windows to very precise points in the interior, with all the dark intensity of fire rather than daylight.

"At dusk the little boy heads out toward the vegetable garden with scissors and basket to snip off some dill, chives and parsley for the dinner his father's preparing in the big kitchen.

"He returns quickly to the safety of the house, his basket emp-ty, and tells his father that he thought he saw a woman at the edge of the forest. She called his name and he ran back to the house. Though her voice was friendly, he was frightened.

"'If someone we love comes back from the grave, should we be afraid or should we welcome that someone even if we're sure it's a ghost, Daddy?'

"'The question is,' the father answers, 'how do we know when we're seeing a ghost? There are times when we dream of someone and then years later have the same dream and the reappear-ance of that memory-person who's also now a dream-person, dream-person who's also now a memory-person, pierces us like a needle going through two folds of the same skin.'"

"Just now, while his son was outside, the father goes on, he was standing at the counter by the window with chef's knife, cutting board and vegetables, but instead of doing anything or even looking at anything, he was daydreaming. He was at a wedding, fixing his tie in a mirror, sometime in the middle of the third era of his life — his third mutation — when a woman brushed by. Her dress was blue and black and the rustle that it made as she brushed by created a little breeze, faintly piney, and the little pine-breeze also carried the aroma of skin and hair with their traces of shampoo and soap: scent of the entire chemical person that can be sniffed, which you later remember as an emotion.

"The aroma-emotion of memory: like the blood the brain smells when the nose is struck.

"He knew that he'd seen a ghost. She died long ago, yet she just swept by!

"Goes down the stairs to the wide glass doors: a note left with the doorman tells him to join her in the park.

"Cross the street, deep in the park at once. There she is in the distance, walking along the path. The desire to bring her close doesn't bring her close and neither does his look into the distance, which resembles desire. Image in the distance blows away from him like a dry leaf, crisp and curled at the edges. Can feel that he himself — the force of his movement toward her — is what's blowing her down the path. Inability to approach her weighs him down with grief and he moves forward as if walking were weeping. Weeping, as usual, doesn't bring relief, it only brings more weeping. The deeper into the park, the more inconsolable. Finds a bench and sits. Dries his eyes, blows his nose into a big handkerchief again and again until his head clears and the sky along with it. A blue night sky with stars in it, everything excessively bright and crisp, like an image seen and corrected before we see it.

"Inhales deeply and catches the aroma of pine on a breeze trapped in a circle under heavy pine boughs above the forest floor. Closes his eyes and imagines that she's next to him.

"Warmth, breath, smoothness of skin.

"A tiny infinity separates them, impossible to cross without a kiss.

"'Look at the stones I've gathered for you,' she says.

"She holds out her palm.

"One stone is a smooth, pebbled blue, another cocoa-colored and streaked with saffron, another a little mountain, with a mountain's heather-purple distance right in her palm, another a tiny night sky shining with mica.

"He knows that he knows the meaning of these stones, yet it escapes him.

"'Keep one in every pocket, no matter how many times you change your clothes, or we'll never find each other again,' she says.

"Expects to feel the weight of the stones in his hand, but doesn't.

"Leans forward to kiss her, eyes closed. Face crosses the tiny infinity into a little, tingly zone of memory and falls into a vacuum of wakefulness.

"Can't get it back.

"Lost to us absolutely, as always, when we're not in it...."

•

The Television Genius is awake and agitated, sitting up as best he can.

She (Valeria) must, absolutely must promise him something! No matter what she thinks she understands, no matter how she believes she's broken the code, she must never ever try to explain the so-called Memory Channel to anyone! Let them keep rummaging around in their wine cellar of clichés, let them think his soul got lost in itself like a coal miner with a remote in his hand instead of a lantern....

June arrives, hoists Valeria up, kisses her on the cheek and says, "Let's let Daddy rest."

In a second Valeria's puckered yellow bathing cap and June's tight white racing cap are bobbing side by side.

Mother and daughter holding one another, laughing, playing games.

Father sleeping, horizontal.

Still later: father suddenly gets to his feet: a terrible instant when he seems too weak to stand, sways while wife and little daughter rush instinctively to the near edge of the pool, elder daughter and her new friend start forward like lifeguards when they spot a child floating face down despite its yellow inflatable vest and green rubber alligator. Little daughter springs up out of the pool, mother swims frantically toward the side ladder, Flora and the thin young man are already only a few steps away — hands out to catch him before he falls.

Teeters, rights himself and maneuvers around a row of fully extended lounge chairs. Steadies himself by leaning on a greenish plexiglass tabletop where a few dark green towels are folded. Picks up a towel, makes his way back, unfolds and smoothes the towel out against the full length of the chair and sits down again, exhausted.

Mother and daughter go back to their splashing.

An hour later they all leave together: the ailing man now in blue terry beach jacket and floppy white hat, his steps weak and slow.

9

WHEN we begin broadcasting where do you plan to stay?" June and her dad have showered, toweled off and changed and now they have drinks and they're settled in beach chairs by the pool. They've swathed the Television Genius in a bulky dark blue wool sweater and soft, earth-brown corduroy trousers, a blue and brown carriage robe over his thin legs and his boyish test pattern baseball cap wedged absurdly on his head.

Flora's upstairs with her newfound friend, their faces together over keyboard and screen. Valeria's in the pool alone. As always, no one can stop her and her father most of all wouldn't want to if he could.

"If you like, stay at my place, that's all I'm saying. I'm only five minutes — no, two minutes — from the site. The place is so dangerous at that hour something horrible is guaranteed to happen. 'If no blood is spilled we'll give you a refund.' That's how sure they are! What they don't know of course is that there's a storyline B and a storyline E and so on already in progress, every one of which is headed for a terrible crisis. Mark my words: soon you'll be hearing the word *cheenyus* every time you hear some idiot talking. 'It reminds us of the sheer youthful cheenyus of David's famous Ugly Period'...."

Ernst likes his own turn of phrase and June joins him in a laugh that polishes a rusted edge off their shared voice tone.

"No, I'm wrong. 'Wrong again.' As fast as Choonie can drive my little buggy, no more than one minute, tops! Unless" — looking at his son-in-law — "you prefer a hotel? I'll set it up for you whatever you like."

Suddenly Ernst's Otto-and-Arnold accent has gotten more pronounced.

June says that she wants to stay with Daddy. She needs his support. David doesn't understand the crisis they're in. Doesn't understand and doesn't want to. Never did want to, even when he was healthy.

"While the cheenyus is dozing," Ernst puts in "Time keeps chugging along. . . . 'Even if it's always a comedy, what's hidden inside it is never a comedy.' And, I hate to be the one to tell you, but Choonie may be getting just a little bit tired of living with the buried thing that isn't funny. . . ."

"Daddy!" Valeria calls out, her untroubled face smiling over the rim of the pool.

Was her dive good? Did she stay under long enough?

Her eyes glow when she looks at him. Clear skin, cheeks below her goggles beginning to look sun-reddened in the light of the poolside lamps. The game of question-and-answer, the game of looks exchanged across a distance, are a bridge that another person can never tread on. He thinks this will always be true. Even later, when he's a ghost who appears occasionally and without warning on the screen. . . .

He just catches Ernst saying in perfectly unaccented English, "Are you kidding? The place was furnished, but I got rid of all that crap. There was *shit* in that place. Some idiot paid a fortune for it, but it was shit. No, I gutted it and shipped over all my own stuff. You'll recognize everything. It'll feel just like home. It is home now, I guess. It's the other one that's empty and that I'll have to fill up with expensive shit!"

His father-in-law carries his big stomach as a broad barrel of forward weight, his face as broad as another person's ass, the grey beard also broad, the head near-bald and there's the ever-present cigar, lit or unlit. June is trim and athletic. And yet their shared identity is apparent — not only in the voice tone, but in other things that are harder to name, the third or fourth thing that always exists in or between shape of ear and its angle of projection away from the head, irritatingly meaningful way of shrugging the shoulders or cocking the head, sly expression on the lips that signals a particularly nasty or stupid joke in the making — a bridge no one else can tread on and which becomes even more inviolable when they lapse into German. Without the Television Genius having noticed it, June's shifted over to the footrest of her father's ribbed lounge chair and they're so close their molecules have mingled into a single plasma. June is laughing, talking more animatedly, with more arm movements and sheer vocalizing, than at any time in recent memory.

June and her dad unpack their laptops and play on them like children at their toy pianos.

Valeria calls out to him again and this time he gets up without wavering and descends easily into the shallow end of the pool. They play at flipping her over and over, high in the air, a big cartwheel and splash she can never get enough of.

The pool water's heated to the point where a delicate egg dumpling could poach in it and he's able to rest comfortably with Valeria in the farthest corner, where distance and the unstable glow cast up from the pool makes the image of June and her father detach pleasingly from June and her father. Makes Valeria and her father wonder simultaneously if the pleasing element in things is always exactly equivalent to our distance from them. Our ignorance of them? Deeper into experience, the less pleasure? Less pleasure, more knowledge? Forget one thing as we learn the other? Forget who we were, for example. Headless and longing for our head. Nothing but a head longing for a body. Necessarily unpleasant? Always at all times the human head is nothing but what it looks at. Another way: what we see is what we live and only occasionally are we living with our own image: and in that case our own image is just another example of what the head sees. At the freakish instant of seeing itself in the mirror an exchange takes place. Walks away from the mirror with a new image-head. As if we were the thread aiming with bad eyesight toward the needle opening: needle must be threaded and thread must go through needle opening

209

— since they were made one for the other. But the need to get to the other side mutates. To look at the needle opening is to aim the whole self at it — and to aim the whole self at it induces a special relation to the ambiguous reality that permanently hovers at that photon-thin boundary line.

The alien creature we scan the universe for dozes fitfully in every room of the house.

Window with one pane of mirrorglass with one watery spot you can look through like a window.

Ghost of the self stares back at us from the dark lawn as emptily as moonlight on water.

Transparency and opacity change places too often to know the difference.

So unlike yourself, a hive of pure activity. Full as an ocean: particle geysers shoot off it perpetually, yet it remains full. Stare at it as if its interchangeable immortality of electrons can become your own. . . .

Now he's ready to speak, but Valeria's left the pool and fallen asleep with her goggles on, wrapped in a green towel, next to her sister and her sister's new friend, also wrapped together in their own oversized towel, a testpattern rainbow of primary colors.

•

Little Valeria, napping under the sun gathered in the hills and winding pretzel-loop paths of her green towel, is telling her father another story as if she were a kindly nurse lulling to sleep a child in the hospital.

"Once upon a time," it goes, "there was a little boy who was ten months old. His blue little visor, blue shorts, little white shirt. When he calls Mommy! people hear the pathetic honking of a goose searching for the pond where its family and all its lifelong friends and neighbors have long since bedded down for the night. Pacing along the edge of the pool he sees mommy and daddy sleeping calmly in their chairs. A tall man, not his father, jumps up and shouts as soon as his tiny robot moves with bouncing steps, as if hypnotized, toward the sky-green water. His own mommy

and daddy aren't worried. They know he'd never leave them for the blue shadow at the bottom of the pool.

"When he gets to the other side, he suddenly sees how far away Mommy and Daddy are — as far away as the other shore of a lake — and begins honking, Mommy! Mommy!

"No one sees him.

"On the other side of the pool the word 'distance' has nothing to do with space. It's more like time, but that's not it either. On that side all the chairs are aligned toward pool and sun. On this side the chairs face away from the pool into a dense and shaded grove of mangroves, sea grapes and cactus. A very tired man — long and yellow with red lips and a thin grey beard — is stretched out slightly twisted, like a wet towel that's fallen on the ground and gotten dirty. Lifts a weak hand and tries to wave toward a point beyond the trees.

"The little boy looks up and sees a girl waving from a distant terrace and calling, 'DADDY! DADDY! IT'S TIME FOR YOU TO COME UP AND EAT! I'VE MADE YOU A HEALTHY LUNCH! COME UP AND HAVE YOUR SUMMER VEGETABLE SOUP WITH GARLIC AND DILL — YOUR SOURDOUGH BREAD WITH OLIVE OIL AND LEMON — YOUR GREEN TEA AND SOUR CREAM PLUM CAKE — AND YOU'LL BE CURED!'

"Later, the little girl's mother is swinging her in circles and singing her favorite songs. The father swims by, turns his head and the little girl sees that this is not her father. They've taken his head away and put on another, younger and healthier one that looks something like photographs of her father when he was young, but not exactly. It's not her father and it's not even his ghost. Her mother comforts her, but her sobbing is inconsolable...."

Valeria wakes up and is relieved to see her father alive and sunning himself in the deepest corner of the pool. Snuggles up against her sister's warm hip and falls asleep thinking of ways to use the so-called Memory Channel to keep her father alive.

10

THE young man can't believe he's here, in the villa of the famous Television Genius, in the midst of his family, seeing how it all happens: Flora, with her legs tucked under her on a green leather couch, watching tapes of last season's shows and writing longhand in one of her father's big sketch pads; Valeria on the floor, playing with her laptop and looking unaccountably taller and older than she did yesterday; June and her father, heads together like conspirators; the man himself just a corpse of his former self, asleep and dreaming on the terrace — the sounds of the night before him and of the television behind him canceling into an odd tranquility.

.

From inside the lighted cube of the livingroom, the image of the dozing or near-dead genius is darkly visible.

Whoever looks toward it can see it. As if "Life" = a perpetual projection of its image into visibility. Available to however many tune in. Neither increased nor exhausted by its projection? Or used up with our radiant visibility and mutating uncontrollably through our undefended absorbency.

.

Mind floats out over the pool and hovers there long enough to absorb the internal blue light and the trilling and whistling of the dark night just outside its boundary, and then it's asleep.

Five, ten, thirty cycles of floating and absorbing have already passed.

Mutating self drifts up high into the ether, into the path of one of the electronic currents always circumnavigating the globe, registering on the sensitive skin of a dish antenna and the mutating self sometimes mistakes itself for a warm, Earthly breeze.

Somewhere far away, in a little university town in New England, in a pleasant condo apartment overlooking a cold swimming pool, a no-longer-young-but-still-attractive woman with a hard-to-place European accent is in her green pajamas, sitting on the floor in front of an unusually large screen, watching with profound nostalgia a noisy little car race from Nice to Monte Carlo, drawing a straight line through two-hundred-and-thirteen-thousand curves.

The driver is handsome and well-dressed. A handsome British playboy with a sense of humor and a love of adventure. Every week at this time he has a new adventure and hops in his noisy little car. It's a happy life, but tonight there are peculiar memories. Once he had a wife, an unpleasant father-in-law and two beautiful little girls.

First you're young and everyone else is young and then there's an imperceptible mutation.

Drive fast enough and the wind blows off your hat — then your head — and memory along with it.

Little by little the invisible forward racing of the tires under him make him feel that he's running away from home, like a little boy running as if he wants his exhausted legs to go as fast as the wheels of a car. Running away from mom & dad and the older brother who tried to drown him in the family's blue plastic wading pool in its green little back yard plot. Held him under just a few seconds short of exactly matching the image of the little body floating face down that made someone else famous.

·

The longer he drives the more certain he is that he's not headed for Monte Carlo, but for a famous donut shop in a once-flourishing college town high up in the mountains of New England where he last saw his brother, sitting with his legs pretzelled anxiously around a stool post, drinking coffee, scribbling something in his eternal drawing tablet and muttering to himself.

.

The speeding driver's brother is in his boyish blue baseball jacket and red baseball cap and he's drinking hot coffee with two trembling hands, opening his mouth wide as if he'd like to fit it around the whole round opening of the ironstone mug, extending his lower lip to form a kind of saucer. But that doesn't stop him from spilling his coffee and scalding himself.

The waitress hands him a paper napkin so he can wipe his mouth.

It seems like kindness, but back in the kitchen she jokes with the skinny cook and then they stand at the door and stare at him through the glass porthole.

.

Two beautiful little girls come in with their handsome, silver-haired granpa, a famous newscaster and weekend farmer, who steers them toward the takeout donut counter, away from the looping double helix of the lunch counter and the childishly dressed man scribbling feverishly and trying to eat his coffee.

While the sisters try to choose among crisp plain fried, crunchy cinnamon sugar, raspberry-jelly-filled, blueberry-jelly-filled, sweet raised cake dough, honey glazed, chocolate with icing, sugar-powdered and at least half-a-dozen others lined up in their fragrant bins, Granpa is positioning himself to block their view of the man who may be young and strangely aged or middle-aged and oddly childish — slurping his coffee, watching an ancient episode of *The Persuaders* and telling his story to a toothless farmer eating a peppery and scalding bowl of corn soup.

He's saying that his brother left him behind a long, long time ago and that he's been searching for him ever since. His brother's a famous TV star — and if they don't believe him all they have to do is search the channels. Search the channels, but be diligent about it. His brother may be a famous TV star, but he's also a *secret* TV star and sometimes his program only appears as a tiny inset inside another, more popular and *stupider* program: what they call an "interior" program and you have to be very alert to find it. He's found his brother many times on television, but never in so-called real life. That doesn't mean he isn't real! On the contrary, his real-life invisibility may be the only proof of his reality. Or is it the other way around?

What is a person? What is a person any longer? Isn't this the question we should be asking ourselves? What does identity depend on? We rely on memory to know who we are from one minute to the next. But memory is nothing. Moment passes while you're memorizing it. Next moment too. So all it's possible to remember is the thing we never memorized and, therefore, our idea of ourselves depends on memories that took shape without ever having been remembered. Still, everyone has an identity. And, if everyone has an identity and it doesn't depend on memory, then it must depend on something else. Something new. There really must be a new basis for identity.

Matter can't be destroyed or invented, isn't that true?

Sit down at the computer.

Little dancing pixels on the screen that are your thoughts.

Sent out to others at will.

Your presence in the worldwide plasma of pixels.

All those little impulses that used to be you.

Amplified or diminished by your proliferation in the world?

Where does all this fresh electronic matter come from and what does it break down into?

The farmer goes on eating his cooling corn soup and the youngish-oldish man goes to the wall phone hidden in the same dark alcove as the toilets, makes a call and is surprised to find that his childhood pal, Ollie, is still at the same number. Hasn't been able to get past the age of thirteen and is still living at home with his mom and dad, whose eternal arguments will always penetrate the hedge-row between the houses with a goose-like honking and nasal baying.

Ollie doesn't remember him at all and has to be reminded that they ran away from home together ten, twenty, thirty times — spent all their waking hours together, till each became for the other the mirror-face more familiar than his own.

"Until for some reason I became sick of you. Suddenly your bean-face revolted me, as if I were growing a second head and didn't know how to cut it off. I stopped taking your phone calls and gradually we stopped being friends — but I've always been haunted by the ugly thing I did to you."

Ollie wonders if, with this phone call, they've decided to exhume his character and allow Time to start up again. . . .

His long-lost pal says that he needs help finding his missing brother so-and-so, the secret TV star. Brother's been sending him clues, but he's too dumb to figure them out.

Ollie says that his old friend's brother is no "secret star". He's seen his brother's dumb program and that's all it is — just a dumb program. There are no "clues" on that dumb program. It's just a tiny dumb program on a tiny dumb station.

"It's like so tiny you practically have to have a *combination* to find it — like two hundred and eight revolutions to the left, then back four hundred and sixteen to the right, another one hundred-and-four to the left — and then there's your brother's dumb program!"

.

The British playboy's brother is on his stool, legs re-pretzelled around the stool post, signaling for more coffee.

While the waitress is filling his mug, he says that he wants her opinion: would it be possible to have a program where each character would be free to move in time without dependence on the time-movements of the others? Each character the inventor of his-or-her own time — no matter how it would force the plot to bend and twist around itself? And to show on screen the individual grooves of Time that lead up to the precise moment — the history of everything leading to the sentence we're pronouncing — proving how absurd it is to believe that two people can co-exist in the same time and space.

She doesn't answer and he sighs and says, "No, I agree, it would be too confusing. It wouldn't be popular."

"Let me ask you this then," he says. "Do you think that television is an inherently rational medium, bound to conventional narrative logic? Or is its true nature something else?"

He loses himself in the difficult tangle of a thought, then picks up the thread.

"Must never forget that the essence of television is its popularity! It's popular, but it's not a 'popular art form'. It's not an art form at all! How many times did they badger me about that? 'This is a *business* — more like a *donut* business than an art form.' That's how I ended up on a stool in a donut shop! All my *genius* ideas for television were *stupid* ideas! To have the illusion that your viewers are going to curl up with your programs inside their heads, like a reader written into what she's reading...."

His short stack of wild blueberry pancakes is set down in front of him and while he's eating he's looking up at the screen, where his long-lost brother, driving a green sports car on the Riviera and dressed like a gentleman amusing himself by having adventures, has his foot on the pedal but isn't talking, depressed by what he's imagining.

Camera pans down from road to ocean.

Because the screen is blue the mind floats out over it, the way it goes out the window on a summer night to listen to the strange bird-and-frog sounds coming from the pond.

.

The ailing Television Genius on the terrace wonders why the mind can't just continue floating out. Why it must return, like a swallow that skims the far-off ponds and water meadows and comes zooming back night after night to the same remote, rank perch under the overhang of the garage roof.

If the mind could follow its digressions to the end, couldn't it drift on beyond death?

Is the voice that calls the mind back from its digressions the voice of life or the voice of death? And is it wonderful or terrible that whatever reality we happen to be in, there's always another reality waiting for us outside it?

11

THE young man comes up behind him.
     Looks at him on the dark terrace.

Is he asleep?

He's wondering why he was sent here. Was he really sent here to do this? Is it possible to do this and go on with your life? Go on as if you've done something good? As if you now have a place in History?

While he's trying to read the genius's thoughts and can't, the genius, without wanting to, knows that the young man is staring anxiously at his thin and foldy neck, a sharpened gardening tool hidden behind his back, trying to work up the nerve to cut off his head.

•

The stroke is tight and swift as a golfer's, finding a ball hidden in deep grass and driving it into the next century.

Pauses on the final upswing, at an angle that reflects the minutely sprinkled not-quite-darkness of a universe receding from the memory of a universe the aging brain is having trouble remembering.

•

Heavy apothecary jar of streaked and swirled marbles falls to the floor. Thick, greenish glass shatters on impact, making it impossible to guess correctly the weight and number of marbles contained in the jar and to win the tiny electronic camera with a chip in it capable of recording and transmitting at least 118 years of private, invisible events. Candy striped swirls, subtle onionskins like clambroth skies, sulphides with tiny creatures hunched inside, speckled and pockmarked blue, chocolate or red clay Benningtons roll every which way along the grooves in the terrace tile, some splintering into beautiful needle-teeth determined to find their way into the flesh of toe or heel.

One particularly beautiful marble rolls all the way indoors and takes a careful hop into the dark toe-hole of a dusty brown loafer under the bed.

•

Self looks around and is amazed to discover it had so many selves.

•

Somewhere a child looks out its hospital window and sees sparkling bits of mineral and crystal, rainbow splinters speeding across the dark sky, twinkling as remotely as the voices of children playing in the street.

12

A HUNDRED, two hundred galaxies spin by, setting the infant laughing without stopping. It's the velocity of forward spinning of images itself, not so much the specific content of the images, that outraces the mind and gives a rapturous pleasure.

The weaker reality bores through the stronger and continues printing itself on the retina until an even weaker force bores through the first. The retina in this way becomes the repository of all the displaced realities that have passed across it, while the texture of the world grows weaker, dominated by persistent and repetitive signals that in themselves hardly matter at all.

13

THE *little boy runs out of the house in his red baseball cap and shiny blue baseball jacket. His heart is pounding because whatever frightened him has left the house and outrun him, waiting somewhere on the dark street ahead.*

He meets another lost child, tiny and unbearably intelligent, like a star that's only twinkling so hard because terrible forces have made it contract to a near-infinite density.

The tiny child skips along next to him like a dog that's happy to be off its leash yet would never dream of straying too far from its master, making wild pretzel loops across lawns and behind hedges, emerging far ahead, then doubling back to catch up in reverse.

The two boys run down the plunging slope of the street with the feeling that their legs are bicycle wheels and that there's no way to stop the plunging rotation of the bicycle. Down at the bottom of the tilted avenue they hit a bump and fall off into dark water. Swimming stirs up the river and arouses a sleeping current that sweeps them away from land. Street and city float out of reach, at an odd angle to the sky.

"Space unswimmable; the struggle to wake up useless; drowning as inevitable as if it had already happened."

Later it becomes commonplace for them to tell the story of how at the last second they were rescued by aliens. Face down, grabbed up by a fragile little arm, breath is forced back into them. Without a second to spare they're transported to a place that's supposed to be another planet but resembles a shabby mining town a little less or more than two-hundred-and-twenty-one miles southwest of Selenium Flats.

Their heads are cut off by a surgical procedure so radically new it seems primitive.

Sharp pain that brings tears to their eyes, a hundred, two hundred times worse than the instant the probe digs into sore gums.

"Dig! Dig deeper! Let the blood flow!

"Our daily prayer, which we don't acknowledge, the only one that's ever answered."

Then there's a sudden, stupid feeling of happiness, a sudden release and fall out into nothingness, like the quiet second you let go and fall off the back of a speeding motorcycle, the bulging forehead drawn toward the bulging road.

They wake up with new identities and with the feeling of having been reborn without ever having been born in the first place.

14

Big *Waldo and Little Waldo are alone together in the kitchen.*
"*I'm sorry! I'm really sorry, Daddy! I didn mean to do it! I promise! I won't do it again! I swear! Please! Please don't hit me again! It hurts me! Please!*"

He can see that his dad's hesitating. Anything can happen. Say something or shut up? Their eyes meet and he can tell right away it's a mistake.

"*Ow-ow-owww!*"

Three, four, five sharp little jabs to the back of the head with the point of a knuckle.

"*Ow! It hurts! It hurts me! Please, Daddy, stop!*"

"*Get up off the floor!*"

"*Owww!*"

"*I said get up!*"

"*I cay-yunt!*"

"*Listen to me, Waldo,*" *Big Waldo's voice is thick with emotion.* "*I don't want you to get the idea that I enjoy whacking you. I myself have no reason to whack you. And it's not necessarily for anything you did now. It isn't even necessarily for something you did yesterday. It's more for what I know you're going to do tomorrow. Are you following me? I'm whacking you because I want you to remember what'll happen if I come home from work a month from now and have to deal with this shit. Do you understand me?*"

Little Waldo is sobbing and Big Waldo takes that as a yes.

15

A LL *you have to do is baste it a little, honey."*
   "It needs to be basted?"
"Yes."
"Let's see."
   He takes the deep casserole out of the oven, lifts the lid. The strong aroma creates a lake of serenity. Everyone in the universe smells the same aroma and feels a happy, quiet anticipation with a tantalizing undertone of melancholy, like the memory-aroma of nostalgia, the tempting whiff the nose gets of the ghost-meal the brain hasn't found a way of eating again.
   "Baste it while I warm it up?"
   "Mm-hmm. That's all it needs, sweetheart."
   "You could've just made some burgers. Burgers would've been ok. You didn't have to go to all this bother."
   Though it doesn't come easily, he takes her around and kisses her. There are tears in his eyes.
   She stops herself from saying that she was thinking of inviting Ollie, the bean-faced kid who lost his job at the network. She was thinking that Ollie could move into David's old room and that he could even be a good influence on Junior. But her brain switches tracks and she says without a hitch that it suddenly came over her this afternoon how lucky they were to have each other, just the three of them! Thought to herself that they were absolutely perfect the way they were. Didn't need another soul for company. When that feeling came over her she junked her plan to nuke some fish balls and went looking for those old recipe files of Gramma's, the ones that are all stained and stuck together cause she cooked from

224

them so much when they first got married and hired out as hands on that gigantic goat ranch way up near Walnut Grove in Minnesota. They had those fourteen heavenly seasons up there, but then that awful thing happened to the farmer and his wife and they had to hightail it out of there. Things just seemed to go from bad to worse and the recipes ended up gathering mildew'n'mouseshit down in one basement after another.

16

WALDO *and June are in the kitchen again.*
 "*How do spare ribs with black bean sauce sound, Junie?*"
"*Sounds alright.*"
"*So I should get that?*"
"*Uh-huh.*"
"*What else?*"
"*Whatever you like, Waldo.*"
"*How about some shrimp fried rice?*"
"*Shrimp fried rice?*"
"*Yeah, you usually like that.*"
"*I do? Okeedoke, then.*"
"*Steamed dumplings. Some of those.*"
"*Skip that.*"
"*Skip it?*"
"*Skip the dumplings.*"
"*No dumplings then. OK. How about the butterfly shrimp? How*z *that sound? Junior could eat some butterfly shrimp, I'll betcha.*"
 Waldo cups his mouth and calls toward a doorway in the far, shadowy corner.
 "*Junior?! How*z *some butterfly shrimp sound!*"
 "*Jesus, Waldo, the way I feel about that little creep right now, he can eat shit for dinner.*"
 Mimics Waldo's way of cupping his mouth, calling out even louder and more sweetly.
 "*Oh, Joooon-yuhrr, how*z *some butterfly SHIT sound for dinner? Sound good, sweetheart? Huh?!*"

Starts cackling so violently that the cackling at once breaks down into coughing, coughing into sobbing, and the railing breaks long before the skidding vehicle approaches it.

17

JUNE *is at the stove, stirring a stock pot of dense red goo with a wooden spoon. Every stir releases a chili-like aroma that makes the unhappy cream-and-caramel mutt under the red formica table sneeze as violently as someone clearing his brain of a lifetime of bad memories. Sneezes again, jingling the rings on its red collar, and imagines its head sailing off so that it can turn into another dog — an old white shepherd, fat, peaceful and mud-stained, that's wandered down out of the snowy woods and quietly made itself at home.*

"You know what I'd really like? What my dream would be?"

Suddenly Ollie sounds ten years old.

"No, honey, what?"

"I'd like us to have a big house in the country somewhere with lots of animals."

"My Mom has a house like that, only it's in New Mexico."

"With lots of animals?"

"Oh sure. My Mom's always had lots of animals. You an me an my Mom in one big house with all the animals. Would you like that?"

"Yes! Of course! Would there be dogs and horses? And cows? And rabbits and geese? And turtles?"

"Geese 'n' turtles 'n' rabbits 'n' cows 'n' horses 'n' dogs — yup — and goats. My Mom's got this thing for goats!"

Shakes her head and can't stop laughing at some goat-event Ollie can't imagine.

"We can't have our own place, cause that would cost a lot of money, right?"

"Yes, it would. And we have no money. That's why I'm de-pressed. That's why I'm in such a terrible mood all the time, sweetheart. We don't have it and we have no possible way of get-ting it. So you'd better go show your face in there before the Blob comes back to life."

Ollie joins Waldo on the couch and, before his gaze settles clearly on the image, he hears a familiar television voice that at the same time is a nostalgia-laden memory-voice.

"Certainly we have no parents in the ordinary sense. And yet we feel our parents abandoned us and that wherever we are we're aliens. Whether or not we choose our destiny is something no one can answer, and certainly there are many who consider us fortu-nate and who even long for our strange condition. Nevertheless, tears sometimes overwhelm us, like the desire to say something that can't be said."

18

LATE *at night Waldo says to June, "you wanna hear a great idea for a book?"*

"Hmmm?"

"Wanna hear a great idea? This would make a great book! I thought of it today while I was driving back and trying to wriggle out of my uniform without going off the road. But I couldn't do it so I was trying to take my mind off the horrible stains that were still on it from last night's job. You know how difficult it is to communicate? How sometimes it seems like every single time you open your mouth you're starting from scratch? So, wouldn't it be great, wouldn't it sell a million copies…."

"There already is such a stupid thing, Waldo, honey."

"But I haven't said anything yet!"

"A language that everyone can understand. They already have it, Waldo. It's exactly because everyone can understand it that you don't necessarily think of it as a language."

"Can't be a language that's invented." he pouts, "cause that would be just one more annoying thing to learn."

"But it's already right there under our noses, Waldo, as common as salt."

"If you're thinking of something with numbers, then you'd have to do calculations. Mine doesn't need calculations."

"Worked that out a long time ago, Waldo. The mathematical aspect, which is almost the same thing as saying the musical aspect. And once you have the musical aspect of course that translates automatically into the electronic aspect."

"You did?"

"Ages ago. Remember when you used to see me sitting in the corner and you thought I was drawing?"

"Well," he laughs shyly, "I said it was a good idea, didn I?"

"I didn't just have the idea, Waldo. I wasn't just another dreamer having her moment of genius out there in traffic. I worked it all out. I filled a thousand notebooks with my charts and tables."

"Gee, Junie, I had no idea." (Demolished.) "Do you think I could look at it sometime?"

"You can look at it now. But I'm not all that sure it would sell a billion copies. I don't think it was a particularly good idea. It might even be a pretty stupid idea. Stop for one second and think, Waldo. Do people really have trouble communicating? Is that really the problem? Or is it just one of those things we say so often we've forgotten that we don't know what we're talking about. Don't you ever have the feeling that we communicate too much? Jesus, Waldo, sometimes I communicate so much it feels like falling out a window. There you are inside yourself, all self-contained and cozy and tight in your box, and then you start communicating and you keep going and going and then you're not in there anymore and exactly where are you then? You're out there vibrating in the ether with so many other waves and vibrations no one can count them — or you're crawling like a worm through some underground cable or you run up against a steel building and feel your forehead go bang and then your head spreads out so thin against the surface that there's no way you can tell your squashed particles apart from the squashed particles of every other yammering head that's come out of the ozone and banged up against it. Are you following me, Waldo? Don't you ever flip through the channels and wish you had the power to make them all shut up? Wonder what would happen to them and to the world if none of them could ever say another word? Is that an example of too little communication, Waldo?"

Waldo is looking hungrily at the containers on the night table where he smells a salty and fishy core of warmth and flavor steaming within their congealed masses.

"Think I'll just have another little nibble." he says.

"Go ahead. Finish it. Eat it all. I lost my appetite."

"How come?"

*"Cause you reminded me that there's something I have to say
and that it's not worth saying unless everyone in the universe hears
it at the same instant. When I was young I used to think that if
I wrote a novel everyone would eventually read that novel — I
wouldn't have to do anything to make them read that novel, they'd
just end up reading it the way a sneeze travels around the world
— and that after everyone read that novel reality would be different. No other novel would ever be written that didn't in some way
derive from my novel and a cell might even mutate in the human
brain. All through my childhood and up until the time I was thirty
or so I was working on a novel called* Blondie and Dagwood in
Hell *and it was a cartoon version of my own life. Listen. Here's
a sample: Blondie and Dagwood are having soft-scrambled eggs
and bacon and homefries browned and crisped with good Hungar-
ian paprika with strands of sautéed and caramelized onion mixed
in, nice and salty and a little peppery, coffee, cream and buttered toast with bitter orange marmalade and Dagwood's going
on and on about his boss, Mr. Dithers, as usual, and Blondie's
finally had it and she says: 'It's always them, the ones who are
capable of happiness, whose lives get gobbled up. They get their
throats cut, they disappear and their skeletons are found centuries
later weighted down with chains, or arranged neatly right there on
the forest floor when some mound of dirt and leaves gets washed
away. While the other ones, the wrecks, the walking dead who
forgot to get buried, the ones like you, get taken care of. Demand
to get taken care of by the happy ones. And they do it. We drain
their lives as if it's our only reason for living. So, if I were you,
I'd forget about Mr. Dithers. I'd go into the kitchen, make myself
another big, sloppy sandwich, an' I'd lie down on the sofa with
the sandwich in one hand and the remote in the other so's I could
do everything I'm good at without having to move.'*

*"It took me forever to let go of the idea of a novel that everyone
would read. Even now it's a little depressing to realize that there
isn't — there can never be — a novel-messiah the same way there*

*can be and always is a new television-messiah or technology-mes-
siah. Is it television or just electrons that's the sneeze that goes
round the world, Waldo?*

"*Let's say there's still someone with a novel inside her, someone
whose weird novel is her, who tries to feed that novel into the donut
machine. Either it won't go through or else it will and then what
you have is more donuts. I think it's fair to say, Waldo, that the
more everyone says that art and popular culture are now almost
entirely blended into one indistinguishable-but-pleasing goo, the
more absolutely the idea of art and the idea of a popular language
are now two completely different ideas and any artist who believes
they're the same doesn't know it but her head's already been cut
off and surgically replaced while she was dozing at her desk.*"

19

THE *old washing-and-drying unit is always on. Laundry's al-ways being processed one way or another and the sound of laundry processing is the sound of life in this house.*

Visitors never notice the perpetual churning and buzzing of the background— or even the occasional violent rattling and thrash-ing as if the unit's about to rip loose from its moorings and lift off into orbit. The visitors sit here unconsciously and those who live here are unconscious of what's going on around them, like tap water poured into lake water.

.

Head turns in its spacesuit to look back at the galaxy just orbited, the same way the visible turns to stare at the invisible that created it.

.

Noise at every point in the kitchen, no matter at what distance from the washing-and-drying unit. With three exceptions. There are three precise points where, if the instrumentation of the head is angled correctly, there's dead silence.

Tune the frequency of the head by minute degrees.

Listen longer, giving the head an odd rotation, like a dog anxiously regarding door or window, and there's a fly-like ZZZ-ZZZ-ing that breaks down into the unhealthy cough of the an-cient coffee maker in a famous donut shop in the mountains.

.

As we become what we watch, what we watch is already mu-tating, most likely into one more real reality never seen before on Earth. And a cell mutating in the watching brain is like a virus plotting its own replacement.

20

ONE *night Ollie slips out of bed. He's headed for the kitchen,* *where he wants to sneak himself an extra helping of leftover* *sauerbraten and strawberry pie, when he's stopped short in the* *darkness just outside the open doorframe by the croaking voice of* *the woman he loves.*

"They said," the worn-out voice manages to say, "'Apparently *you were a mess most of your life, but however much of a mess* *you were you're too messed-up now to play that mess, so we can't* *at all promise what role you'll have in this. We may slip you into* *a minor role somewhere so that when your name appears in the* *credits people will wonder if that fucked-up woman was you. But* *it will be your script and it will be your story and the series could* *go on forever!'*

"But it never happened! No one knows my story, Mommy! I'm *in a place where no one ever sees me and it's just like hell!"*

Ollie comes forward a few more steps. Can see into the fluores- *cent over-brightness of the kitchen. There's June in the far corner,* *sitting on the chrome-and-red-vinyl telephone stool.*

"All my life I only wanted one thing. And I never got it! Never! *I've never gotten it from anyone, Mommy! From the youngest* *age, I never got it! I always wanted it, but I never got it! All I* *ever got were these tunnels. They're not even tunnels, they're holes* *right in the middle of your life. In the middle of your day, while* *you're sitting and eating, while you're with other people, Mommy* *— in the middle of all that you're falling into a hole, into the* *pit — and they all think you're normal! They all see you sit-* *ting there, even though you're somewhere else! You're somewhere*

else, but where? Where are we really when people can see us but we're not there? One existence more real than another, Mommy, do you know? They're all watching you smiling and chatting — and somewhere else you're rocking back and forth, humming and banging your head against the edge of whatever's nearest and has an edge — and somewhere else you're already buried but still sobbing.

"What? No, Mommy. No! No, don't say that! Don't! Oh, no, no, Mommy! No! Oh no! I didn't mean it that way! No — god — oh no! No, I didn't mean that you — oh Mommy you know how much I love you! I love you more than anything! I can't even tell you how much I love you, I love you so much! You were the best mother in the whole world — you were the best friend in the whole world! You really were. The whole world thought so and I thought so too! Oh, forgive me! Forgive me, Mommy! I didn't want to hurt you! Oh god, I shouldn't have called! I shouldn't have called, but I had to ! I feel bad, I feel really bad, Mommy! No! No! Don't say that! Don't cry, Mommy! I feel like shit! Oh god! God!

"No, look, I'm calming down! I am. Listen. Can you hear it? I'm getting it together now. Mommy? You hear it? I'm calmer now. But the doorbell is ringing — I think it's Big Waldo. Waldo Senior is coming home. He doesn't use his key. He has a key, but he doesn't use it. 'Cause he likes me to come an let him in, that's why! He likes me to welcome him home at the front door! He likes me to prove that I'm thrilled to drop whatever I'm doing and come to the front door to welcome him home. Yes, Mommy! It's just that I can't stand what I'm feeling. My children think I murdered them and now they're on every channel you turn to! They've got fabulous new heads and they're able to talk and make faces better than they used to, but they still call me a murderer! No one knows my side of it, Mommy! You've got connections! I don't care if they put me on at three o'clock in the afternoon! Or at four a.m.! I'd rather be on when the airwaves have a feeling of solitude. I love the dark forest of middle-of-the-night TV and the creatures you find wandering there.

"I think the whole world would tune in forever if they could watch me re-enact all the filthy things I've done…!"

She's hung up the phone, but her mouth is still going through its wet spasms of over-excitement.

It's depressing for him to find that all feeling of attraction has drained away and that she reminds him of nothing so much as the one memory he has of his mother, red-faced and screaming, mouth open wide and twisted to one side, crazed with the frustration of not being able to bite pieces off the side of its own head, which at that moment she couldn't tell apart from the thick typescript sticking out of her handbag.

"Even if you're a nightmare," Ollie thinks, staring at June, who's gazing through him like someone pretending to carry on a conversation while secretly entranced by the quicksilver streaming of youthful, beautiful faces of whatever mini-narrative happens to be on TV, "even if you're a memory — even if you're the nightmare memory that comes exactly at the moment when we're finally beginning to feel our own freedom — when the lingering grief of childhood begins to fall away and we're mutating into someone else — even if you're the memory-demon that comes back to spoil everything — I want you to know that I'm not the good son. The one who'll take you in and nurse you till you don't seem quite so cracked. I'm the son who'd put you away forever!"

Her eyes come into focus. Her look makes his hand go instinctively to his throat and he thinks: "Let this blow strike me: receive the full force of this blow: draw as many blows from her as possible so she can slip back into her hell!"

21

AFTER *months on the road searching for his brother he returns home for a rest and finds his Gramma arguing with an unfamiliar woman in the blue-carpeted front hall. The woman, whose hair is even blacker than his Gramma's, done up not in a frightening ice cream cone, but in flattened metallic ripples, has violet lipstick so thick the lips project out an inch off the white-white face.*

"Jesus, Ma," the younger woman says, "you only shaved off half your moustache! You left half your moustache on your face!"

"I did?"

He can tell from the zombied monotone of her wild soprano that Gramma's on something new and potent. And he can tell from her eyes that her brain's on a separate adventure.

"I thought I got it all. You mean I didn't get it all?"

"You look horrible, Ma! How many times have I told you not to shave while you watch!"

"Can't shave while I watch?"

"No!"

"But then I'll miss my program. I won't know if they found that little girl! I won't know if she made it back through the horizon — or through the hellish region of dark vacuums — or through the heliopause. I think I missed that episode already. Do you know if the little girl is back with her family in the house overlooking the goose pond where she used to go looking for baby toads, tree frogs and turtles?"

Is the younger woman supposed to be his mom? Not only doesn't she look like his mom, she doesn't look like any mom anywhere. Doesn't look like a woman or even a person. Looks more like a reconstituted corpse, with a head that hasn't quite gotten the hang of sitting up straight and swiveling on the neck.

New Mom (if she is his mom) reminds him of someone who used to bend into his crib. Face and hand were loving, yet the gesture was frightening. Or was it the gesture that was loving, hand and face that were frightening? This is a memory of no one, yet it haunts him. And now this ghost-memory has returned as a living corpse that hasn't gotten used to its new head.

22

THE *great horizontality of evening.*
No breeze and the last fiery cloud, the erect one, standing straight up overhead as a tower of burning frequencies, begins to lose its charge and blend in with all the rest. Its messages drain off and die out unheard.

The weight of the day.

Everything light already risen into the thin air of the sky.

As the dark residue settles into the mass of the Earth, birds on their antennas receive signals through their talons and give out odd little cries whose code they themselves haven't figured out — while out in the fallen leafbeds there's the squeak and rustle of mutating identities.

23

ONE *night, from a hill that's like a bulky green potato, he stands for minutes long enough to be hours observing the way moonlight flows from the little stream into the little pond. The light that travels forward and the light that takes its place, like a wheel whose revolutions have come loose from the circle where they were bound.*

After a time he starts down the hill and stops to listen to a bird swimming in the moonlit pond and then rising up out of the water. Sits on a branch drying its wings and making frog-like noises that ascend along the spine into the short bristles and soft curls at the back of the neck , ending in a difficult sequence at the apex of the bare apple tree.

.

Another night, far away, sitting alone at a restaurant table with pen and folded green paper that needs to be smoothed flat, he tries to remember but can't. Tries, but can't dig it out of the paper with the sharp point of his pen. Wonders if (once he returns the folded paper to his pocket, its thoughts unfinished and not having found their form or rhythm) he'll ever find it again. Unfolds it, tries to smooth its creases flat and thinks about his father. A father himself now, he feels that his father ought to be but isn't waiting in the house for him to come back from his walk up the hill and down to the pond. What's worse, he hardly remembers him. Who was he? Who was he really? And, whoever he was, how long did he remain who he was before mutating into someone else? a) Know what we know only while we know it. (Oblivion only requires the slightest unscrewing of head and memory pops off like a bottle cap.) b) And even while we're in it we and it are already becoming something else.

Before re-folding the sheet of green paper along its original creases and slipping it for all time into its home in his jacket pocket, he isn't able to write anything about his father's presence, only his absence, and instead finds himself writing that the first dark creature that crosses the light sky is a signal to all to help the night arrive.

24

THE *floating dock, moored to a plank around the bar, dips away with one deep undulation as he steps onto it.*

Each one taking this step fails to notice the slight difference in the two planes — the weak, unstable attachment between one plane and another — takes an ordinary misstep and comes close to tumbling, signaling the invisible gap between two realities.

Suddenly we're in it.

Stand on the dock, staring at the dark lake that yields a dark image. Floating, yet stable. Anchored, yet with a drifting instability.

Something in us wants to cry out, but, as always, we don't do it and another reality is set afloat, like the ʒillion-ʒillion pixels born on how many screens held in how many hands at the same instant.

Those inside, behind the neon KINYON'S KAVERNS sign, elbows on the bar, heads pointed slightly down and forward, looking at an angle that travels through their drinks and into the vacant space behind the bar below the mirror where the dark window is reflected, black glass that has the blackest blood red dissolved in it, backs of heads deceptively youthful, faces aged by some inhuman process that nevertheless wears a hideous human look, are thinking (and they're right) that the young man out on the dock is outside the situation, just as they feel their own insideness (inside this situation, outside every other) and the inside-or-outsideness of everyone everywhere.

"We burrow into a life — any life — and carry that with us forever as our definition. Extraordinary how what comes to be known as 'our life' accumulates around us. The world rushes by us as a perpetual outside of impossible possibilities, carrying its

distance close enough to stir the fibers of a sleeve. The having-burrowed-into-a-life is clearly written on our faces, especially to someone outside every situation, inside none, like the young man on the dock, looking at the dark lake as longingly as an actor without a series, lying on the hardwood floor, under the screen that used to be his home."

The empty dance floor looms large and shiny behind the railing, the color of light in beer. It really is a lake and we don't go out onto it except when there's music to keep us afloat.

The bar is lit only enough to look like an attractive inside to anyone unlucky enough to be trapped in the darkness outside.

25

EVENING *comes on rapidly and with it the withdrawal of the world from the skin. Cooling air brings distance close: the temperature of the eye's relation to the world now becomes the body's whole skin.*

What stands here now is not him, but his isolation in the world.

Keep staring at the lake as an antidote to memory. Memory dies with each minute turning of the head, as the head turns like a screw-off bottle cap and death occurs when forgotten experience accumulates to a certain critical mass.

Stares out, head tilted slightly upward, following the track of a few stray crystals that were dropped from a donutshop sugar bowl and are dissolving in the night sky.

Forest keeps its green, but hidden, and what's green and hidden emits a long cry in short drills, while something black — a black bird or insect with green wings — struggles rapidly back and forth across the water, going EEP! *PEEP-PEEP!*

Last weak orange light drains out of grass and picnic tables as the real night of the forest seeps into the lake.

How thoroughly darkness takes over the forest! Forest takes over lake: dark lake and forest take over the universe.

"Here I am by the lake, staring stupidly for hours on end. Into darkness. Oh! Mother! I'm the child abandoned! I'm the child murdered! Alive in the woods and afraid to reveal myself, lest they abandon me again! Lest they murder me again! Don't they look for us only so that they can abandon and murder us again?

"Memories haunt us of having flown at low altitudes above the Earth — of having glided with an odd lateral movement over

the ground — and we're puzzled by our knowledge of the ceiling's cool plaster.

"Talking about my grandmother to someone, I suddenly have to cover my face to hide my weeping, yet I'm not at all certain that I had a grandmother.

"I fell asleep and dreamed. And for once I didn't have a nightmare. I wasn't locked inside my little black box. I wasn't buried somewhere, waiting for someone to descend to the ocean floor with a powerful light and robot retrieval arm."

The darkness outside makes the interior of the little tavern glow with a warmth it doesn't have. And this unreal glow from a real source reaches the young man on the floating dock at the same time as a thrilling old melody that's lost and gained many meanings with time.

He retreats up the green hill and stands for a long time looking at the distant little building's glowing windows against the dark matter of lake and trees and wondering how he came to be lost in the eternal outside of the flickering distant point of the eternal inside.

26

A MAN *in deepest indigo jeans and almost-as-deep-or-even-deeper indigo-and-green plaid shirt is striding across a meadow to the fenced-in enclosure back of his barn.*

A chestnut horse with an irregular white diamond on his forehead is visible in a more distant meadow, grazing under trees.

Crossing the field into the deep focus of the panorama the man pauses at the crest of a gentle elevation above a hollow that may once have been a pond, choked purple and yellow with reeds and wildflowers.

Buzz of a tractor. Thing itself invisible. Hidden like a wasp behind a window blind.

The little plane buzzes and drops into the hive of tufty evergreens where sound waves reform its image in the mind.

Hollow and sharply rebounding as a hammer on wood, a dog begins to bark for private dog reasons .

Foreground ZZZ-ZZZ-ing of insects in the low-lying grass, level and enormous. Clicking and trilling in the deeper undergrowth. Other sounds diminish or intensify, diagramming the random multiplication of moments on a level map of space, but the microwave life of insects is collective and continuous.

Breeze brushes the tanned back of the man's neck just above the collar of the blue/green plaid shirt like the ghostly prickle of a far-off look: hand goes to neck and one ear feels the coolness of the forest's gaze.

Here and there an insect is receiving a persistent cell phone call in the grass.

Messages are chirping everywhere and it's easy for the head to imagine that it's receiving too many for it to handle. As if it's the only head alive in the wobbly globe of space-time, all lines passing through it.

He has with him a sack of halved apples for the horse. Calls the horse by name. Horse looks up: ambiguous spark of temptation lost in indifference. Ambiguous spark encourages the man to continue waving a fragrant section of apple. Horse goes back to his grazing. Grazing is the horse's day's work: under coarse, tasteless blades and unappetizing matts, there's a thin layer close to the ground where whatever's tender and aromatic must get cropped precisely in order not to chew tough earth with its wood chips, straw and pebbles. Once the horse has found this delicious layer, the trick is to keep at it — chewing on a level plane — even if some fool is flashing a cut-open apple with its white flesh and green aroma streaked with sugar.

Man stands there with his apple, feeling rejected. This horse-rejection reminds him of something, but he doesn't know what. Redoubles his efforts. Pretends to eat the apple. Loud chomping noises and mouth-watering apple aromas reach the horse on cool forest breezes and inspire him to turn 90° and sidle away — down toward a swampy spot where a thin stream is flowing half-hidden toward the flowering sump.

Stands forever turned away, drinking and grazing.

The man throws his apples in the stall and starts back down the slope toward his house, thinking that all we do is unmask our yearning with our so-called gifts. (And the more our yearning is unmasked...?)

27

ALONE *in the isolated smoker's corner of the Japanese res-taurant, near the aquarium and the red folding screen that conceals the entrance to the bathrooms, eating his tile fish poached in sake, drinking plum wine the color of yellow raisins.*

The meter that's always on, measuring the kindness, the in-difference, the cruelty of others, its needle waving wildly from instant to instant, settles calmly on the young waitress's sympa-thetic gaze.

Night after night in the same corner, eating, drinking and smoking.

Sometimes, when it's late and there's no one else in the restau-rant, she joins him at the table.

When she was young, she says, her parents traveled through the States on business. She was lonely and always dreaming of home and she remembers thinking: "If we live in memory, where are we? where are we really? Is memory longing crawling back-ward? Crawling on all fours like an infant? Longing memory that crawls sideways? And when we're living in longing and memory is that our real self living? As if our real self could live out its life unknown to us, like a character on a program we never watch but who's living exactly the same life as we are. The real self is per-forming far away, while the one in the flesh, the one your parents see, the one they feed and pat on the head and think is the one-and-only, is nothing. The same or different from the one that en-joys its pizza and has frequent, wearying orgasms? Isn't it true that there are times when the flesh-self is nothing but a photoelectric cell whose only job is to transmit information to the remote, real self?"

This is what she thought then, as a child. Stupid or not, these unanswered questions were important to her and, to be honest about it, still give her life its impossibly twisted pretzel shape.

The no-longer-young young man says that, once-upon-a-time, in a beautiful Japanese restaurant at the densely wooded intersection of two small highways somewhere southeast of Albany, he was having dinner with his mom & dad of the moment. His dad was Visiting Professor of Television History at RPI in Troy and his Mom was Station Manager of a Total Television station in Western Massachusetts and they were having one of those amiable, collegial dinners that turn the child of civilized parents against civilization: the superficial disagreements mask such fundamental agreement that the disgusted child develops a taste for whatever is senseless and uncivilized, preferring the Neanderthal gesture and the bedlam of unintelligible yammering to an overload of lukewarm civility. Discard it all in the purple-brown run off of the nearest river and never come back to look for it.

Always leaning out of the common, family moment.

Leaning out of their moment, do you necessarily lean into yours?

Leaning out of their moment, you fail to lean into any other moment and end up in a moment that belongs to no one.

The famous pinhole in time.

Hard to find your way back.

Live out a whole irretrievable lifetime there as a not-quite-famous TV personality whose existence depends entirely on the existence of another, more popular program in whose interior your program is buried.

Remembers leaning out of his family's moment and noticing a beautiful Japanese girl leaning back out of her family's moment: mother, father, two other couples eating and laughing, a festive occasion, and the beautiful daughter alone with her mountainous dessert, the vanilla-ice-cream-sponge-cake-chocolate-sauce-rum-sauce-and-whipped-cream "Mt. Fuji," gazing with deep focus through the dark windows whose long, square edges seem curved because of the oblique angle of the view into the curve of the intersection and the whirling spindles of the trees. He remembers sensing that she was thinking of someone she loved but who didn't love her. And he was able to follow her gaze through the window and knew that she was thinking miserably that the desire to be loved is a fatal mistake. "It's the hunting dog that always gets eaten by its prey."

28

THERE *he is, isolated in the wraparound window of a restaurant, visible to anyone approaching across the broad, divided square of the agitated intersection. The intelligent, miserable look of a misfit graduate student. The young Television Genius who already sees his ideas headed for the donut machine. Holding his head with one hand as if to keep it from rolling away.*

29

STARES *out into the intersection, then suddenly bends over mint green paper, glossy, with no resistant or absorbent grain to it. Folded in four for years in his pocket, now it won't lie flat on the table next to an oversized white bowl of half-eaten capellini in spicy red sauce. Flattening it with one hand, he attacks it with his pen as if carving something into it. Against the bright late autumn light of the street (a residual but glaring brilliance softened only at the orange edges of the stones) he's trying, between bites of cooling pasta, to work out a code for the cartoon version of his childhood, a comedy that looks like a tragedy or the other way around, depending on the viewer's position in relation to the screen.*

What is it that catches the eye? The unique gesture we've seen before.

A figure brushes close to the window and the eye follows it across the blinding X of the intersection to the far pavement where those in shadow are about to step forward into the sunlit foreground.

Cold sun of autumn burns in the window, for the eye only.

A window between one reality and another is sufficient to create a reciprocal unreality. Heads stare from one side at the other, so much more crystalline — saturated colors precisely embedded in its outlines — marveling at the precise abstraction of another world; and from the excessively visible world heads stare into the ambient swirl of the other, so much more explosive and exhilarating than the one they happen to be planted in.

Someone crossing the intersection, invisible at the crosshairs of its blinding X and wearing dark glasses against its glare, has the impression that the man in the restaurant window is on television, broadcasting live. A familiar anchorman, the one with tired, human eyes and a greying little beard, whose mouth sometimes gives a tiny, involuntary spasm of excitement and whose humor never quite gives way to the melancholia that is its wellspring. Papers before him in a subtle order of crumpled disarray, pen in hand, his face and body address the world with a sidelong posture.

30

THE *stroller in sunglasses gravitates toward the restaurant window, a sheet of glass as thin and sharp as a guillotine that passes through the neck without the head having noticed it. With your new head you acquire programs already in progress.*

Wherever one stops and stares, dozens gather.

Stand there wondering when they started broadcasting from this buzzing, agitated intersection.

Now the stroller comes out of the glare, focuses and sees that it isn't the familiar and beloved newscaster, but someone new and younger, the one they say is the future "Television Genius."

Television Genius looks up, biting his pen, as if absurdly looking for his thought beyond the sunny intersection shining like water. Can't tell how many are out there in the glare, their heads leaping off their shoulders like particle geysers when the sun's robot rays dig into whatever gets in their way.

Says that now that he's out in front of the camera, in public view, he can imagine what it's like to be a talk show host at home, depressed over raspberry-jelly-filled donuts, cinnamon-sugar-crusted cider donuts, un-sugared cider donuts, a wedge of sour-cream-apple-walnut coffee cake and coffee, watching TV and seeing his own dumb head smiling tomorrow's smile with more of a real self's vibrant life than he feels sitting there in his livingroom. Talk show host, no longer young, recovering from his fourth miraculous neck surgery, is thinking about immortality. Wondering: if he's feeling dead, what good is the supposed immortality of the TV screen? Mineral immortality without feeling alive has something important missing from it. And: how do we end up sitting on the couch pretty sure we're alive but feeling dead? Time and gradual loss of memory may explain it, but that would mean that memory makes us feel alive and everyone knows that even the most lifelike memory never resurrected anything. More likely is the self's gradual loss of its secret other self. Secret other self dies perpetually throughout life and the self experiences many deaths of its own. Doesn't die entirely. Remains tethered to the self with the possibility of resurrection. What is it that can bring it back to life? Can it spring back to life spontaneously or do we need to induce its resurrection with our coded rituals? Self's secret other self a sort of condensed soup destined to stay sealed in its little tin packet because the first self is the only one who has a clue how to reconstitute it. Desperately wants it reconstituted but doesn't want anyone to know the secret recipe for doing it. The living corpse mistakenly sealed in its tomb prays for someone to open the door, yet refuses to reveal the combination of the lock.

.

A man ill and prematurely aged is walking with a cane.

One leg stiff and one like jelly.

One step rigid, hitching up one side of the body, the other oddly slapping, as if the sole were detached from the shoe.

Crosses the intersection at a snail's pace.

Stops short in sunlight as if he's heard someone call.

"David!"

And then again, "D a a a-v i i d!" as if from far away.

He plunges forward into blazing water and for a second the glare erases him from the view of every diner in every restaurant window.

Now he's made his way across and is standing with all the other onlookers crowded around the window where the future Television Genius is broadcasting live.

All around the lake it's sunny. Sun on the surface spreads out into a single disintegrating particle. Below it, a child is drowning in the squishy vegetable matter his foot always recoiled from in horror. Puzzling to the long pickerels and transparent sunnies, the parent desperate in his canoe or kayak, about to dive in.

The prematurely aged man thinks he's the only one who hears the young genius talk about the first grief and the far worse, unexpected one that comes later. The sensation of swimming up toward someone after a lifetime of grief and separation.

After a time, he says, the sensation dies down and we stop calling as if expecting someone to pick up at the other end. Likewise, the head stops turning on its neck, certain it's heard a cherished voice calling from another room.

31

THE visitors have been ferried out to the satellite island across the treacherous Plumbicon, a narrow channel cut out by successive hurricanes where three islands used to be one, leaving behind a twisted splice of currents and rip tides.

Now they're out on the vast and sloping lawn below the pool, beyond the shrubbery and the beds of tropical flowers, in a semi-circle of hooded blue cabana chairs, drinking and listening to the Television Genius's father-in-law give a speech that might also be a eulogy.

"Now that you've seen a little of what David is doing, I don't think you'll be worrying anymore for a second even about what direction he's taking! I see at least three faces here — and if Dick would for a second show some sign that he's breathing, I could say *four* faces or even five — that know as well as I do that every failure we've ever had was the result of listening to your good advice and that for us a good review has always been one that says: 'Watching the so-called Between-Channel channel is like attending your own beheading. After half-an-hour you can't find your head. Your own head is missing and someone else's head is on your shoulders!'

"This was always the *cheenyus* of the man. Or have we forgotten that already? When he wasn't even twenty — my god, I can't even *believe* now the ugly stuff he had everybody watching! I myself, when my dauder Choon first came to me and told me she was in love with this guy I never heard of — this kid she met on a train — and she made me look at hours of his stuff, I hated it! I thought this is the ugliest garbage I ever saw! This stuff is disgusting. But in six months I could have formed a club of no more than twelve guys as backward, as out-of-date, as *out of it* as I was. I think everybody here forgot already how *gruesome* his early work actually was — and how popular. That was his famous 'Ugly Period'. And with the so-called 'Memory Channel' we're seeing in some way a return to the greatness of the 'Ugly Period'. Two years from now you'll be complaining about all the imitations of this stuff you find so hard to swallow. In every stupid Sunday Supplement of every stupid newspaper some idiot with a fax machine for a head will be repeating something he heard on one of our 'invisible' little so-called interior programs as if he just dreamed it up himself. And you'll be begging us to fry up a million donuts exactly the same as the ones you were just spitting out.

"You and everyone else will be saying how *brilliant* it was, what a *cheenyus* it took to make this leap. You'll be saying, and really feeling you're having an original thought, that it's as if the invisible band of the television spectrum had been made visible. Inside what already exists as a landscape, a continent of possible experience, he discovered a vast, hidden kingdom. Think of it like this: now every dummy with a set of ears attached to his skull suddenly has the possibility of hearing the inaudible dog whistle for which we happen to own the patent.

"There's never been a time in human history when what we think is a fresh idea occurring only to us at that very instant hasn't *already been uttered* by someone else. But it isn't very often, gentlemen, believe me, that someone owns the patent to the obscure pre-utterance that later becomes a *popular* utterance!

"Already because of you we missed the boat maybe half-a-dozen times on stuff like this! When he said for example 'the next wave of nostalgia is always-at-all-times already in them' you wouldn't listen. Or you didn't know what the hell he was talking about. And you still don't understand (and I probably don't understand myself) what he meant when he said (what seems like a century ago) that they feel their own non-existence. 'It's because they feel their own non-existence that they worry so much about reality mutating around them because of the supposed unreality of television.' Raise your hands everyone who understands that. 'The force of unreality is always stronger than the force of reality and is always changing it. But what do we actually mean by the 'reality' of a person? As soon as we're born we begin to receive signals, to radiate signals and to accumulate garbage.

"'The accumulated family garbage and work garbage and everyday garbage that sits down in front of the set for some relief from itself — where's the harm if that begins to mutate? To become less "real"? I could make an argument if I put my mind to it,' he said, 'that a person is just an imperfect form of television. That television is what the human soul has always aspired to. Designed to be a model of what we'd love to turn into, but can't. We see a repetitive, retrievable life there that may or not be the immortality the soul has always longed for. And the simple, everyday act of looking out of the body at it means we're always trying to get there but can't quite do it. As if the secret key is getting through the bog of stupid content. Stupidity of content is deliberate and meant to keep us from getting there. It could be said another way. It's visibility itself we're watching when we watch TV, every program a plastic sandwich bag filled with wave-particles of light. But the plastic sandwich bag is all we talk about, never the mystery inside.

"'We're born into the world clutching at a finger and sucking on a nipple, but after that we can't stop sipping on that ice cold cocktail of electrons. . . . Even worse: we're like smokers who clip off the cigarette and smoke the dark little nicotine-sponge of the filter only.'"

When his speech ends the closing festivities are over and when the closing festivities are over everyone departs the island quickly, without having had a glimpse of the Television Genius who's supposedly dozing in a healing near-coma on the terrace.

32

A MAN wakes up on the terrace, in full sunlight yet covered with a thin blanket the color of a newborn peapod, a glass of iced tea and a lightweight pair of yellow field binoculars on the table next to him.

Someone is waving from the pool.

He picks up the binoculars and sees her clearly, carrying into the nearness of the optical field the beauty of her distant image: little shock of black hair, white face, red lips.

But why on earth is she calling in *German?*

His daughter explains that it's only *baby* German and that all Mom is saying is that Granpa is hungry and that it isn't good for Granpa to go so long without eating — so she's sending him up and she'd appreciate it if they could scrape something together.

Now Granpa Ernst comes clearly into view, orange towel around his thick neck, waving up to them as he takes a fat-old-man's stiff hop from raised boardwalk down to sand path, his body brilliantly taking over the functions of the brain so that the broad, bearded face can smile up at them at the same instant the hand goes up and waves, the leg takes its youthful jump and he calls up, unmindful of the loudness of his bellow in an accent that's suddenly so thick it's like a potato and oxtail soup that's boiled down so far it can't be swallowed.

"I could eat right now a Prague fillet of beef with crisp fried onions and sour red wine sauce! with some peppery, paprika-fried potatoes even! and some bread dumplings and red cabbage! And for dessert, my god, what I wouldn't give for some

ASCHER/STRAUS

of my mother's pfankuchen! You know why? Because my mind hasn't been this sharp since a hundred years ago — when I had my headquarters in Bucharest and I could say really that I owned Eastern Europe because every idea I had was a cheen-yus idea! And now — with a little help from her Poppa, who's got his head screwed on again — our little cheenyus Choonie has solved everything! You can go back peacefully to sleep now for a thousand years, David! Believe me! I hope at least you've got some cold *Pilsner* up there!"

He gives another wave and disappears at a near-trot under the palms surrounding the villa.

262

33

THE pool water is heated to the point where a delicate egg dumpling could poach in it.

The beautiful young woman climbs out and is dismayed to discover that the long shadows over the pool have grown cold despite the hot sun still shining behind the hedge-and-tree horizon. First self shivers with the evening chill while the second, image-self shimmers for others in its coldly glowing blue suit. Daddy is not waiting as he used to, soft towel flung wide and wrapped around her quickly, absorbing all cold shadows from the skin and drawing them up before they can settle in the core.

She rubs her own hair, back and shoulders just as if her daddy were doing it, throws a robe around herself and hurries toward the narrow opening between the sea grapes and the wild olives.

Head turns as leg and foot are about to take the long step down from boardwalk to sand path. Looks back and sees the corpse of her dead father rise up from a horizontal lounge chair, place two long hands in an unnatural gesture along either side of the head, as if holding it in place, then walk without wavering. Corpse trails her slowly at a distance.

34

THE beautiful child Valeria, who already looks like another Valeria (neither the Valeria she's going to be nor the Valeria she once was, mutating so fast not even the same Valeria from one day to the next), lying on the carpet, crossing things out and scribbling things in with her stylus, shaking her head as images change on the screen, suddenly stops and looks toward the kitchen.

35

DIDN'T see him go in, but there he is, back turned, bent over the stove in his blue Japanese robe with drooping sleeves. As old before his time as a child discharged from the hospital, incurable and given up for dead, home while others are at school and making memories for the adulthood that may never happen. The adulthood that, if it did happen, would eliminate the impossible alternate life already present as something lived.

·

The man in the blue robe carries a small sauce pan the few steps from stove to countertop. Thick socks don't make a sound on tile.

Bent low over the counter, he's gingerly tasting something hot and red with a soup spoon. His lips recoil from the spoon and approach it again with caution. At the end of the bent curve of neck-into-head, lips hover for a long time like a nervous animal before settling around the spoon.

Makes his way slowly onto the terrace, spilling only a little of the red, soup-like stuff onto the tile.

Sits down by difficult degrees at the round table and starts eating.

A tropical moon is making the black sky look blue and at the same time the beauty of the luminous blue projection makes the skeptical mind see through to a transparent blackness.

A pale curve of villas stands out through the trees with a familiar excess of plastic definition and, down at a straight diagonal in the middle distance, the rippling blue pool gives a cold shock against the surrounding green.

Swallows a few spoonfuls of liquid with visible swallows and tries to speak but can't. She watches him swallow, a slow and painfully self-conscious process, with the hand going repeatedly to the throat as if the liquid is too hot for the injured and healing tissue.

Long interludes in the struggle to eat and to be human, during which the gaze struggles against the drooping angle of neck and head and every attempt to speak ends in a cough.

He makes a gesture and she brings him water. He coughs, drinks more water and tries to speak again with no more success. Another gesture, more ambiguous than the last, but she understands and brings him his laptop. He begins tapping at it immediately.

36

B ENDING close to the cold skin of face and shoulder, she
follows his typing as it appears on the screen. He writes
that it seems to him that a very short time ago he was living on
what used to be a farm outside one of the hill towns southeast
of Albany. He went out early one morning and walked up beyond the old chicken coop and found a depression in the tall
grass of the slope leading up to the woods as if a heavy body
had been resting there for a long time before it was dragged
away. There was a horrible mat of blood: right about where
the head would have joined the body. And around the bloody
depression the grass was tall and unbroken.

Now, only days later, he's an old man and she's a tanned
fifteen-year-old, calm and smiling in a mint green sweater,
with wavy hair and a profile so tightly drawn to its own
outline that you can hear space snap off around its edge,
like what the head hears when it leans forward and bites an
apple.

Her face reminds him of another face that used to look
straight out of itself into the distance, as if staring out the
window. He used to wonder: how is it possible to look
straight ahead out of yourself to a fathomless point whose
only limit is whatever happens to intercept it and at the same
time to have a seductive inwardness. Never to left or right,
always straight ahead with burning concentration. Can almost see the energy leaping up in little particle geysers out
of whatever pliant material happens to get in the way of the
end-point of her gaze.

Now the image is different. Within the same crisp outline a look of compassion that resembles grief — but for whom or for what?

"Of course by now everyone knows about our mutation. But when did it begin? When did it begin *really* and in what was it hidden?" he writes. "The self's other self's secret way of conjuring itself up again time after time, the virus capable of replicating itself, turning into life, ceaseless repetition interrupted once too often, the sentences acquired long ago and recited as a magical way of maintaining a stubborn continuity: all forgotten. Certainly long before the horrible time that comes to everyone, when you can no longer work as you used to — can't think (not in the way you call thinking) and instead are in a perpetual state of near-dozing.

"Times, also, when sleep doesn't feel like sleep. You're awake, but can't move. The part of you that's awake detaches from the part that can't move and travels out over the world as a television camera. Staring with eyes that can't close, the world below like an aircraft carrier you can't quite land on. Exhausted, you *want* to sleep, but can't. Imagine you're thinking, because thinking makes you feel good. The sleeping-thinking self flies its own little plane and looks out the windshield, like the feeling of having written we get from reading.

"The dreams we have then are not like the dreams of the first dozing head. Or the objective dreaming of the head's other head or even any of the head's other head's many other heads, far away from us, but undeniably ours since childhood, like the bleeding out of memories when the cell membranes have broken down.

"Doesn't get better, it gets worse.

"Worse and worse.

"Begins as a subtle change in the rhythm of our moods.

"Once upon a time we believed in happiness and struggled against any impairment to it. Later, we came to see that an impaired happiness was our fundamental state. And when there was no impairment we felt something like nostalgia. As if the struggle for an unimpaired happiness in which we passed our life was in fact happiness. . . .

"Haunted by a sense that the remoteness we've always felt in things is our own.

"And this sense of distance, the hallmark of our existence on Earth, gradually becomes real and unbridgeable.

"Sense of isolation becomes isolation.

"Space we sense around us actually does become the space around us.

"Idea we play with becomes invention and invention becomes physical reality and newly invented physical reality changes who we are.

"Under cover of an individual yearning for intimacy we collectively searched for distance — until Distance was installed as our deepest sense of intimacy.

"All the bridges we build to the world separate us from the world.

"Ghosts in our own world, we gawk at the world as if we could touch it.

"A realm that's neither here nor there. Real, but only while we're in it. Dissolves completely, no more substantial than sugar stirred into a heavy ironstone mug of scalding donutshop coffee, with the slightest rotation of the parabolic dish."

·

The ghost of her father is as stubborn as her father used to be. Insists on getting his own glass of water. But somewhere between outside and inside he vanishes. From the terrace, she doesn't see him at the kitchen counter or refrigerator and later she goes in and falls asleep on the rug under the television screen, face sideways on her forearm, dreaming of her father as a younger man, smiling and waving as he wades across the shallow edge of a lagoon, its blue water rippling over transparent stains of green vegetation and orange minerals, his sneakers slung around and slightly bowing his tanned neck.

·

Later, there he is again, in the darkest corner of the screened-in terrace where there's an abrupt view into the most transparent illumination of the swimming pool, blue and timelessly electric as a screen without need of a human figure. The sobbing head that he's holding is so far down between his knees that it might be something that's come drifting sorrowfully back toward its body out of the night.

37

ONE evening, David and Flora are taking a walk. An unearthly fragrance of flowering life on Earth drifts over as breezes rise before sunset and the sky casts up a lemon-blue radiance beyond the pines.

Her beautiful face, close enough to kiss, enters him with its perfume. But a second, colder aura around the skin instructs him one more time in the pathetic ecstasy of what's impossible when the vulnerable neck stretches out its long stem and head, head stretches its face, face its lips for a kiss that may or may not happen.

They've reached a shaded grove of pine and wild olives and they stop and unfurl their blanket within the little basket of light and shadow eternally woven and rewoven by the movements of the ants that can be heard forcing their way over and under the fallen pine needles and sharp little olive leaves. "Evening on Earth at its most earthly and beautiful," David thinks, "makes us feel that even though experience is ours, it isn't our experience. The disk of collective experience is always turning and sometimes it settles over us while we're out walking and we experience a little shudder of coincidence."

When they're settled he says that he has a long story to tell that he should have told her before.

He wants her to remember back to when she was fifteen or so and traveling with her mom and dad by train. He himself was no more than thirteen, traveling by train across Florida, up the west coast, through the Panhandle of Florida and Louisiana, across Texas, headed toward some secret destination out west with his mom & dad of the moment — demented Tardigrades — the evil slime that wakes up after a trillion years of mossy slumber and claims you as its own.

He remembers sneaking away from them while they were drunk and cackling, going into another, more peaceful car to have a minute to himself — curling up out of view, nibbling from a bag of frosted blueberry donuts, crumbled and a little stale but nice and sugary, and thinking how quickly and thoroughly whatever reality we're in replaces the open rustling of the world. And as soon as we stop feeling the open rustling of the world, virtual reality is near.

Began to wonder: is "virtual reality" something out of the ordinary? Or is the only time we live in a world that *isn't* virtual the instant we bump into something. The mind is always hovering between interior sense of self and idea of an external world. World hovers in self, self in world, so that we can exist in the world and have the sense of containing it. Therefore virtual reality is the reality we live with every day. It *is* reality, inside and out, with the exception of the very narrow band of touch. What is new is the ability to turn what was always implied in our relation to the world and to every art form (where, for example, is the reality of the printed page? or the movie screen?) into one more game for an age of dummies that doesn't resemble any other age of dummies.

He was trying not too successfully to sort these thoughts out, as well as all the train's rattles and oscillations — at the same time paying attention to the fluid exchange of panoramas, the visual sluice of the tumbling image-world brought about by the train's forward plunge into absolutely everything, but always at a glancing angle to it — when a set of sentences came to him that had to be written down exactly as they occurred. Only he had no pencil or paper and could only keep repeating his sentences over and over, hoping to memorize them.

"The first image possesses a coherence and a sense of inevitability that we systematically destroy. We discard the mysterious coherence and inevitability of the first image and then try to think

our way back toward it. Brief totality of perception, then the long mess we call reality. And the only thing that holds the mess of reality together is the lingering conceptual unity of the first image in the mind, no matter how discredited by what comes later. This is at least as true for people as for things. Know everything about each other in the first second, but don't want to know what we know and the rubbish of detail we heap over it can never quite be cleared away. Life goes by, haunted by the weak memory of what we think we once knew."

He remembers staring out the window at all this stuff flying by, focusing on some stable fragment in a thousand unstable ones and trying to memorize it, all of it falling apart in memory while the eye holds it together or the other way around. To a certain degree, each instant of experience is like the stone your boot kicks and which you bend down to pick up and slip in your pocket because its polished, pebbled blue or cracked and streaky lavender catches your eye. Slip the cracked or polished pebbles of experience into your pocket — only to find out later that the little yellow pocket knife you always carry with you has disappeared along with the pebbles, having worn a hole in the tired lining.

Have to take into account the possibility that the pebbles of experience may be reluctant to be pocketed. May prefer to stay in whatever new world your boot kicked them into. Like the woman who turns her head while driving along the local road that runs parallel to the railroad track, senses that someone aboard the train is staring at her and is troubled by the consciousness of no longer acting invisibly in her own singular world.

He remembers stuffing himself — first with the crushed blueberry donuts, then with some sort of flattened sticky sandwich — frantically looking and thinking, feeling all his ideas slipping away, as if one second your self is yours and it's inside you, revolving where it belongs while you stare out through it like someone taking aim with rifle and scope, and the next second you're like an unmanned aircraft, nobody home behind the spotted windshield as it arcs in flames to-

273

ward the gravitational drainpipe of some inhospitable planet.

That's when he saw her dad: across the aisle, face close to the window, concentrated beam of the overhead reading light lighting up white hair and white sweater, from time to time noting something down with pad and pen or murmuring into a tiny cassette recorder. While others couldn't wait to get the curtain drawn shut, impatient to tear open their bags of ruffled and barbecue-spiced potato chips and begin reading their novels and papers, her dad never stopped looking out the window. Also unlike most passengers, who sit wherever they're put and don't seem to mind if they're looking at the world or at a buff metal panel three inches from their noses, her father had chosen his seat with care: directly in the middle of the long window, with nothing but a narrow strip of window frame to interrupt the view.

He remembers being drawn to this man and staring at him for a long time from his huddled position in the dark. Just as the man in the white sweater stared insatiably out the window, he stared at the staring man to the point of dizziness and thought about him to the point of absurdity. Thought also about the self and where it is while staring. Seemed to him obvious that the self (*his* self) was no longer inside itself in the usual way while it was staring. Yet, equally true, couldn't reconstitute itself as a living self at the target end of its gaze. So where was the self while it was staring? And was there a difference between staring at a TV screen and staring at a white sweater lit up by an overhead reading lamp? Could there be the same desire to ooze out into that glowing external blueprint and live there forever? His thought process became more and more obsessive and deranged and he even began to fantasize that the man in the white sweater, staring insatiably out the window, was thinking the same thoughts he was: that is, a more lucid and beautiful version of his own muddled ideas, without even a stub of a pencil and stained and crumpled cocktail napkin to write them down.

But, if their staring and thinking had something in common, then had he really crossed this man's path at random? *Meant* to cross his path? But why? A satellite just now cycling back into proximity after aeons flying out into the longest groove of its elliptical orbit? Seedpod dropped in the water, carried by bird, turtle or aquatic mammal: years later anchored little mangrove island stares forever at the goings-on in the near-distant yacht harbor.... How strange to be such a mess and yet feel certain that you're *meant to be this man*! But how do you stop being yourself. Where is the gate to being and unbeing? The coherent image waits for you within its frame, while you lie on your stomach staining the carpet with pizza sauce. . . .

Later he saw the same man with his family: beautiful wife and daughter. A kind of love he could no more understand than the language they were speaking. He remembers very clearly that they did not have sandwiches or snacks from the snack bar. Remembers the green aroma of apples carried over on air conditioning currents and he didn't even have to lift his nose to sniff it. Bread and cheese. A bottle of white wine. Hot chocolate from a thermos and cookies of some kind.

Hours later, when her family had long-since finished eating and every light was out, he figured he'd better crawl back to reality — the reality that must be reality's most real reality because it's too dumb to be anything else, the one that bites our neck and makes it itch, the one we've plopped into with its human coelecanths that, every time we cast out our little line, come reeling in for us to gape at during their billionth demented rerun, the one that disgusts us so much that we dream up two-hundred-and-seventy-five other ones.

He was already at the door, looking back into the car that was as dark and peaceful as if he'd never been there.

Stopped for a second to look at the beautiful daughter's sleeping face and felt willing at that instant to do whatever was necessary to change into someone else.

He pictured himself jumping off the train as it clung to the inward curve of a turn and hung over a ravine — flying down and smashing himself on a sharp jumble of broken rocks and metal junk — head sheared off and soccer-kicked away from the neck — waking up later in a hospital with a new head.

In the twinkling micro-memory-second that ticks inside the second that ticks inside the watch but lasts forever, he was just beginning to live in his own future, but his agitated electrons had already begun to wake her and her agitation began to wake her parents, his hand touched the automated panel that makes the door slide open and in another instant he was back in his own car, where the lights were still burning and his so-called Mom's cackling and coughing were at their highest pitch. His dad, who was now called "Freddy" though he had at least four other equally valid names and didn't truly know who he was himself, nibbled nonstop and hardly ever said a word, which did and didn't make sense considering that he looked starved, with no chin and something odd about his neck. The story was that he'd died, not once, but three times in the course of his idiot life and that he'd survived each death *but not as the same person.* His brain was so fucked after the second death-and-resurrection that when they gave the corpse its little jumpstart he had trouble keeping his identities apart. At least three identities were scrambled up inside him in no particular order, yet he continued to appear on national television, testifying in two notorious trials. And this was the man (drinking and chewing and endlessly trying to clear the fluids that collected every fifteen minutes or so in his severed and mended throat) he was supposed to call "Dad."

·

While he's wondering what makes us start talking and what makes us stop, the world ebbs back into its own microscopically sharp and distant focus, ZZZing as if all the selves that had come scurrying up near the surface while he spoke can be heard wriggling back down into their burrows.

·

Now he smells her perfume again and inhales deeply whatever comes from her but has no weight, her face hovering close for a kiss that feels as if it will never happen.

She says that she has only a vague memory of traveling with her parents before Valeria was born and became the family prodigy, but can't fit herself into his memory of her family traveling on a train. She has no "childhood memories" and doesn't have the kind of memories that other people claim to. What others call "memory" is alien to her. It seems to her that she remembers very little that isn't colored by her father's long coma and illness, his premature burial-in-life, and wonders if every corpse was a walking corpse before it was a corpse. As if life's way of preparing us for death is to kill us before we're dead. The corpse we've all seen (the corpse we ourselves have sometimes been) shuffling and shambling along the cold avenue leading as it always does toward the shopping street that crosses. Walking slowly in a worn out quilted parka of a hideous pink or green, pushing a shopping cart as if leaning all our weight on it to keep from falling, crawling toward our second death (or is it our third or fourth?) or trying to get away from it, like someone hurrying home from bus or subway just before dark with the collar of a thin and junky overcoat turned up against the wind, the world's terror behind us, the world's warmth before us.

And don't we sometimes see a familiar corpse talking on TV with exhausted eyes and a face long-since emptied of any human ballast? So familiar we assume it's alive just because it's talking.

How long did they refer to her dad's premature death-in-life as his "coma"? After his first wife died he went into some sort of tailspin. May have begun as a tailspin, but it became some awful disease, frighteningly similar to death, but they never noticed, misdiagnosed it and continued to call it a coma....

But, David says, if he was a corpse all that time and was only waiting for someone to *call* it a corpse, then who knows how long Valeria has been the real Television Genius....

"Wearing Dad's head on her shoulders...?"

Now it's truly evening and the frayed edges of everything are being woven and rewoven with humming and ZZZ-ZZZ-ing by the burrowing and spinning insects who have a long night's work ahead of them so that the world can resemble itself tomorrow.

They think they hear Valeria's voice, the voice of a child

who sounds like an adult who sounds like a child, approaching more and more distinctly through the olive grove, and they stop to listen.

"Let's see if I understood," she says.

"'What does it mean to really be here? To exist? Is the question of existence the same as the question of identity? The question, "Who am I?", now seems to me a very commonplace and practical problem. And can questions of existence and identity be separated from the question of memory? For example: is the one who's here, not stupidly, but unselfconsciously lost in the activity of the day, less or more here than the one who struggles for consciousness and struggles to remember? More we're able to recall, less we were actually alive in the moment? For example: while committing to memory the lake before us, as if in order to paint it later in the studio, are we less or more alive to the experience of the lake at that moment than the father and son propelling their lightweight kayak with beautiful, synchronized movements across it? (Also: is it only others or are we ourselves proof that we're here?)

"Did I get it right, Daddy? Is that what we're going to type in when we get home?"

They aren't sure if they hear a hoarse voice answer weakly, coughing.

They creep forward and part the branches.

An odd radiance is still glancing off the dark ocean in minute but brilliant geysers, tiny jets where invisible rays are digging in with great force.

Valeria is outlined against the peculiar glitter, walking slowly on the shallow sand slope below the grove of olive and pine.

She's looking up adoringly at her father, who's stopped for a second after summoning the will to be alive still one more time and who's now resumed his painful forward progress, one leg drawn up and folding unnaturally like a marionette's, the foot coming down and slapping the ground like the detached sole of a shoe, one hand unsteadily wobbling on a shaky cane, the rest of his weight resting on Valeria's little shoulder.

38

M Y *dearest Valeria,*
Sometimes I wake up and begin my day as if I'm in the middle of my life. If a sentence enters my mind it feels natural to go to my desk and for that instant I can make myself believe that I know how events that come before and after will be disturbed by the addition of these new words.

But by evening I remember that I'm not in the middle.

And when you're not in the middle you're at the end.

And when you're at the end there's very little you should add.

There's a law that the middle isn't allowed to simply keep on going — which is exactly what would happen if I kept on adding the sentences that come to mind.

Is this death itself then? No repository for what you feel is new in yourself. The feeling that your right to add to what exists has been taken away by a law that is a law no matter how you reject the idea of a law.

39

FLORA comes in from her morning run and checks the kitchen monitor to see how her dad is doing while she puts together something to eat.

There he is at his desk by the window, slowly tapping the keys of the old keypad that's always seemed to help him with his writing.

It's another autumn on the lake and he's squinting out toward it as if trying to see with the weak eyesight of memory the panorama vividly before him — its hard green turned oily and spreadable under the pressure of a strong thumb, asparagus yellows melting over oranges with edges so sharp that everything that lands there bleeds.

Squints and keeps squinting, beyond the foreground toward the deep screen where the invisible and inaudible define the visible and audible. Stares and listens, but can't quite tune in the tantalizing static from the edge.

Bends low over the keys as if trying to whisk the crumbs of a buttered breakfast muffin out of the crevices.

40

M Y *dearest Valeria,*
*I wonder if I've invented this memory: on the overnight
train to Selenium Grove you climb up behind me and try to reach
with both arms all the way around me to the keypad in my lap.
They're too short and you end up with both hands on my forehead
— and we laugh, look out the window together and read each
other's mind. You're thinking that you love this wheeling by of
the world and, in the same way, you know that I'm thinking yes,
the world spins by like the potential language on a daisy wheel.*

*"The dark and speeding world is fascinating to the quick eye of
the traveler, as if he or she is being granted a look, immediately
forgotten, at the smashed world of order.*

*"But, if the world of order is smashed, then why does the chaos
that comes leaking out look as sharp and coherent as a TV screen
in a dark tavern?*

*"Beauty of the speeding, unknowable world. (Beautiful, but
why? Because it is smashed?) Each thing and its negative have
hold of one another and are cartwheeling across the shiny dance
floor.*

*"Coherent only because the background universe looks so emp-
ty behind it, the same way there'd be no memory without forgetfulness?*

"The undeniably real can never be real for us, thank god!"

41

VALERIA'S room always has a pleasant electronic hum and glow, its own permanently glowing twilight and insect-buzz of instrumentation. While she's working, all her monitors on and galaxies spinning, she keeps an eye on the screen that shows her father at his desk. When she sees him tapping away like a young man in the first excitement of knowing that strangers are straining to read the sentences that appear and disappear quickly from their screens, it gives her hope — until she looks again and sees that he's given up and moved over to the enormous white leather wing chair, wide enough for two people and low to the ground, and that he's sitting there, doing nothing, his sketch pad open in his lap, head on his chest, mouth slightly open, eyes closed, fingers almost touching the floor. Other times she looks over and the image of the thin, immobile figure, clothing blue and skin yellow, stretched out full length on the bed without a tremor, makes her heart stop beating.

42

DEAREST *Valeria,*
   Sometimes an awful look of annihilation wakes up with us, walks with us to the mirror and then to the breakfast table.
   Why "sometimes" and not always?
   How many corpses of ourself's selves dying one after the other already live in us like viruses? And how many days does one of our corpse-selves do our living for us? How much time does the living self actually spend on Earth?

43

FLORA'S husband, who's always felt that the name "David" was attached to him without being his, after making sure that Flora is asleep, checks the livingroom to see if Valeria's still crossing out and scribbling corrections on her father's old journals and storyboards or if she's finally dozed off on the carpet, then crosses to his father-in-law's room, quietly opens the door and stares at the slumbering face for a long time without allowing himself to go in and do the thing he can no longer remember with certainty he came here to do.

44

IN another country far away, approximately 2850 miles away, a little girl with brown eyes and graceful arms is playing the piano for her father while she keeps a watchful eye on him. Once a commanding figure who traveled the world, for reasons she was never told, now something's happened to him that was called a stroke but may be something harder to name — and it's left him house-bound and mute.

Always at his terminal while her mother is nowhere to be seen, he's addicted to the so-called "*Posthumous Notes of an Ex-Television-Messiah*" that appear regularly on his screen as if from the grave.

Tries to but can't stop his daughter from reading them when she leans on his shoulder and starts reciting aloud what she can't understand.

45

M Y dearest Valeria,
      This morning I was once again amongst the dying or
newly-dead. Horrible breathing in hospital ward or morgue,
where there's always at least one with a flickering blue ring of
flame, trying to gnaw its way back to life. I wake up and there's no
way to tell if I'm on a respirator or if there's already a tag hanging
from my toe.

An old woman (someone I used to love when her hair was a
dark and shining chestnut dome and her eyes were long and warm
between a high and open forehead and wide mouth, someone who
was as necessary to me as a book read from and lived in every day
as if it were an alternate life, which long ago was lost in memory's
mildewed library) starts to explain to me why she doesn't mind
dying.

"Dying = merging with the sweetness of being," she says.

As she struggles to put into words what she means by "the
sweetness of being" the oval pleasantness of her face becomes
the sweetness of being. I stare at it like a child about to lick its ice
cream.

"The sweetness of being" she says, "is the secret additive to
death. Latent in life and brought to life by death, in exactly the
same way that Time is brought to life at birth."

"My head extends forward uncomfortably on its long, bony
neck, the skin not young, all freckled and foldy (head tries to get
into position to kiss the face that has something sweet but old,
old but not aged, about it, like an aging screen of flesh where a
beautiful image of youth is floating), my two hands reach out to

take the face and hold it, draw it close and kiss it, and then I don't know if I'm holding a face or a deep dessert dish piled high with a sweet and towering spongecake-chocolate-sauce-rum-sauce-ice-cream-and-whipped-cream Mt. Fuji. As I spoon it in hungrily I feel like an unhappy child solacing himself while looking out the long window of a restaurant, a window that bends around the whole front porch, his gaze not quite carrying him out into the leafy intersection while the adults are yakking away above him.

"All those fleeting, slippery moments when the tongue happily licked and pursed lips closed over ice cream immediately melting away, thick and sweetened, melting pleasantly down the throat,' she continues: 'we find all that again when we die. We're eternally climbing up a slippery ice cream mountain, licking it as we go, feeling it's about to melt away entirely. But it never does — and this is the sweetness of being...."

Another woman, with beautiful wavy silver hair and childish corkscrew curls, hates the idea. The idea of death as ice cream, of dreaming of finding in death the simple pleasures we had in life, offends her and she calls the first old woman stupid. She's fierce and the fierceness of her expression makes the sweetness of the first woman's expression look stupid. And then her look of stupidity begins to curdle with the sourness of unhappy aging. . . .

Curdling of the self toward death.

Others, many others, also curdling. Why am I amongst them?

During the long instant of death the brain lingers with dismay on the set it forgot to turn off and doesn't like what it sees any more than it likes the face of the so-called healer bending studiously over it with an expression of guilty curiosity.

46

M Y *dearest Valeria,*
     I say to an old man who's dying: "This is your chance to prove what no one has ever proven. If there's life after death, prove it by coming back and lifting one leg of one piece of furniture off the ground!"

The next thing I know I'm a child sitting bored and cross-legged on a little plot of ground with a worm's-eye view of the legs of countless pieces of furniture. Shifting my position and lying on my stomach, I pass the time tearing out clumps of grass and staring at people crowded in uncomfortable chairs under the enormous red-and-white candy-striped tent, all facing forward and paying strict attention.

I fix my gaze on the slender, tapering leg of a lady's writing desk, touching the ground with a delicate fawn's hoof. Suddenly I feel a burst of energy. I don't have the patience to wait for the dying man and feel certain that I can lift the slender leg of the desk myself by staring at it. Concentrate all my powers. My focused will travels out on the waves and particles of my look at the desk leg settled no more than one quarter inch into the muddy ground.

Try to lift it. Exhaust my mind trying.

"Is it too much to ask?" I say, but nothing happens.

"The problem is the weakness of the will. *Wishy-washiness seals our destiny. If only we were capable of one superhuman effort, if we could concentrate our will, alone or collectively, Time could be popped off like a stubborn bottle cap!*

"I'm spinning crazily on my back like an insect that's gotten its first taste of poison — but not one adult is paying attention.

"How long do I have to spin here on this little plot of dirt and grass under the roof of this striped tent, waiting for the leg of a writing desk *to move?!"*

I touch the old man's shoulder and know at once from its sticky coolness that he's dead.

Out in the sunlight on the lawn, far beyond the wavering twilight of the auctioneer's old striped tent, a towering whatnot with rope-turned columns and oddly-placed little round mirrors that reflect the sky's blind pixels (tall and dark as a Victorian mansion sheathed in ancient shingle) is clearly levitating a few inches above the ground.

47

M^Y *dearest Valeria,*
    The more dreams I have the more they become braided together like legs around a stoolpost: won't let go their pretzel grip while the frightened man gulps his burning coffee with distended lip and wide open mouth.

Nearby, the nervous man's brother is struggling for breath in a hospital's calm green light: washes through him like a swimming pool's lattice-of-shadow disguised as lattice-of-light.

Memory has a form but no content and laps back and forth like green waves in an old bathtub.

"Look!" someone says. "Look at the page! As long as you keep looking at this page, as long as you don't close your eyes, you'll stay alive!"

Someone is holding a book open for him to read, while a strong hand props up the head, wobbling on its weak neck.

Over and over he's told that he won't die as long as he keeps looking at the page.

"Keep reading and never stop! Read one word after the other, as if you're counting. And don't stop counting until you reach a billion. By the time you've reached a billion you'll be near the end of the book and by the time you're near the end of the book we'll have figured out another way to keep you alive!"

I'm convinced. The logic of the argument is strong (as long as you keep reading how can you be dead?) and the desire for it to be true is even stronger. The strength of the desire for it to be true makes it logical or is it the other way around?

For once, a raft of truth and logic solid enough to float us past death!

"Keep looking at this page!

"Keep on reading, if not sentences then words, one word after another, recite the words in your mind as if they were numbers. It doesn't matter what they are and neither does their sum. Pausing to add up the numbers to find the sum that would equal their meaning would be fatal. Keep on reading no matter what!"

I become aware that the helpful hand is no longer turning the page, that the head is lolling back on the pillow and that the dying man has therefore stopped breathing. Or, without realizing it, I've dozed off and stopped reading.

48

M Y *dearest Valeria,*
  I was going along alright. I was headed in the right direc-
tion. I was created, but it resembled a birth. I was a child like
any other and my life had a track (so much so that it was visible
to anyone zipping by and looking out the window) but then there
was a horrible interruption. The track of my life was broken just
as clearly as the track of someone who's murdered in the snow. The
footprints go on for a while and then there's blood. An unbroken
meadow of snow lies beyond and then fresh tracks appear — as if
your life had suddenly started up again — far away from where
you fell. The old head may still be there, sinking down under its
own weight and thinking about the new world it's about to discov-
er, as impossible to assimilate as the last. Time too short, world
too crowded, experience too dissolving.

  Of course the tracks that start up again may not be your tracks,
they may be the tracks of whatever it was that murdered you.

  The brain remembers the bloody aroma of the blow to the head
and the brightness of a wide blue basin, as if the place where I
was standing had been hollowed out, water swiftly seeping in so I
could drown there.

  I was beginning to feel like myself again, but something hap-
pened (I don't remember what) that let me know that I wasn't
who I thought I was and that in that sense the track I was on
wasn't really mine. (Logical or illogical: couldn't be my track if
I didn't know who I was.) Far away from what I started out to
do and unable to console myself with the idea that sooner or later
things follow their own path and the path they follow is your life.

Your life is nothing but the track you've followed and, no matter what, it has a form that's all its own and that is the weird pretzel shape of your life. A shape though no one gave it. These ideas were drummed into me, but I never believed them and I lived with the torment of having lost my self and my way without having any idea what my "way" was supposed to have been.

Sniff as much as we like, we can never pick up the aroma we once knew. Self once knew itself the way a nose knows an aroma. "Lost aroma of the self," yet we keep on sniffing. Beheaded, the body gets its head back, but nose and aroma never find one another again.

Is it true that the one emotion that holds all of childhood and therefore all of life is the emotion that generates every night of dreams? The image we always forget on waking and the unnamable emotion that lingers, poisoning the day. As if the self had bitten into the bitter pill of itself, the mouth filled with blood and cyanide....

49

M Y *dearest Valeria,*
  Someone asks what time it is, the stupidest question a human being can ask.

Because of the question it turns dark, everyone in a hurry to get home.

A meadow has to be crossed, no one knows why.

The dream moves forward, flows into the meadow, half frozen. Therefore everyone wading forward, hurrying but tired, and now we carry the weight of water.

Struggling movement of our bodies through frozen water.

+ Terrible struggle of the earth to extend itself.

= Endless lengthening of the meadow.

At last I'm on the other shore, in the next grassy field, only a few others managing to follow me.

I find myself in the distance I was gazing toward and then look back and discover that I've traveled far beyond the point I thought was my destination.

Start back. Don't wait to see if anyone is following me.

Now the pond has spread out over every dry or grassy area.

Pond is shallow, and yet there are places where I can't touch bottom.

No end to it.

I say: "Beyond all endurance."

And I hear your beautiful voice answer with unbearable kindness: "You have a tiny amount of energy left, Daddy, and you must conserve it. The body has super-human reserves of energy. The energy of the will and the brain exceed any possible mea-

surement. But you've used up all these super-human reserves to the point where you're almost invisible. And if you keep shedding electrons, I think you're going to disappear before you finish typing the page."

50

M^Y *dearest Valeria,*
I myself am radiating Time. And the time I radiate is im-mediately translated into the exhausting space of my life.

The length of time it takes to cross a space equals the identity of Space and Time in its simplest form: what speed zips together.

The end result of our centuries-old obsession with staring at things is that the distance at the end of the our gaze has arrived under our ass.

With every look we dig out even deeper the channel of abstraction that history flows through, impressing its shape on the next reality wired together by the next genius.

Make the world with our gaze, but can we unmake it?

And if the brain is growing increasingly impatient with its boring dependence on the eyes — what then? Zip it all together by wiring the brain directly to its source.

51

MY *dearest Valeria,*
Do you remember? How beautiful the afternoon light was. The glistening caramel down the center of the green spears?

Everywhere the glistening green and the glistening caramel.

Looks like color, but it's really light.

Looks like light, really heat.

Heat also "really" something else, of course, but what it is really will always speak to the part of us that isn't really here.

Help me with this too, because now that the leaves are almost gone, now that there's nothing but a little yellow in this world of freezing earth and sodden bark, the lake is blinding through the bare trees and, when I sit at my desk and look out the window, instead of filling in what's missing in myself I find smashed mirror fragments still stuck in place, the edges of their crystals gleaming. What am I looking for in them with my idiot's stare of stern confusion...?

I'm afraid it's true, but tell me if I'm wrong: our life is rarely our life. Another way: everything puts us at a distance from our life. Our life is one thing and we're another. Does that make sense? On the one hand the nameless activity of living and on the other the entity we sense is really us. What is it that, supposedly linking the entity we recognize in private as our self to its activity in the world, actually screens off one from the other?

True or false: sometimes the image of another person's face is where we actually live out our life. And when that image is gone the nameless activity of living and the entity we've always assumed is the self are severed like a head axed from its body. One may survive, but never two together.

52

M Y *dearest Valeria,*
There's no one else I trust to give me an honest opinion.
They say: "The only reason we die is because we wear the same head from childhood to the grave."

Do you believe that?

I know it's true (I'm sure we've talked about it) that the head is a lighthouse: it radiates time in every direction equally and ages without exception everything the light of its gaze falls on. But does that mean that if we could get rid of our head we'd also get rid of time, therefore aging? No head, no time, no aging. Is there some error in this logic? And, if there is, why can't I see it?

What they said to me is: "It takes a split second of courage to have a new life."

"What 'split second of courage' is that?," I asked.

"The split second it takes to cut it off yourself!"

He comes back with a blade capable of doing the job. He's relaxing in a chair, his knobby feet in ugly sandals out on the flagging. Dark hairs on the toes occupy my attention. I'm left lying helpless on my back with the heavy blade pressing on my chest. Don't even know if I can lift it, let alone sit up and then swing it hard enough to cut off my own head!

"One thing is certain: every person who's ever worn the same head from childhood to the grave has had only one life and one death."

And I think he also said: "Every corpse, given the chance, would rethink its options. In the few terrible seconds when life dreams of renewing itself with an extra breath forced through the earth stuffing up its nostrils and mouth, it reconsiders its decision not to start over with a new head, even one that wouldn't recognize the original one staring at it through a restaurant window...."

Tell me, Valeria, is it proof that I'm dead that this idea makes so much sense to me?

53

OOK," says the beautiful child with kind brown eyes and skin that reminds her father of an autumn tree with too much gleaming fiery orange in it to call it brown. "Look how the low yellow plane of fallen leaves draws the eye in above the forest floor to a point where the soul feels it's inhaling a damp and bitter yellow-leaf aroma!"

"Yellow-leaf aroma and dark *root* aroma also?" her father says, sniffing as if testing the air.

"Mmm," the little girl frowns, trying to distinguish possibilities. "Dark root aroma and raw *potato* aroma? Is the aroma of raw potatoes, damp and cold in their skin, the aroma of the earth they come from or the aroma of my grandmother's cellar? Not the cellar of a long grey house cantilevered above a surging river and a campground hidden in a forest of blue spruce and hemlock on a winding country route southeast of Albany, not far from Malden Bridge, but on an ancient street in the crowded borough of a great city, underneath a house as tall, dark and narrow as an antique whatnot with round mirrors that reflect the sky's blind pixels. Aroma of whole potato-in-its-skin the same as the aroma of *cut* potato? And who is it that said that the aroma of *mashed* potato is the aroma of oncoming snow? Potato and ozone mashed together with some hot milk, butter and salt."

Together they manipulate the touchscreen, happy to be sharing an adventure.

"A heavy ironstone mug of coffee."

"Heavy ironstone mug of *scalding* coffee," the little girl corrects, laughing.

"Right. And a plate of…?"

"Glazed blueberry donuts!"

"She's having her morning coffee and donuts and trying for the three-hundred-and-first time to make sense of her father's old logs and journals. Over the years, dozens of publishers have tried to get him to tell his story."

"Won't work this time either though."

"How come?"

"How come? Because his journals are a senseless mess, that's how come!"

"Not because the real story is the one we never want told?"

"That too."

"The real story is always lost or destroyed…."

"And sometimes we *think* it's lost or destroyed and it's there all along as an interior program."

54

YOU'RE *silly*," the beautiful child with long graceful arms
and a musical nature says to her father, laughing. "No *way*
the woman can salvage her father's old junk — not if the old
interior programs they've managed to bring up into the foreground are any example! Better off letting it sink back into the
interior of the stupid program it was hidden in!

"The only way to know if the so-called Television Genius's
journals make any sense would be to go back and follow the
thread from the beginning," she says.

"How it began is the one thing that can never change. Isn't
that true, Daddy? Or is that just one more certainty we can't be
certain of?"

"We can never remember how it began," her father says, all
at once looking as sad and old as if the self's self had become
its latent other future self. "We like to think that what gives us
the power to conceive of our life as having a coherent form
is knowledge. But the truth is that what holds life together is
ignorance. The longer life goes on, the more people we meet,
more stories we hear, more things we see, more information we
gather, the more life piles up and sticks together in an absolute
and glued-together mess: our life and no other. But the mind
can't hold it. Mind can't hold its own life. Made for us by others
in ignorance. We live in a world made unknowingly for us by
others and the world made by others is our life, but the mind
can't hold it. Throw it all out. Reduce it to a hard little rubber ball it can surround with its hand and throw far away. The
cartoon of the world in the head and the head living out its life

302

in the abstraction of the world it's able to live in. Forgetfulness clears off the crowded table and scours it so that there can be a few crumbs of memory left on the scoured table.

"If we occasionally experience the sweetness of the moment, if we wake up and see the clear fractions of light in the tree-like hedges, in the next instant, when the head turns three degrees to the left, consciousness is gone. And the children playing in their pool in the shadow of the hedges are always forming memories they won't remember. Isn't that so?"

"Let's see," the musical child says, dropping to her knees to manipulate the screen.

"*'My journals are a senseless mess!' the television genius says, ambiguously dead-alive, but still capable of despair. 'Beyond all cure!'*"

"The four of them ('television-genius' father, youngest daughter Valeria (supposed *future* Television Genius), elder daughter Flora and her disgruntled husband David) are sitting in front of the set watching *The Invisible Ghost* for the fifty-fourth time, each with his or her meal on a folding snack tray. Flora and her sulking husband have divided into two enormous helpings a colossal platter of rare prime rib dressed with both a rich bordelaise sauce and a rich hollandaise sauce, potato that's been mashed generously with butter, heavy cream, parsley and garlic, then baked until it forms a brown and salty crust, candied baby carrots and sautéed wild mushrooms; Valeria has a giant bowl of fat cheese ravioli with a spicy fresh tomato sauce; and the ghost-like father has a bland, unappetizing square of poached scrod, plain boiled rice and steamed vegetables.

"They've just begun to eat and to watch the ancient film about a man who goes into a homicidal trance every time he looks out his window at night and sees his dead wife staring up at him from the lawn and everyone is blindly spearing forkfuls or spooning in steaming little mounds of food, staring straight ahead and trying to follow the invisibly flickering action.

"The ghostly, resurrected Television Genius is eating solid food for the first time since he's come back to life and takes an eager mouthful at the same paying close attention to the homicidal husband, far from young.

"Aging, homicidal husband, tall and weary, goes to the window.

"Inclines his head forward and at the same time parts the curtains with one hand.

"Camera glides past the tall husband's oddly elongated neck, forward-tilted head and outstretched hand and takes over his glance down.

"Glance becomes ours and we can feel the invisible husband anxiously peering over our shoulder.

"Now, together, we're glancing down between curtains parted by our hand.

"See the ghost on the lawn.

"Full figure of a woman, stiff and spectral in starched linen, staring up.

"Our gaze glides down closer.

"See only the eyes, which see only ours.

"Only the shortest distance between our two gazes, which see nothing but each other and therefore change places freely.

"We look up from the lawn as if hypnotized and catch sight for a second of the hand we take to be our husband's, allowing the curtain to fall closed.

"Inside the room we drift away, take our distance from the husband and see him reel back from the window as if stung. Stares fixedly into the darkness at the other end of the room, through the dusky rose-in-trellis wallpaper and deep into the house where, in a small, overstuffed room, someone waits nervously to be murdered.

"The son-in-law is watching the prematurely-aged man watching the screen. While the scene is unfolding and the geometry of glances is being drawn, the prematurely-aged and resurrected Television Genius, mouth full of food, forgets to chew and swallow. Only when the scene is over does he take a drink of spring water, a little rice, an overcooked cauliflower florette, chew and swallow again.

The son-in-law waits for him to take another over-eager helping of fish and then asks:

"Why is it, Dad, that the language of looks — so important in film — has never been successfully translated into television?"

"For an instant the father's face still shows a touching pleasure-in-eating and a bemused, analytic interest in the purpose of his son-in-law's pseudo-question. When he starts to answer, no sound comes out. Face turns white, but no one pays attention. Body knows the danger it's in and stands up weakly, supporting itself with one thin arm and swaying with the effort of sucking air. Ordinary shallow breathing of weak lungs becomes strangulated gasping. Terror of it goes immediately to the eyes, which look to Valeria for help.

"Valeria rushes to the telephone. David and Flora go to the father and David gets behind him to perform the Heimlich maneuver. While Valeria struggles with the operator, she hears David explaining that he still has his hands nervously at his sides because he isn't completely comfortable performing the Heimlich maneuver. He's never actually witnessed anyone *execute* the Heimlich maneuver and has no idea how to do it properly.

"David feels that he's already beginning to smell something unpleasant: the faint whiff of the human when it becomes too human. Despite the strong force of the weak body's struggle to stay alive, sucking in the tiniest thread of air with a terrible noise, he feels it's a corpse before him: without a coffin, but behaving like a corpse struggling to lift the impossibly heavy lid.

"The son-in-law reaches around the corpse with his strong forearms, makes a fist, locks the opposing hand on the opposing wrist and gives a sudden crushing jerk up against the rib cage.

"Corpse feels its fragile scaffold of weightless bones drawn high up in the air.

"The crushing hug is repeated over and over, fragile body lifted up, bruising its ribs without opening the air passage.

"Corpse breaks loose, takes a couple of wild steps as if chasing an elusive bubble of oxygen, son-in-law follows, gets a good grip again. Corpse and son-in-law dance a few strange steps together, pivoting away from chairs and snack tables.

"Corpse sees someone enter through the bright milky portal of distance. Valeria comes close and the son-in-law relaxes his grip long enough for the corpse to scuttle down the hallway to the bathroom.

"Corpse is at the sink, two thin arms spread out as weak supports, head down, trying to get something out between horrible breaths. Sees its thinness and isolation in the mirror. Utter isolation in the mirror seems to have something to do with its awful thinness. Every speck of matter in the universe, it seems to the corpse, is isolated and embedded in darkness the way his image appears in the mirror embedded in bright and empty light. Corpse is certain at this instant that a mirror held up to any isolated speck of matter would reflect and deny equally the empty darkness around it: reason why the dead astronaut, ejected in his protective burial suit, always wakes up long enough to take a picture of the universe, an empty snapshot he can carry with him in place of memory.

"The son-in-law's flushed face and wild eyes appear in the mirror over the corpse's bowed back and bent shoulders, determined to get it in his grip again. Valeria is there as well, tucked into a corner, round face lit up like a little candle.

"Corpse isn't certain, but it seems that as its last breath leaves and the body grows weaker, something else grows stronger and kicks its legs. Keeps on kicking even after the horrible struggle for breath stops, as if the soul's desperation may be the only thing strong enough to outlive the body.

•

"Later it finds itself sitting on Valeria's bed, head all the way down and Valeria's arm around its shoulders. The obstruction is no longer there and it's drawing full breaths into the constricted honeycomb of the lungs, a sharp pain where the ribs have been crushed. Flora is in the doorway, strangers are in the house and emergency vehicles are parked on the lawn and on the road, their tinted dome lights visibly flashing through the curtains.

"Far off and up in the hills barking dogs are testing the pliancy of a pleasantly dark and summery world.

.

"The woman is looking out over the railing from the deck just below her father's study window. Tiny golden flakes of late leaf-remnants blow her way yet remain in the distance, unable to arrive in the near meadow, dissolving somewhere in the bright space above the far-off barn and woodshed."

"Does she hear a voice, honey?"

"What kind of voice, Daddy?"

"Well, a voice that makes her turn. Not necessarily a loud voice — it might be the voice you hear when you're washing dishes, somewhere in the splashing and spattering of the water tones. This ghost-voice is a little like the watery reflection on the surface of a shiny plate dripping in the drain rack. The reflection swirls oddly. Something shimmers there that shows a universe swirling in a different direction from the one streaming down the sink drain. You feel that neither world accounts for the other and you think: 'What is this bright, swirling image from our ghost-world? What is it the ghost of really?'"

The child with the orange/brown leaf-tone skin frowns and reaches for the controls.

"I hear the voice of the father's nurse, the old woman with the round face and silky skin who reminds him of the beautiful grandmother he knows mainly from the creased and faded snapshot he carries: in the shaded foreground of a field absolutely lost to memory his grandmother is standing in a pale cotton dress with dark buttons from collar to hem, hair darker than it ever was in life, holding a little boy's right hand with her left, her right hand instinctively coming across to touch his fingers: curly-haired little boy in striped polo and white shorts with shoulderstraps gazes straight out into the eternal present of whoever happens to be looking at the photograph, shadows of foreground figures pointing off toward the upper left corner where, in deep focus, the lithe, miniaturized figure of a young man barely old enough to be the child's father is leaning against the hood of a domed sedan afloat under dark leaves and branches on the invisible horizon of the middle distance.

"The woman turns away from the point in the distance where the golden leaf-flakes keep dissolving before they arrive and smiles up toward her father's little terrace, where the nurse, with her silver fluff of hair, round face and silky skin whose wrinkles are broad, smooth and pleasantly concentric, is calling her in for lunch with a voice that's warm and inviting.

"A quiet scene at the table. The daughter has never looked more beautiful, more radiant. What is the mysterious emotion that's making her glow? It resembles, but may not be, an un-sentimental grief-in-advance, a grief without melancholy, dark but oddly tranquil. Grief for her father who's still living makes her bend with gravity over his plate when she carves his enor-mous saddle of rare rib roast into bite-size morsels. Gravity and tenderness darken her hair. Glossy and chestnut, it flows in a full dome over her head, away from the perfect oval of the face above the loose, forest green sweater. Her brother-in-law across the table, complaining to the round-faced old nurse (who receives his complaints the way pond-water receives whatever happens to fall into it) about his day's meaningless work, day-after-day of meaningless work, drinking glass af-ter glass of dark Rhône wine, catches his sister-in-law gazing distractedly out the window and feels an emotion he isn't able to name. The intoxicating, ambiguously erotic perfume of her hair reaches only him, not exactly the same as the eternal aro-ma of near-farness that's haunted him since childhood, and for a second he feels something other than the bitterness of having been passed over and left behind.

"Toward the end of the meal, the ghostly father asks for pen and paper and, pushing his dish of caramel custard aside, be-gins to write convulsively.

"Immediately, we're able to read what he's written. . . ."

"Wait a second, honey, how about trying it like this?" the

precocious child's father says, putting new images up on the screen. "It's only after the father's been helped to his bedroom by the kindly nurse that the two daughters and the son-in-law get up from their places at the table, bend over the memo pad and help each other decipher what the old man's written."

Now father and daughter are sitting on the floor together, manipulating the screen as if with one hand.

55

M Y *dearest Valeria,*
Answer me if you can: was I a failure? They say that my
so-called "Fifth Leap Forward" was a success, while I myself was
a failure. How could my work be successful and I myself person-
ally a failure? Because it's true that I did not succeed in creating
the virtual equivalent of knowable reality, as I'd promised. And
therefore (because there was no "infinity" of sites to monitor) it
was impossible to validate the idea that the mirror universe would
by definition attract more viewers than the universe.

None of this came to pass while I was alive. Does that mean I
failed? Was it impossible to succeed? If only our first life is life
and only the world is the world, then anything else is a virtual
world and every virtual world is doomed to be incomplete. Am I
wrong? If something that's rolled into the crack between two floor-
boards is left out or if the crappy library of stuff blown into the
lattice of a chickenwire fence isn't catalogued, then it's not the
same world, isn't that so?

One day a Young Genius in the Office of Public Entertainment
convinced his bosses to let him throw a switch — re-animating a
set of global cells that had been in place for aeons but which until
then had been used only for reasons of national security. The idea
seemed so obvious to the Young Genius that he couldn't believe
the system was just sitting there unused!

Others, of course, carried out the Young Genius's so-called
dream. I myself became one of the others, eventually mutating
into the stooge and the lackey of the brilliant young man I used

to be. The task of my adulthood, like the task of every adult-hood, was to pervert the genius of my youth.

.

My sensation on waking feels like illness but isn't illness, un-less "illness" is our name for the condition we're always in, but don't always feel.

Little spark dying away.

I lie in bed inside my own body. Alive only once and therefore not at all.

A living person sometimes wonders if he-or-she's woken up dead, just as there are accounts of corpses feeling strangely alive.

As you know very well, what animated us once-upon-a-time is not what animates us now. We are not — repeat, are not — alive on the same principle as before.

Some mornings I wake up feeling as if they've pulled the plug and yet, even with the plug pulled, I'm able to lie in bed thinking, like a radio with a set of powerful backup batteries.

Lie in bed with the certainty that, even if I could move, no amount of movement would help me arrive at my destination, not even in the soap-spotted mirror hanging open at an angle over the bathroom sink, long, bearded face, red and soapy, eternally shaving itself in it.

Look down from the woods toward — and know that I can't arrive at — my small, lamp-lit bedroom with its beloved books, paintings and music, wound on their spools with no one to release them.

From my bed I can't reach the yellow shadow of the woods where the aroma of rich earth, animal fur and fallen leaves star-tles the sleeping brain directly, like steam from black coffee in its heavy ironstone mug.

Room and woods stare one at the other, unable to arrive.

Answer this also if you can: just as we draw life from what's created for us unconsciously by others, do we animate the space around us? Does it die with us? Another way: are the things we live with alive only in the sense that they're alive with our idea of them or are they really alive? (Another real reality, neither "it"nor "us," yet alive only as long as we are?)

If only the aroma of the world were the world we could be sure we're living in it! So why is it, Valeria, that it's the non-aroma of the world we seem to crave?

There's this too and I can't explain it: I've always been haunted by the knowledge that somewhere an exceedingly kind woman has been grieving for me, like a nurse with a dying child.

56

IT'S late, the father's kissed the child goodnight and he's already standing in the doorway, worn out and ready for bed, but the child's still on the red-and-blue carpet in front of the screen, obsessively playing with narrative combinations.

"I wanted to put in the sound of trees along the sand path," she says, looking up and seeing that he's still there. "But I forgot to do it! And now it's too late, isn't it, Daddy? There's no way I can go back and put in the sound of trees, is there?"

"Well, sweetheart, we can solve that technically in a couple of seconds."

"But when we reach a certain point...?"

"Yes, there is a certain point that, when it's reached. . . ."

"Can't go back and change a thing? Can't change a word?"

"We're free to do what we want. No one can stop us from scraping away something we suddenly find too built up and there's no technical obstacle to darkening a spot that's grown too light because of everything that's accumulated around it. The problem is not what we're permitted to do. The problem's like the one in life: at a certain point (if we're at all honest) we're forced to admit that the life we've lived is the life we've lived. Every pretzel loop detour, every stumble over a broken lip of sidewalk, every hole in consciousness, every stupid move and waste of time brought us to where we are, for good or bad. Go back and iron out one little kink in memory, change the teentsiest dot in the path of connected dots, take away one beautiful, lavender-streaked pebble the booted foot kicks skipping and bouncing in front of it or avoids stepping on with an odd, hopping step — and not one dot after can be the same. Accumulation of accidents is what we think is necessity. Life accumulates, like the positions of cows folded and dozing in meadows we drive by, always perfect.

"The only question: is it possible that the atmosphere around a life sometimes doesn't exert sufficient pressure on its boundaries to give it a shape? And that life in that case leaks out in all directions, wherever it wants to go. Boundary of identity in general, of course, is not so crisp as we like to think. Always a little leaky. Leaky in its transitions from one state to another, the way the bright edge of light around the body becomes too much like the diffuse light of daily space in the transfer from film to video. And when the body leaves the screen entirely for the open air of life it drips like a three-hundred-and-fourteen-pound sack of ice cubes....

"And another thing. I don't know (does anyone know?) if the days of a life are continuous. When one day ends does another, absolutely separate day begin? If a separate day begins, why such a sameness to our days? But, if the days of a life are continuous, why do I sometimes feel like a different person from the one who used to be living my life? A continuous sameness of life lived by different selves or the other way around? It's confusing. If the same self is living a continuous life, a recognizable you at the core no matter what, then why doesn't that always feel true? It seems to me that my self and the life it led were not always the same. Something stumbled, stutter-stepped, jumped forward, hopped sideways, tripped, recovered itself, dodged and occasionally made a brilliant dash around the perimeter, but I'm not at all sure that my 'self' and the life assigned to it made any sense together. . . ."

"So I *could* add it but shouldn't? Just leave it alone. At this late point it might be like sticking my head out the window to see where I've been and having the delusion that I'm getting a panoramic overview — a genius-flash of panoramic *knowledge*, when all that's really happening is that my head's been lopped off by the sharp edge of a train speeding the other way..."

57

THE grandmotherly nurse with the smooth, round face calls out OO-Hoo! from the little terrace outside the upstairs study and Valeria looks up and waves.

.

David and Flora, out on the lake, paddling their swift, yellow lightweight kayak and plotting their next moves, see Valeria and her father having lunch with the nurse up on the little terrace. David looks through his binoculars and tells Flora that it seems to him that the corpse is lively and talking.

.

Valeria is reading aloud to her father a passage from one of his old sketch books. No matter what shape he's in he never gets tired of listening to his ancient scribblings, wheezing with excitement whenever his turn of phrase strikes him as particularly irreducible, true and sharp, his aphorism memorable, his word-picture rhythmic, economical and painterly: shorthand strokes of reality and super-reality pretzelled together with ideas never braided in such a way before on Earth.

"Left unattended a pair of old sneakers will live forever under the bed, with only dust and lost bits of paper for companionship. A white clay pipe with an elongated stem, a red and yellow metal toy that twirls convulsively when you press down hard on a blue plastic knob and corkscrew shaft, a not-quite-empty tube of blue-green shaving gel, a pair of white leather baby shoes that may have been hers, a tiny cast-iron cap gun stamped BIG CHIEF on one side and MADE IN USA on the other and the amber plastic bottle that contains the clay-colored triangular pills that absolute-

ly must be taken every eight hours all have no predetermined limit to their lifespan. Our idea of immortality is based on these daily encounters with the inanimate. While every thing that's ever lived lasts just long enough to prove that life is programmed to end."

•

Another quiet dinner. David and Flora, June and Granpa Ernst keep a close watch on the Television Genius, who seems to have lapsed back into corpse-hood. Returns to life only when Valeria feeds him. Opens his mouth to receive the food and then stares at her pathetically while she mashes the little cube of salmon, the halved sweet potato into baby food, her forehead grave and frowning like a child problem-solving at her terminal, unable to finish the story she's been working on for weeks.

After Valeria and the nurse have led the Television Genius upstairs everyone tries to read the wild hieroglyphics he's left behind on the notepad by his plate, as jerky and mechanically non-human as a liar's lie detector graph.

Flora translates the blotted notepad-scribbling, not at all sure she isn't adding her own language.

"'The tired waitress puts a heavy ironstone mug of coffee in your hands as if strong coffee is just the thing to calm you down, but it doesn't stop your legs from pretzelling around the nickel-silver stool post or your head from feeling that it would be happier on someone else's shoulders.'"

They conclude that, after all this time, Dad is still trying to plaster-over a hole in the story he let fall and roll away a long time ago.

58

THE screams come from upstairs. Sounds like the nurse, but, when Valeria gets there, the nurse is sitting transfixed on the chair outside her father's door as if she'd made the mistake of parting the curtains and returning the gaze of the ghost staring up from the dark lawn.

Valeria opens the door and sees the soles of his feet yellow as old paper, body shrunken enough to be hidden behind a tall and crooked toe.

Draws closer, but not too close. From a corner angle the body seems elongated: an elongated arch from ankles to shoulders. Nothing but an arching scaffolding of ribs, fragile and wing-like, covered with a thin putty of flesh: wing-like scaffolding extends into hands, one of them horribly bent double under the dead weight of the body, wrist bone apparently broken: looks more like a prehistoric bird-or-reptile fossil than the body of her beloved father.

59

BETWEEN the rubber casters of the computer caddy and the curved steel frame of the low leather chair where he liked to work below the desk-surface, drawing tablet in his lap, the head already has its mouth clamped on the chair's polished steel frame and has to be pried loose.

David touches the corpse's wrist and is alarmed to find a faint pulse. Looks at the chest and sees no movement. Reluctantly presses an ear up to the side and finds himself cradling the body as if he'd like to bring it back to life. Hears nothing. Relieved, he tries unsuccessfully to get the head to sit squarely atop the neck and shoulders.

When the medical team arrives he still has his hand on the oddly sticky shoulder that seems to have some warmth in it, trying to keep the body sideways for no good reason.

·

The nurse isn't looking at the body. She's trying to keep her mind off the fact that there's an extraordinary amount of blood dammed up inside every living creature that's sprayed out when the throat is cut and then gurgles into whatever will absorb it, traveling forever as a dark-edged stain for which there's no solution in kitchen or laundry room. She's adopted the posture of someone praying, eyes cast down and hands together under her chin. The coroner's taken off his ridiculous Stetson to get down to the ugly job of making precise measurements of every aspect of the corpse's head, neck and shoulders, impatient with the team of technicians who are having trouble getting the jaw to close. The mouth remains open and dark as a

318

kitchen drain waiting for someone to turn on the tap of life and give it a drink.

·

At long last they take the head away and put it on ice.

The nurse is in the other room, sobbing and saying a human name over and over into the telephone so many times it begins to sound like the name of something that can *never* be human — not the name of Valeria's father or even of the headless corpse, but of a *thing* so deliberately senseless you can't get it out of your mind.

·

The coroner says that they've twisted some wire around the head to get the jaw clamped shut. Right now they'd better get the body on ice as well or in exactly two hours this place will stink. It happens fast, with first cooling, when the eyes are beginning to catch gleams from some colder source of light than the little orange-shaded table lamp, but no one wants to know that.

She has to admit to herself that, already at the beginning, alone in the bedroom, she was lying to herself about the thin, foul whiff of dying. And again later, from a distance, when the green blanket collapsed into the round shadow where the head with its sudden violet stubble should have been, she'd smelled something too.

The mind won't allow it, but can't change it either. Even to this instant it's trying to change the persistent image, but can't.

Retreats to a distance and hits the x-ray button, like a dentist hiding behind a wall.

60

THE force of the moment is always a camouflage. Moment camouflages itself in its own urgency, keeping us from paying attention. But under the urgency? What are the dregs of the moment that settle out? Every moment has its dregs that gain their force only later, like the poisoned part of love that enters your bloodstream when it ends. And these poisoned dregs are what we usually call memory.

61

HER father's room is clean and ventilated and Valeria is sitting at his little desk, feeling alone. Alone, and yet her father is beside her, tiny as a microbe or even tinier, a particle of aroma the mind smells, giving it an idea.

Everything is divisible, even the particle of an idea that sometimes breaks down into an aroma, and the mind gets dizzy chasing the ghosts of matter that appear to it as memories.

What enters the nose from a distance when it sniffs? Brain gives a second sniff, like a train that goes around a bend chasing the tail it won't catch unless it bends around the world. Hunting dog that gets eaten by its prey....

As the body ages it dries out, Valeria thinks, and the evaporation of its thoughts, dreams and memories may be what cools it dangerously toward death.

62

H E'S watching them batting balls back and forth across the net.

Everything is purposeless, pleasant.

"You're *spectating*!"

They've seen him on the parapet. He hadn't realized that the sensation of being alive depends on invisibility. And that the corollary to that would be that being seen would make him feel like a ghost.

The stout mother in tropical shirt and white shorts appears below him. She's forgotten her racquet.

"Have you got your key? My racquet's on the diningroom table."

Talks as if she knows him.

Says they were *supposed* to be playing "Canadian Doubles" — which means Babs against the two of them. Which *really* means, she laughs dryly, it might make more sense to go upstairs and have a martini.

Over on the court, the father — sixty-plus and boyish, with a longish, pleasant face — has just taken a clumsy, lunging stab at a ball fired at him by his daughter. The right shoulder of his white sweater almost touches the ground and his white sneaker lands flat-footed with a hard slap. While he's recovering, shaking his head and laughing at himself, she's already turning smartly on her toe, getting in position to shoot another ball past him with all her force.

Now that he's finally found his way here, that changes everything!, the stout mother calls up merrily to the spectral figure looking down. "*Now* I feel like playing!" Along with her racquet he should bring one for himself (there's a spare racquet and some tennis clothes in the guest room closet). And try not to dawdle! No time to waste. Lost time to make up for, as he should know better than anyone. Always-always time dribbling away as if there were a drain hole. Shower drain, a screened-over hole, sewer drain, an un-sewn pocket in the bottom of life. Sun will be going down soon behind the roof of the villa and, from childhood to old age, there's never enough time to play....

Later they have drinks and make a barbecue together and still later there's a program on TV that someone wants to watch for the three-hundred-and-twenty-third time and the whole family settles down to build their own ice cream sundaes in heavy white ironstone cereal bowls made in western New York state over a century ago. While the others are happily clinking spoon against bowl, piling up little Mt. Fujis of ice cream, fudge, walnuts and whipped cream and enjoying the ancient comedy repeated so often it needs to be repeated again, he feels a sudden sense of panic, excuses himself and goes out onto the dark terrace.

This is the one thing that he absolutely cannot—*must* not — do.

The wandering corpse of the self is permitted many things, but not this.

The light of the giant TV begins to wobble strangely in the glass door panels, the images recombining, oozing into and swallowing themselves like soapy reflections in a drain rack full of dishes where the self sometimes feels sick catching sight of itself dissolving into another.

•

The little boy in the torn blue parka runs out of the house.
Someone follows him to the door, shouting.
On the sidewalk, just beyond the straggling hedge rows, he turns and catches the shine of cold sunlight on the wet teeth of an open mouth.
He shouts back.
Later he's spraying the front of the house with rug cleaner. A

*little later he has a can of automotive anti-rust paint and he's
writing his name in giant cartoon letters on the sidewalk in front
of the house. Toward the corner he sprays a sentence that two sisters and their barking dog, using a pair of field glasses in their
attic bedroom window, read out loud to their mother listening in
the doorway, standing on tiptoe and craning her head on its long
neck as if she could see all the way to the intersection.*

*"HISTORY NOW WEARS TELEVISION AS ITS HEAD,"
they take pleasure in reciting at the top of their lungs, then break
into giggles picturing it.*

*Still later he's squatting in the middle of the gutter, on the bro-
ken yellow line that precisely divides the local street into two images that don't quite reflect one another. He has his hands over his
ears and his eyes are closed. He's trying to project himself into a
future that doesn't feel like a future so much as a memory he's already having trouble remembering. Once he was a little boy, born
already old with the knowledge of what death is and grieving for
the loss of someone beloved. Sharply at the age of two and then
again distinctly at the age of twelve he feels the shadow of a grief
and regret that make no sense. As if born at the wrong terminal
of life and looking forward the way someone else looks back with
sadness at everything lost.*

Resurrected for a life that never felt like a life as others describe.

*Slumped in a rusty garden chair with eyes closed on a cold day
when the little locked-in square of sky overhead is the weak mirror
of what ails you, hands cold, clothes ugly and ill-fitting, memories keep evaporating. The comedy that's always been on is still
on and, even if you don't watch it anymore, life is unimaginable
without feeling that it's playing somewhere for someone else.*

*Sometimes the beautiful face he sees is his grandmother's:
round, with round wrinkles and silky skin, her clean aroma bending close as she wheels him down the hospital corridor.*

Sometimes it's the beautiful face of a girl with dark, wavy hair.

*Sometimes there are banks of hedges, oddly electric not only in
the clusters of tiny flowers that later on become the color of lipstick
on lips often kissed or of a blouse vivid against smooth young*

skin with a little touch of autumn in it, but also in the internally radiant green of small leaves. Dot of color crisp within excessively defined leaves as if the human hand had pulled the electronic drawstring, tightening the edge of all optics.

A few steps down into the sunken garden on the campus of a university that disappeared long ago. (Where is this garden? Where is it really?)

Students are alone and reading or talking in twos and threes, having sandwiches and sodas together or lying back and looking at the sky. Sky looks back and follows these endlessly recombining formations, impossible to remember.

Someone says that the electric green of the leaves and saturated dyes of the flowers are "azaleas." Someone else says "rhododendrons." The girl with dark, wavy hair and soft autumnal skin wishes for something else, a flower she doesn't know the name of and may never have seen. She only knows that it exists because she's wished for it. And an extraordinarily thin and bearded young man in an old sports jacket and torn shoes disappears and returns too quickly with two dozen "liatris" not to have flown above the ground (an odd kind of vertical of flying/walking as if just under a ceiling and smelling its plaster). The color of the flowers are the color of the young woman's beauty and mystery.

When the hedges are at their most radiant, he thinks, the beautiful girl's ideas are the most brilliant. The edges of her arguments are crisp and her eyes are alive with the pleasure of knowing that she, not you, has understood three-hundred-and-twenty-five pages of difficult narration.

Long afternoons talking and arguing on a little grassy slope below the agitated wavelengths of the azaleas or rhododendrons.

Her superior intelligence swims through his.

Her beauty eludes the insipid snapshots of camera or memory.

Sees her again later, drinking a root beer float and reading a novel in a mallside pizza plaza or sitting alone, bent over a table in a museum cafe, studying a newspaper as if she were learning a foreign language, but knows in his heart that it isn't her.

More often she passes him slowly on a highway, behind the

wheel and looking straight ahead. Or on her knees and gazing out the back window as if it offered a view into the future, watching the world and pretending she's a kind of lighthouse radiating time into the universe.

•

The interior program becomes a window it's possible to zoom through into the out-of-doors. Everyone goes out to feel the night air and are confronted at once with the smell and sound of the sea directly below the narrow esplanade.

One of the waitresses shivers and says they're all dressed for summer, but it's cold.

"That's probably because you've never been outside the donut shop before!"

They all laugh and another waitress wonders if that's anything like the depression that comes from not being able to get inside your favorite program all those years.

"Sometimes we imagine we're inside it and sometimes they try to make us feel we're inside it, but that can never be the same thing as actually leaving your room. And when we allow ourselves to know the difference it's depressing."

Now the brother, having recovered his poise, is there again, but not without having aged badly from a pose of mocking youthfulness to a pose of weathered cynicism. He takes off his beautiful English jacket, drapes it around the shivering waitress's shoulders and, sounding like someone who's spent too many evenings watching reruns of The Persuaders, *says "However often it happens, however obvious, it's still strange that another reality is always waiting outside whatever reality we're in."*

•

Now they call him back in.

•

The tennis-playing daughter is approaching, carrying a round and heavy ironstone cereal bowl heaped up with sponge cake, vanilla ice cream, chocolate sauce, rum sauce and fresh whipped cream, a model of Mt. Fuji. But he knows that she'll never reach him and that he'll never taste it.

326

63

PARK outside the gate. Two tires on earth, two tires on grass. Have to be careful not to pull up too far to the right (facing south) where grass climbs a slope and mixes with yellow reeds (hollow except for the rough strokes of sun that glow in them), concealing a deep and treacherous furrow.

To the left of the locked gate a narrow wooden arch leads to a footpath.

Dirt path through a meadow of purple thistles.

Pause in the sun, as if it's possible to take in the moment: long view ahead of woods and meadows, aroma of hot grass and flowers inhaled in waves: deep troughs between waves of aroma may, at the same time that they're troughs, also be waves of sound: packets of agitated energy press the shape of the world around the brain like wet clay.

Listen long to the humming basin of the foreground: filled completely with insects vibrating at different frequencies.

Take a sniff.

Little concentrated teaspoon of grass elixir.

Length of listening and sniffing allows the fall and rise of whirring, rise and fall of trilling to flow in with heat and breezes.

Pools around us as long as we stand still and show no interest. Raise the hand to adjust the focus of attention and they fly off like startled animals, making thrashing noises in the branches, dodging and skipping along the forest floor as if across the entire surface of a life.

Path continues into the forest.

Reach a point on the rutted and branch-strewn dirt path where sound of children's voices carries from the lake. Voices and the odd hollowness that surrounds them. Mineral basin filled with water, hidden behind dark trees bound to it for centuries. Voices softened, hollowed out, cast skyward.

Beautiful shining basin surrounded by evergreens.

Child cries out to another child in the sun. Splashing inside the boundary rope where the robot rays of the sun are digging into whatever gets in their way and shooting up particle geysers of light.

Moment evaporating from life as it's lived and from the memory of each child diving into the next instant reaches you as you approach along the shaded path through the woods, lost in your own evaporating moment of mineral water-and-rock aroma, rock aroma and steaming *leaf* aroma too.

Echo of distant voice sounds ghostly because it is the ghost of memory as it's being lost.

Lost to them.

Found by us.

Lost to us right after.

64

ARC of sand beach. Boundary ropes suspended on childish blue-and-yellow floats.

Floating dock anchored at a precisely measured distance beyond the boundary ropes marks off an eight foot depth. White paint spread in a creamy way on its rough boards. Sunlight gets stuck to roughness of board or creaminess of paint. Warped, it dips slightly at one corner, which stays permanently wet and mirrors sunlight as blindingly as a restaurant window where you're searching for a beloved face across a sunny intersection.

Swim toward this outer boundary.

Past the rope and childishly striped floats.

A few feet from the dock the water is surprisingly warm, but the cold spring that feeds the lake branches unpredictably everywhere. A stroke this way or that and you're over your head in cold water. Set your foot down, find nothing, panic, begin to thrash desperately toward the shallows.

Another stroke and you're standing, mouth just above water, on a bottom that's slimy and matted. A few strokes in from the boundary rope and the water below is nakedly clear: your feet, planted far away amid layered shards of purple rock and darting green fish, have the golden cast of sparkling mineral.

Swim toward the unfamiliar suntanned girl on the lifeguard's chair as toward someone familiar. Lake stops short in this century, while her gaze out over it keeps traveling. Those in the lake think they're its object, but they're only dark blots against the blinding sparkle of the immediate basin of the foreground.

Laughter on the shore, pleasant and weightless. Pleasure of

the meaningless encounter. Project yourself to the shore, sitting on a blanket with strangers, talking and laughing. Who is this young woman? Her look, which means nothing, strikes you like a stray particle of love, yours to enjoy as if it were true, but only so long as it falls on you. Buoyancy of the meaningless moment floats us through life. Self acquires weight only as it swims stupidly away into meaning.

.

Terrible heat of the day turns to thunder. Lifeguard stands up and blows her whistle. He paddles towards shore slowly, watching mothers herd their children toward safety.

Hurried toweling off and packing up of picnic gear on the little arc of sand beach. Pine woods all around exhale a cool aroma thrown up by animals digging toward evening and aroma of the also surprisingly heavy and uneven pineneedle-stuffed sofa pillow that once lay fragrantly behind two lovers' heads.

A few powerboats and sailboats on the water, the rough note of a motor diminishing toward an opening in the horizon.

The complete universe is always spinning within an uneven radius around the one observing.

Distant thunder and lightning press in on forest and lake as a sudden, violent shaking out of wind and rain...the darkening instant leads into the woodland path...ahead of him, a single file of mothers and children hurry through the forest.

Now he's in the forest. The storm reaches its peak just as he approaches the forest's center. The rain that sweeps down doesn't touch him, but the dark wing that passes through the forest, making it sway, is also passing through him.

Hurry along after the others.

Out by the parked cars the universe is bright enough to bring to mind a forgotten state.

Wind dies down into an ordinary rain storm.

Already he's experiencing the quick, thorough swallow of memory.

Drive away from the moment, wondering whether it will have a ghost-life for others.

65

STANDING in the water not far from shore, in the shallow area roped off for children. All green, all darkness stretch in exceedingly thin sheets along the tranquil surface, while anywhere you gaze down into the water you see a lucid block without magnification — all the way to the bottom where a pair of oddly yellow-white feet are spread flat on shards of worn purple-brown rock and mud.

The corpse, as always, is free to wander into the lake and, catching sight of its feet, wonder if this is still one more lifeless resurrection.

"Is this me? Is this really me again?"

The lake's cold currents remain in the bone, yet the water gathering around the legs and the air brushing up against the tiny vacuum around the torso is warm, as if it were summer.

The corpse knows that certain things are true, but never-ever the ones we're told are true.

For example: what we call "wind" is something that starts quite small as an isolated rustling in one dark tree, then spreads through all, carrying the far evergreen shore rippling to your toes. Even the little island travels round and complete with its shaded cottages under the breeze-stirred hemlocks — right to the water by his bloodless feet.

A world continuous, transparent and pleasantly bounded, lake of summer happiness he's never known. Three boats skimming quickly away: one speeding so quietly over the water it seems to have no engine; two boring with noisy difficulty through the resistance of something that can only be human; all three fleeing as if testing the invention of speed, which in every instance feels like the invention of time — for a short burst accelerating the present out of itself in a continuous and perpetual jump of instants — leap-frogging into the future without interruption. Now (for this narrow instant) the past = everything not accelerated with you, the whole anchored world rolls back, world that rolls back toward the little arc of sand beach where a corpse-like figure is teetering as if gingerly stepping on broken shards of rock and slimy snail shells, losing his balance near the splashing children.

The corpse teetering in the shallows can see all the way across the lake. Sees the departing gaze of the young woman in the boat. Knows how quickly he's diminishing while he tries unsuccessfully to summon up memories of his happiness. The harder he concentrates the more groggy he feels and eventually he's overtaken by the familiar pleasure-boredom of childhood, staring straight ahead for hours at a distant fluctuating image within a stable boundary.

·

The corpse has found another life as a thin man with a close-cropped brush of prematurely grey-brown hair, soft and pleasant to the touch, coarsely shaven features within a perfect egg-shaped oval, shoulders and arms exceedingly pale and freckled yet muscularly wired together, eyes humble and voice kindly — a being that might very well receive a corpse into its keeping — crawling about in shallow water with an exceptionally beautiful little girl, a wriggling tadpole in a swimsuit of the palest sky blue.

"You always have your *eyes* closed!" she complains.

No more than two-and-a-half feet high, with dark, wavy hair and fat cheeks, her strong voice rings clear from a distance, across the great breadth of the shallow wading area and even to a tired, bearded man in a blue shirt with red sleeves on the far shore, lying stretched out on a blanket with his head at a strange, uncomfortable angle to his neck, indifferently reading a novel with a shiny red-and-blue cover held above him with two hands and listening to the sharp cries and remote echoing of this complete little world.

"*Mozhna*," the father with the kindly eyes and fuzzy, egg-shaped head says.

"No!" she shakes her head, laughing. "You should have your eyes *open*!"

"*Mozhna!*" he holds his ground, laughing also.

"Open your *eyes*, Daddy! Don't you know it's more interesting with your eyes *open*?!"

The father stops crawling and splashing, stands up, shades his eyes, looks out across the lake and says in his own language, "Yes, but *beyond* the first evergreen promontory? The flowing, lazy sparkle of *what*? Just like the beautiful pixels dancing across the screens of every nursery."

"Just one more unreality made real-unreality," the little girl answers in English and they plunge back into the water, laughing and paddling, the father making noises, spouting geysers and acting younger and sillier than the daughter.

They leave the water, holding hands.

She breaks away, back toward the lake, laughing.

"Another *five*! No! Another *ten* minutes, Daddy!" and dashes back in while he stops to watch, then goes back up the sandy little slope to the big lavender rock by the trees where they've left their things and begins toweling off, rubbing his short crop of grey-brown hair this-way-and-that-way as a bath mat.

In a minute she runs up to him and he wraps her in a big blue towel, rubs her dry, puts his arm around the whole bundle and kisses her head.

"*One* more minute, Daddy?"

He laughs and she runs back in, splashes with her face out of the water and flat on the surface, looking at the sky, runs out and says, "No, the *green* towel now!"

He lifts the green towel.

"No, Daddy, the *blue* — like before!"

He swirls the blue towel around her.

She frowns. "No, you were right, the green towel is better."

He changes the blue towel for the dry green one, they get their gear together and leave.

66

DOWN the forest path leading away from the lake — through the shadow of the forest — and then out into sunlight where the path clears the woods and cuts a furrow through an open field of purple thistles.

The father has his arm around the tiny figure wrapped in green.

His step wavers for an instant, a misstep, bending oddly and sliding, the pale, long foot about to shoot out on a rounded pebble or the rolling cylinder of a twig as if the wandering corpse who'd chosen this body as its temporary house had suddenly asserted its weakness with all its force.

The parking area outside the gate is carved into hard ruts, mined with the exposed edges of embedded rocks and pitted with deep potholes.

The father sweeps the child onto his shoulders and manages to hold her there while he carries chairs, towels, robes and picnic hamper all the way to their old blue van — far away and up a slight, more sunbaked slope, near some yellow reeds.

In a second the van kicks up dirt and gravel and lurches into the empty curve into the depths of which the child had just been gazing from her father's shoulders.

00

THE child with long, graceful arms of an autumnal hue finally gets tired of rearranging her images and goes looking for her father, who, it suddenly seems to her, has been asleep far too long in the dark back bedroom.

0

ALL the children in the world have been sitting in one room or another with their moms and dads laughing together over the newest, most senseless program.

"OK kids, time to turn it off and get to bed."

"Already, Daddy?!" who can say how many precocious sons and daughters cry out in unison.

"Just another minute!" the youngest pleads.

"Another *five* minutes!" the oldest laughs.

"Yes, I'm actually beginning to enjoy this thing," the mother says, and they all continue watching.

·

Little girl with autumn colored skin cocks her head and asks what kind of bird it is that starts to sing at this late hour.

"Who else could it be?" another child says. "That's the *evening* bird! The one they've given a stupid name to!"

"No, not one bird," other children argue. "Mysterious evening bird, of course, but no one really knows what the voice of the evening bird sounds like, so there have to be other birds too."

"Dozens of birds!"

"No, *hundreds*!"

"All the birds in the world?"

"Yes," they all agree, listening.

They must think someone's ailing and they've gathered under the window to cheer her up.

As many birds as there are leaves, starting with the giant Red Oak in the yard outside your window or the Regans' enormous Elm that may or may not still be there.

Misnamed black-and-grey evening bird, male and female cardinals and a pyrrhuloxia too and families of mourning doves and too many varieties of blackbirds to figure out.

Girl with autumn-colored skin rushes to get her little tape recorder as if she hears something different from the other children in all the rhapsodic singing and guttural gracking and thinks: this is how I'm meant to spend my life: translating the coded equations tangled in the branches. And, if I can do that, will I be the one who at long last solves the problem of Time?